BLOODLINE

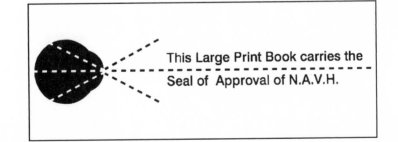

This Large Print Book carries the Seal of Approval of N.A.V.H.

BLOODLINE

MAGGIE SHAYNE

WHEELER PUBLISHING
A part of Gale, Cengage Learning

GALE
CENGAGE Learning™

Detroit • New York • San Francisco • New Haven, Conn • Waterville, Maine • London

GALE
CENGAGE Learning·

LIBRARY OF CONGRESS CATALOGING-IN-PUBLICATION DATA

Shayne, Maggie.
   Bloodline / by Maggie Shayne.
    p. cm.
   ISBN-13: 978-1-4104-2061-9 (alk. paper)
   ISBN-10: 1-4104-2061-2 (alk. paper)
    1. Vampires—Fiction. 2. Large type books. I. Title.
PS3619.H399B57 2009
813'.6—dc22   2009030435

Published in 2009 by arrangement with Harlequin Books S.A.

Printed in the United States of America
1 2 3 4 5 6 7 13 12 11 10 09

BLOODLINE

1

My first thought upon waking was that maybe I was dead. It wasn't until much later that I realized how accurate that initial, intuitive and seemingly irrational notion was. It popped into my consciousness as soon as consciousness itself appeared. It made no sense. It was based upon no reason. It was just there.

I must be dead.

And just as quickly as it had come, the thought was gone again.

I wasn't dead. I was cold. But it was an odd kind of cold, because it didn't make me shiver or feel uncomfortable, it was just an awareness of the fact. I was cold. And I was wet, too.

I opened my eyes slowly and blinked to wipe away the blur of sleep, for I must have been asleep. It was dark. Newborn darkness, though. It had that sense to it, though I wasn't sure at that moment how it was I could sense newborn darkness from any other kind. It wasn't something I would have thought came naturally to ordinary people. And it was certainly nothing I'd ever noticed before.

Or had I?

Oddly, I didn't remember, but I dismissed the slightly queasy feeling that notion brought to my stomach and focused instead on my surroundings. The immediate ones first. Beneath me, dirt. Solid packed, damp, but not muddy. A few scraggly patches of crabgrass and dandelions struggling for survival here and there, and looking proud of their triumph in such inhospitable conditions. All right, then. I was on the ground. Not flat ground, but a hillside that sloped precariously downward to a stretch of pavement at the bottom. And on the other side of that pavement, another patch of ground, sloping upward — a mirror image of the one on which I lay. And above them both . . . a ceiling?

A bridge.

I was on the sloping ground beneath a bridge.

On either side of the bridge, rain poured from heaven's open spigot, soaking the road at the bottom, except for the part of it that was sheltered.

Why, I wondered, am I lying outdoors, on the ground, under a bridge, in the rain, at night?

Naked.

Refocusing my attention on the things in closest proximity, I noted the damp sheet of cardboard that lay over me, like a makeshift blanket, and noted further that, aside from that, I wore nothing. It had that wet-cardboard smell to it, and as I flipped it off my body, I thought my skin did, as well.

I started to shake. Not from the cold, because the cold didn't bother me and that had me worried. Maybe my nerves weren't working just right, but at any rate, I was scared and I could feel panic creeping like ice water through my veins. I closed my eyes, firmed my spine, held my breath, then told myself, "Easy. Just take it easy. Just take it easy and figure this out. It can't be all that difficult to figure this out."

Nodding in response to my own advice, I opened my eyes again, and this time I looked down at my own body. I was long, and I was thin. Perhaps athletic, I thought, and it scared me that I didn't know if that was true or not. Maybe I was just sickly. Although I didn't feel sickly. And my body seemed more lean than skinny.

In fact, I felt . . .

9

Strong.

I opened my hands to see if they worked, then closed them again. I studied my slender arms, lengthy legs, small waist and hips nearly the same size, and my compact, round little breasts, as if I'd never seen them before. And then I noticed a lock of hair hanging over my shoulder, and I grasped it, lifting it to look and feel and smell it.

It was copper in color, the kind of hair they call auburn, I thought, and it was curly and long, long, long, just like the rest of me. But also like the rest of me, I had the feeling I'd never seen it before.

I stood up to see how long my hair was, and also to move around a bit. Maybe if I woke up more thoroughly, this fog in my head would clear and I would know who I was and what I was doing here in the middle of nowhere on the cusp of night, naked and alone.

So I stood there, noticing that my hair reached to the tops of my hipbones, until a sound jerked my attention away from it. Something running, scampering off in the distance. My head snapped toward the sound fast, and I felt my nose wrinkling and realized I was scenting the moist air. My eyes narrowed, and my mind thought, *Rabbit.* And then I saw it, scurrying from one

10

clump of brush to the next, far in the distance. Perhaps as much as a half mile from me.

There was no possible way I could see a rabbit a half mile away in the dark, in the rain, much less identify it by smell.

And yet I had, and I realized, as my senses came to life one by one, that I could hear *many* things and smell even more — the flitting of a little bird's wings and the scent of the leaves in his nest, the hushed flight of a moth and the smell of the fine powder on his body, the bubbling of a stream somewhere beyond sight and the smell of its water and even the fish that lived in its depths. I smelled autumn. There were decaying leaves, their aroma so pungent and wonderful and evocative that it overwhelmed almost everything else. It was comforting, that scent. I heard the sound of cars that had not yet come close enough to see, and I could smell their exhaust.

My brows drew together, and I pressed my fingertips to my forehead. "What am I?" I whispered.

Lights came into view then. Headlights, as a vehicle rolled closer and closer on the road below. I started to move carefully down the hill. My feet seemed extremely sensitive to every pebble, and I sucked air through

11

my teeth, tasting everything it carried in its breath, but I hurried all the same.

I stopped halfway down just as the car rolled under the bridge, and I heard the brakes engage as the vehicle came to an abrupt stop, still ten feet from where I stood.

I didn't move toward it. I just stood there, naked and waiting. There was something tingling up the back of my neck that felt like unease. Like a warning.

The car was black. Big and black. An SUV, I thought. An expensive one. My eyes slid toward the manufacturer's logo on the front of the thing, and I saw laurel leaves encircling a shield, with blocks of color on its face. I thought I should remember it, though I wasn't certain why. As I stared, unsure whether to move closer or turn away, the driver's-side window, which was deeply tinted, moved downward just a little. A man's voice said, "Get in."

The chill along my nape turned icy. I shivered, and everything in me went tense and tight. I felt as if I were coiling up inside myself in preparation for flight, though I didn't know why I should feel the urge to run. I ignored the impulse, but still I didn't move.

And then, through the tiny gap in that window, I saw the black barrel of a gun, pointing right at my head, and the voice was cold this time. "I *said* get in."

The spring that had been coiling up inside me released all at once. My body sprang into motion as if propelled by some outside force. I turned, I lunged, I leapt, soaring from the embankment to the pavement beyond the bridge, behind the car, where the rain was pounding down. Barely had my feet settled on the macadam before I was moving again. I accelerated into a dead run, the speed of which astounded me.

I heard tires spinning behind me, and then gunshots, three of them, so loud I thought my eardrums had split, but no pain came with those shots. The bullets, though certainly fired at me, had missed their mark. And when I dared to glance over my shoulder, I saw those headlights falling farther and farther behind me as I ran.

That didn't make any sense at all. The car was chasing me, speeding after me along the same stretch of road. And I was on foot, running through the pouring rain. And yet I was pulling away.

Almost as an afterthought, I veered left, away from the pavement, and sped over uneven terrain, through an open field that was lush with grass and far easier on my tender feet. I ran until the car was long out of sight, and then I kept on running, because there was an ecstatic rush to it that I couldn't understand.

I leapt over boulders and limbs that appeared in my path. I jumped over the stream I'd heard from so far away, expecting to land somewhere in the middle of it, but clearing it instead. I ran alongside a doe that I startled, and while she flared her nostrils and bounded away with her white tail flying its warning, I passed her, and kept on going.

God, what *was* this? How was this *possible?*

Finally, when I began to tire at last, I stopped and again tried to take stock of who and what I was, but I found nothing there.

Tabula rasa. The phrase echoed in my mind. *Blank slate.* It was as if whatever I had known or been before had been erased.

So instead of searching within me for answers, I took a look at my surroundings, because I would need, I thought, food and shelter and probably some clothing, if I hoped to survive long enough to figure out anything more. Those were the immediate requirements. And they were easier to face than the emptiness inside my mind. Thinking on that brought me to the edge of panic, and I had the feeling that, should I give in to it, I might never return.

I had run into a stand of forest, a woody little paradise, its floor lined with fallen leaves, and its trees awash in russet and scarlet and gold. I walked through it now, following my senses to its edge, where I could look out and see what lay beyond.

Another stretch of pavement, curving into what appeared to be a small town. I saw a tall pointed church steeple. I saw several oversize barns, and lots of little houses. They were clustered together in some places, farther apart in others. Smoke wafted from chimneys, and I smelled the wood burning, and the oil, too. But my eyes fell on one place in particular, a place well beyond a cluster of homes. I didn't know why. It was far away in the distance. A red house with white shutters. It had a red barn and a lot of green land around it, all of it enclosed by white wooden fences.

And then a flash in my mind. A man, kissing me. Unfamiliar, powerful, wonderful feelings rushing through my body. Lips on mine. My hands tangling in dark hair.

And then it was gone. Gone, just that fast.

I wanted it back. I wanted more of it. But it had receded into the deep black waters inside my mind.

Sighing in disappointment, I returned my

15

attention to that little red farmhouse. It was *that* place that drew my attention, though I had no idea why. Another place would have been far easier to reach. That one, the one that caught hold of me and held me in its grip, was well past the rest of the town, situated on a hillside and only visible from here because of the angle at which I stood. The town itself was close at hand. That place . . . that place was miles from me. Isolated. Lonely.

Calling out to me.

I had to go. And I had no idea why I was so compelled.

Yet, I rationalized, I'd had no idea why I'd felt a sense of panic when that car had stopped. And *that* feeling had proven accurate. So common sense dictated I should pay attention to my feelings. If my senses were somehow heightened beyond normal — which certainly seemed to be the case, since I could see and hear and smell things I shouldn't be able to — and if my physical speed was also magnified — which it clearly was, since I had outrun a deer and a Cadillac . . .

Yes. A Cadillac Escalade. That was what that car had been. I smiled a little, slightly gratified to think tiny things were coming back to me.

But the point was, if all these other senses and strengths were somehow heightened, then maybe my intuitions were sharper than usual, as well. Though I couldn't, just then, have said what "usual" might have been for me.

I would, I decided, trust my intuitions. I would go to that red farmhouse — no, I would go to its barn, which would be safer. That would be my shelter for the moment. And from there I would plan my next move.

So I walked down the slight grassy incline, away from the autumnal beauty of the woods, to the curving country road, and then, keeping to the softest part of the shoulder, I began walking, naked, toward that tiny town. And as I walked, I began to feel aware of a demanding, urgent hunger unlike any I had ever known before.

21 Years Ago

Serena blinked the drug-induced haze from her head and glanced up at the man in the white lab coat, with the stethoscope around his neck. He wasn't looking at her, but at her chart.

"Where's my baby? Can I see her now?" Then she smiled a little, through the fog. God, they must have given her a lot of drugs, she thought. "I'm already saying 'her,' when I don't even know for sure, but I expected her to be a girl. Was she? Is she perfect and wonderful? How much did she weigh? Why haven't the nurses brought her in to me yet?"

The doctor lowered the chart, replaced it on its hook at the foot of the bed, and then he came closer and reached down to pat her hand. Not hold it, just pat it. He wasn't smiling.

Something clenched tight in the pit of Serena's stomach. And suddenly she didn't want to hear what he was going to say.

"It was a girl, yes. But . . . I'm very sorry, Serena. Your baby was stillborn."

A sledgehammer hit her squarely in the chest. She fell back against the pillows as every whisper of breath was driven from her lungs. Her hand clutched her chest, because she couldn't seem to draw more air back in. And then the doctor pressed his icy hand to the nape of her neck, pushing her head forward.

"Put your head down and breathe. Just breathe." He hit a button on the wall behind the bed and snapped, "A little help in here," then yanked something from his pocket, snapped it and held it underneath Serena's nose.

The ammonia smell hit her and burned,

making her gasp and jerk her head away. And then she was breathing. In and out. Breathing. As if nothing had happened.

"That's better." He glanced up as the door opened and a nurse entered. Pretty, blond and young.

Serena glanced at her only briefly before shooting her gaze straight back to the doctor. "It's a lie," she said. "It's a lie. My baby was not stillborn."

The nurse came closer. "I know how hard this is. I'm so sorry."

"My baby was *not* stillborn," Serena repeated. And she locked eyes with the doctor. "I heard her cry. *I heard her cry.*"

"You were heavily sedated," the doctor said, with no hint of sympathy in his matter-of-fact tone. "This isn't uncommon, this delusion of having heard the baby cry. I know it's hard to understand, but it's fairly normal."

"I heard her cry," Serena said again. And then she noticed that the blond nurse couldn't meet her eyes.

"I'm ordering a sedative," the doctor said as if she were no longer in the room, then he returned to the foot of the bed, grabbed the chart and scribbled something on it. "Get it into her, stat."

Serena sat up straighter in the bed. "I

don't need a freaking sedative! I told you, I heard my baby cry. I heard her!" She shot her desperate gaze to the nurse. "I won't take a sedative. I want a phone. I want the police. I want to know what you people did with my baby."

"Your baby was stillborn," the doctor said again.

And very subtly, so slightly that she couldn't even be sure if she was imagining it, the nurse shook her head as she held Serena's eyes.

"Get the Valium," the doctor ordered.

The nurse — her name tag said Maureen Keenan, R.N. — hurried out the door. Serena wondered if she had really seen the silent message Nurse Keenan had sent — and whether the doctor had picked up on it.

No time to tell. He left on the nurse's heels.

The second the door closed behind him, Serena scanned her hospital room, but there was no telephone in sight. Getting out of the bed, wincing at how sore she was, she went to the window and pressed the slats of the blinds apart so she could see outside.

The sun hung low in the sky. The parking lot lay beyond her window. She was on the second floor.

20

God, where was her baby?

She heard the door opening and dove back into the bed.

Nurse Keenan was back, syringe in her gloved hands. She came close to the bed, leaned down and clasped Serena's forearm.

"I really don't need that, Nurse Kee—"

"It's Maureen, and I know you don't need it," the other woman whispered. "But you do need to listen and do exactly what I tell you. I want you to wait one hour. Pretend to be out cold, because this shit should knock you right on your ass. Understand?"

"But what's going on? Where's my baby?"

"I don't know. I just know you need to get the hell out of here. One hour, then go out the window. Dangle from your hands, then let go, so it won't be as far to fall. Maybe five feet. There will be a backpack in the bushes with everything you need. One hour, then go. Fake it till then."

Footsteps came tapping along the hall, and Maureen quickly slid the needle into the pillow and depressed the plunger. "You're out cold. There's a clock over there." She inclined her head slightly. "One hour, then get out. Your life depends on it."

The door opened, and the doctor walked in. Serena closed her eyes and let her head sink onto the pillow as if she were completely relaxed. She made her breathing slow and even and deep.

"Did she give you any trouble?" he asked.

"Only a little. I talked her around. I think she likes me."

His cold, gray, unfeeling eyes were still on her. Serena could feel them, even though hers were closed.

"She shouldn't give us any more trouble tonight," the bastard said.

"It's hard on her. Poor thing, thinking she heard her baby cry. What do you suppose is behind that?" the nurse asked.

"You were there, Maureen."

"Well, not in the room. I mean, I was in the unit, but not —"

"So? Did you hear a baby cry?"

It sounded almost like an accusation. Or maybe a challenge.

"No, Doctor Martin," Nurse Keenan replied, in a tone that held no life. "I didn't hear a thing."

Serena knew it was a lie. She knew it right to her soul. Maureen Keenan knew. She had heard Serena's baby cry, and she *knew*. And she wanted to help.

Serena wasn't imagining anything. She hadn't been hallucinating or deluded or reacting to drugs. Her daughter was alive. She was alive!

And if it took Serena the rest of her life, she would find her.

2

The Present

Ethan's first chore in the evening was to see to Scylla and Charybdis. The draft horses were big enough to qualify as monsters, though he supposed naming them for sea serpents was a bit of a stretch.

He smiled at the notion of his companions as the legendary creatures from the tales of Ulysses — guarding his solitude, the way their namesakes had guarded the Straits of Messina.

As he strode through the deepening darkness, along the path that twisted from the house to the stable, he heard them blowing a soft welcome from within. They sensed him coming. They would sense danger, as well, and paw and snort their warnings. They seemed to understand that there were some — many — who wanted him dead.

He was almost to the stable and deep in thought when he stopped walking and lifted his head, suddenly picking up the clear scent of another of his own kind.

Another vampire. Close.

A Wildborn? Or one of the Bloodliners, like him? One trained to kill, and sent out to hunt him down and destroy him, as all escapees were hunted down and destroyed?

Standing utterly still, he honed his senses, feeling for the presence, sensing for any sign of a threat. The horses hadn't pawed or stomped. They hadn't blown in anger or snorted, the way they would if danger were near. Why not?

The presence was that of a female, and the only emotion coming from her was fear. She felt him, too; he could sense it. But not deliberately. She wasn't scanning the airwaves for his vibration. She'd found it by accident. And now that she had, she wasn't probing his mind, the way he'd taught himself to do with others since he'd stolen blood from the labs at The Farm and transformed himself two years ago.

He didn't feel any hint of danger or menace. Even so, he tugged the pitchfork from its nail on the wall as he entered the barn. It would stab deeply, and she would bleed out well before the dawn brought sleep and its attendant healing power.

He stepped inside, his nose filling at once

with the pleasing aromas of fresh, high-quality hay, straw bedding, honeyed oats and the scent of horseflesh, sharp and rich.

Scylla snorted softly and swished her tail. Not a warning, but a message that something had her wound up. Excited. Anxious, perhaps, but not afraid.

Easy, girl, Ethan thought at her. *I already know someone's here. Just not exactly . . . where.*

He rounded a corner and met the mare's eyes. She shook her mane, then shifted her gaze and bobbed her head up and down.

He nodded, then glanced at the stall beside hers, where Charybdis stood munching a mouthful of hay as if he hadn't a care in the world. *And a lot of help you are,* Ethan thought. Though he knew if there were any real threat, Charybdis would be kicking down the stall door. Instead, the stallion only blinked at him and then went back to chewing.

Ethan shifted the pitchfork into his other hand and walked without making a sound toward the tack room's red wooden door. It was closed. *She* was on the other side. The closer he got to the door, the more certain he was of that.

He glanced at the pitchfork in his hand and wondered what sort of weapons she

26

might be intending to use on him. A gun? Some sort of electric-shock device, like the ones he'd been forced to wield against other innocent captives at The Farm? A blade, razor sharp and big enough to behead him? Was he insane to be walking into the tack room with only a pitchfork?

He didn't see that he had any choice. If one of the Wildborns had found him, he had to kill it before it spread word of his existence, and that of his kind, to the rest of them. And if it was an assassin sent from The Farm, then the same reasoning applied. Kill or be killed.

He couldn't be found. He'd made a life for himself, and he intended to keep it — at least long enough to find out what had happened to his brother.

Because James had left, and Ethan still didn't know how or why. Some of the captives said he'd been made over into a vampire and sent out on a mission for the organization to which they all owed their lives — such as they were — the Division of Paranormal Investigations. But Ethan preferred to believe his brother had escaped and survived, just as he had done. And now his goal in life was to find his brother and make sure he stayed safe — and free.

But right now he had a lurking vampiress

to contend with.

Slowly, he opened the tack room door.

His gaze shot right to her, as unerringly as if that extra sense of his had attuned itself automatically and instantly to her aura. He saw coppery curls, scads of them, and pale pink skin. She was sitting on the floor, her back pressed into a corner, her knees drawn up, her head bowed down, her long hair covering everything other than a glimpse of rounded buttock, a bit of knee here, shin there, a bare foot peeking out beneath it all.

He'd only known one woman with hair like that in all his life. She hadn't been a vampire then. She'd been just another one of the Chosen, another captive being raised on The Farm. Just like him. A member of the Bloodline.

She lifted her head slowly. One long, slender hand rose to push that glorious hair away from her face, and she speared him with the luminous emeralds that were her eyes.

He held that gaze, tried to read her jumbled, confused thoughts, and finally he spoke. "Are you here to kill me, then?"

Lashes, thick as black ferns, swept downward to hide those eyes from him. "Why would I want to kill you?"

And then her lashes rose again, and she

met his gaze with an impact he felt in his chest. There was fear there. And there were a lot of other things swirling in the depths of her eyes, as well. But one thing there wasn't, and that was the recognition he'd expected to see.

"I don't even know you," she went on. And then, biting her bottom lip, she added, "I don't even know . . . *me.* Not even my name."

As the words hung in the air between them, she rose slowly and stood facing him, her hands at her sides. She was naked and beautiful and vulnerable in every sense of the word. She was not the wild child he'd known.

At The Farm, she'd been untamable. Unbreakable. She would argue about the lessons they were taught, day in and day out. She would disagree. She would refuse to be as mindlessly obedient as they were supposed to strive to be. Oftentimes the Bloodliners would be ordered to perform a task that had no reason, made no sense. Twist the head off this squirrel. Eat this handful of maggots. Stand outside in the middle of a blizzard, barefoot, for twelve hours.

She, unlike all the rest, had refused.

They'd deprived her of sleep. They'd

29

increased the dosages of the drugs they administered. They'd kept her in the isolation room, eyes taped open to see the insane images flashing across a wall-size screen, while the headphones strapped to her ears screamed indoctrination into her head.

It had been torture, what they'd done to her. And he probably didn't know the half of it, because he hadn't witnessed it. It was all rumor, whispered among the frightened, obedient, mindless captives. They would kill her, it was said, if they couldn't break her.

At least he'd had sense enough to *pretend* to submit until the chance to escape had come at last.

And now, here she was, a vampiress, a Bloodliner, who didn't know him and claimed not to know her own name.

What the hell had they done to the indomitable shrew he remembered? What had they done to Lilith?

21 Years Ago

Serena closed her eyes and remembered again the sound of her daughter's first congested, lamblike cries. So fragile, so fresh.

She watched the clock from beneath lowered lids, and she didn't get out of her bed until the very minute Nurse Keenan had told her to. And then she pushed back the covers and tested her legs, putting her weight on them slowly. They didn't buckle, so she got all the way up, then turned to fix the bed, tucking pillows under the covers to simulate a sleeping patient. She pulled the curtains all the way around the bed, moving them as quietly as she could. Then she scanned the room again, in search of anything she could take with her, anything that might help her in her flight. But there was nothing.

The nurse had told her that she would find everything she needed in a backpack outside. She was just going to have to trust that that was true.

Stiffening her spine, she went to the window, silently pulled the cord to raise the blinds, then flipped the window latch and pushed upward. The window opened easily. She'd expected it to be more difficult.

Leaning over the sill, she looked down. It didn't seem like such a long way. She was barefoot, wearing only a hospital gown. But if she was quick, she could escape unnoticed and duck out of sight. Maybe no one would see her.

She swung one leg over, and then, sitting on the sill, swung the other one outside. She twisted to face the window and, lying on her belly, shimmied down, gripping with her hands and finally lowering herself, dangling there. Closing her eyes, taking a deep breath, she let go, pushing off just slightly, so she wouldn't smash into the wall on the way down.

Her feet hit almost instantly, in less than a second, and it wasn't much of an impact. Her knees gave, she landed on her backside and bit back a yelp of pain, and that was that. She had to blink a few times to get it through her head that it really had been just that easy.

Maybe there wasn't some giant conspiracy going on. If they were truly lying to her about her baby, wouldn't they have taken greater precautions to keep her from escaping? Wouldn't they have locked the window, at least?

Serena had landed on a grassy lawn, with hedges bordering the sidewalk that meandered past. She didn't see anyone around. Swallowing hard, she got to her feet, then moved to those hedges and, parting branches, searched within them.

The large green backpack was right there. She spotted it almost immediately and yanked it out, then peeled back the zipper. Inside she saw clothes, shoes, a file folder. There was more, but she felt compelled to hurry. To get dressed and get away from this place.

A car door closed, startling her, so she zipped the pack shut again and drew back into the shadows.

She caught sight of an alcove around the corner. It was blocked by hedges and the angled walls of the hospital building itself. Not entirely, but maybe enough. She hurried to it, and saw benches, tables and ashtrays. It must be where the staff took their lunch breaks when the weather was good.

Serena yanked the clothing from the bag, moving rapidly now. A pair of jeans came out first. There were panties beneath them, and several large-size maxi-pads like the one she was already wearing, postlabor. She pulled on the clothes underneath her hospital gown, then grabbed the sports bra and T-shirt from the bag, and put them on, as well. She was in such a hurry that she wouldn't have taken the time for the sports bra, but her breasts were swollen with milk, and heavy and tender and sore. It would help. So she took those few extra seconds to put it on without removing the hospital gown. And then she untied the strings holding the gown in back, stripped it off and stuffed her arms into the T-shirt sleeves almost in one motion. There were shoes in the backpack. Flip-flops. She shoved her feet into them, wadded up the hospital gown and stuffed it into the bag, then zipped it and headed for the sidewalk. Walking fast, barely able to suppress the overwhelming urge to break into a run, she left the hospital far behind her.

Soon, sooner than she could have believed, she was walking on a busy sidewalk, past shops and restaurants and convenience stores, and no one was paying any attention to her.

They would be, though. Someone would notice her missing from the hospital. And it wouldn't be long. But what would they do about it?

There was a ringing sound. A phone ringing. Close.

Frowning, she realized it was coming from inside the backpack, so she stopped walking and yanked the sack off her shoulder and dug around inside until she found a brick-size mobile phone. She pulled it out, extended the antenna and held it to her ear, terrified, looking around in search of the caller. As if he or she were close. Watching her. God, she was scared, and she wasn't even sure why.

"Did you get clear?"

She recognized the voice. It was the nurse who had helped her. "Yes. I mean, I think so."

"Where are you?"

"I . . . I don't know. On a street." She looked around. "Near the corner of Main Street and Elm. I'm standing in front of a jewelry store."

"Okay, listen, there's a bus stop about a block ahead of you, on Main. Do you see it?"

Serena looked one way, then the other, and spotted the bench inside the plastic weather guard. "I see it."

"The bus should be pulling up any minute now. Get on it. Get off at the third stop. I'll pick you up there. I'll be in a red VW, okay?"

"I don't — I don't understand what's going on. Is my baby alive? Why are they lying to me? Why couldn't I just tell them I wanted to leave and sign myself out? What —"

"The bus should be there any second, Serena. Don't miss it. There's money in the same pocket where you found the phone."

"But —"

"Your baby's alive. Now go. Catch that bus. I'll explain the rest once you're safe."

The phone cut off. But Serena had heard the only words she really needed to hear.

35

"My baby's alive," she whispered. A smile pulled her dry lips, feeling alien. "My baby's alive," she said again, and she began walking again just as the giant bus lumbered into sight and pulled to a stop. She was running for the bus stop as the air brakes hissed and the door cranked open. She tucked the phone into the backpack and slung it over her shoulder as she got aboard, pausing at the top of the steps to fumble in the backpack for money. She found a wad of bills and a handful of change, dropped some coins into the receptacle and then made her way to the first empty seat and sank into it.

As soon as the bus lurched into motion, she felt a rush of relief, relief that grew with every bit of distance she put between herself and the hospital. The relief of knowing that her baby was alive was making her almost giddy. And the fear of being pursued was gone, as well.

She wondered what was behind all this. It must be some sort of baby-stealing ring. They were probably planning to arrange an expensive adoption to some wealthy couple and make a small fortune by selling her child. The doctor must be in on it. But all her nervousness was probably overkill, wasn't it? And the nurse was no doubt just being dramatic. After all, it wasn't as if they

36

would want to hurt her, was it? Why would they lie to her if they were just going to . . . kill her or something?

She was okay. She was free. Maybe once she started digging, started getting close to finding her baby, maybe there would be danger then. But surely not now. She was away from the hospital. She was meeting with the one person who might be able to tell her what was going on. She was fine. And she was going to get her baby back.

The bus stopped. Serena went back over that phone call in her mind. The third stop. She was to get off at the third stop. So there were two more to go. She used the time to examine the contents of the backpack more carefully. The file folder contained medical records — her baby's time of birth, weight, length, head circumference, blood type.

Blood type — marked with a star. She read the notation beneath it. *Child possesses the Belladonna antigen. Extremely rare. Government notification mandatory.*

She frowned, not knowing what that meant, then felt eyes on her. Glancing up, she saw the man in the seat across from her look away quickly. She closed the file folder and thrust it back into the bag just as the bus stopped again. The man got off.

Serena took a surreptitious look around

as the bus began moving again, saw no one paying her undue attention, and again pawed through the bag. There was a set of keys, with a tag on them, like a luggage tag. The address on the inserted card read *72 Montgomery Ave.*

Finally the bus stopped for the third time. Serena zipped up the bag, got up and slung it over her shoulder, then made her way to the front, down the steps and onto a sidewalk in the suburbs. The bus pulled away as she looked up and down the neat, unlined road. And then she spotted it. A little red VW Bug, parked across the street alongside a playground. It was a convertible, and the top was down, giving Serena a clear view of the woman behind the wheel. As it was no doubt meant to do.

It was the nurse she remembered, Maureen Keenan, no longer in uniform or wearing a name tag. She lifted a hand in a friendly wave as she saw Serena.

Smiling in relief, certain she was about to get some answers, Serena looked both ways, then began to cross the street. Just as her flip-flops hit the pavement, the little red car exploded.

3

The Present

There was something about the man who stood across the tack room, staring at me. Something that made things deep inside me begin to stir and tingle and . . . *ache.*

Did I know him?

I saw surprise in his eyes, followed by suspicion and a hint of fear, though why he would be afraid of me, I couldn't begin to imagine. I hadn't expected that reaction. I thought he would either try to kill me, as that other person had, or offer to help me. That he would fear me made no sense.

I let my eyes move up and down, inspecting everything about him and wishing something would elicit a memory. I felt a longing — and something else — and I wondered why.

He was tall, and his rolled-up shirtsleeves revealed hard, hairy forearms that my fingers suddenly yearned to touch. His shoulders were wide and strong. Strong enough to hold my tired head quite easily, I imagined. Strong enough to ease my worried mind, too. Why would a man like this one be afraid of me?

And yet, that was what I felt.

My gaze ran over him again and again, as if drinking him in, and the more I looked, the more relieved I felt, though it made no sense. My attention lingered on his face, because I was suddenly helpless to look elsewhere. He was a beautiful man, with eyes as dark as melted chocolate and moodier than a storm cloud. So much in those eyes — restless, reckless things, but hidden just enough that I couldn't identify a single one. His hair was gleaming black and long, its natural waves captured and bound in a leather band behind his head.

And again, that flash. My fingers burying themselves in hair just like that.

His hair? Was this the man I was kissing in the one and only memory remaining to me? But there must have been millions of men with hair like his in this wide world.

And yet it was to this one I'd been inexorably drawn.

His clothes were nothing special. The pants were olive green with numerous pockets. The shirt was a tan button-down.

He wore a wristwatch with a wide silver band. I caught a glimpse of something beneath it — something blue on his skin, and my eyes focused there, as I tried to see more.

He turned his hand, just slightly. Just enough so that I couldn't see the mark. But even as he did, I turned my own hand palm up at the mark on my inner wrist. Blue ink, in a series of short lines, some thicker, some thinner. A bar code. Could his wrist bear a similar mark?

"Tell me what you're doing here, in my stable," he said.

His voice touched my nerve endings, rubbing roughly over them until they quivered and stood erect and expectant. The sound of it, and the feelings it elicited, drew my eyes back to his. "I'm hungry," I said. My voice sounded plaintive and weak, like that of a small orphan child, begging for crumbs. I felt irritated by that, so I spoke again, my tone deeper and stronger, deliberately so. "I need shelter and a place to rest, and . . ."

"And?"

"I don't know. Something . . . drew me here." I wasn't sure whether telling him the truth was a good idea or a bad one, but the words spilled out of me without my permission all the same. "When I saw this place

41

from the distance, I felt compelled to come here. I knew it would be . . . safe." Blinking twice, I lowered my eyes, unable to hold his as I whispered, "Is it?"

"I'm no threat to you, unless you're one to me."

I hadn't realized I'd been holding my breath, until his answer let me release it. "How could I be a threat to anyone? I told you, I don't even know who I am."

"How can that be?"

A sob rose in my throat. Stupid, that his one obvious question would be enough to send me beyond the edge of control, but it did. Suddenly I just couldn't take any more. I wrapped my arms around myself and lowered my head, ashamed of my tears. Of showing him such weakness. I sensed that it wasn't something I did easily, and it angered me, but not enough to give me the power to stop it. "I don't know. I don't remember."

Sighing deeply, he stared at me for a long moment, and then, as if making a decision at last, he quickly took off his shirt and held it out by the collar, offering it to me.

My hand trembled as I took it, never looking up very far. "Thank you."

"You're welcome, Lilith."

I had been pulling the shirt around me when he said that, and the name, Lilith, made something tickle deep within the core of my brain. It brought my head up, made my eyes narrow and strain, as if I were trying to look through his skin and bones to see into his soul.

"What did you call me?"

He seemed to wish he could bite the word back as soon as he said it. I could tell by the way he quickly averted his eyes, leaned the pitchfork against the wall and began to fidget with a harness that hung from a peg. "I have to call you something," he muttered. "It seemed as good a name as any."

I pulled the shirt the rest of the way on and buttoned it. Then I scooped my hair out of the collar. His shirt came to my upper thighs. It was only slightly longer than my hair.

"You said you were drawn to my house from the distance. Do you remember anything prior to that?"

I nodded, allowing him to believe he had distracted me from the matter of that name. A name that felt . . . familiar. "I remember . . . a little. And I have no reason not to tell you all of it. But I'm tired, and I'm *incredibly* hungry."

"All right." He nodded twice, and said it again. "All right. Come on to the house. I'll get you something to drink." As he spoke, he turned and started walking, taking my arm lightly as he did.

"I need a meal, not a drink," I told him. My stomach was growling. "I need meat. A nice rare burger or a steak or —"

He stopped walking and stared at me. "You said you don't know who you are. Do you know . . . *what* you are?"

I frowned at him, having no idea what he meant. "I'm . . . a woman. An amnesiac. A . . ." I couldn't think of anything else, and I could tell by the look in those brown velvet eyes that I hadn't said what he'd wanted me to say. "What?" I asked softly. "What am I?"

Even then, though, I think there was some inkling. I could outrun a deer. I could see for miles. I could hear things no ordinary person could hear, smell things only a bloodhound should be able to smell. I began to shake, and I lowered my head, looked at the mark on my wrist, felt tears welling up in my eyes. My knees seemed to weaken as I whispered the question again. "What am I?"

My legs turned to water, and his arms came around me, fast and sure, to keep me from falling.

"I feel so weak."

"I'm sorry. I should have seen it sooner.

44

Come on, Lilith, I've got you now."

He scooped me up as if I were a child, and I gave in to the weakness that was overwhelming me and let my head rest on his sturdy shoulder. I closed my eyes. Softly, I said, "I don't even know your name."

"Ethan," he told me. And that, too, caused a powerful ripple in the still waters of my mind.

"Ethan," I repeated. "Thank you, Ethan."

"You may not be thanking me later," he said.

I frowned and searched his face, but he kept his eyes forward as he carried me out of the barn into the darkness of the night, and then along a winding path toward his house. Soon enough, we were inside. I felt the comfort of warmth enveloping me as he closed the door behind us. I smelled a wood fire and looked around for the source, but we were only in the entry hall. He kicked off his shoes without putting me down, then continued into a modest living room that welcomed me like a hug. The furniture needed only button eyes to resemble a family of teddy bears — plush and soft and brown. Green and gold and russet throw pillows littered each piece like the fallen autumn leaves outside. The fieldstone fireplace held a dancing blaze that painted my face in heat and light, and above its gleaming oaken mantel, there was a painting.

I stared at it, unblinking, my tired eyes suddenly finding the strength to stay open.

It was a woman, a nude woman, with coppery curls like ribbons draping down her body. Twined around her was a giant snake, and she looked as if she adored the thing. She had more curves than I had, and I had no idea whether her face bore any resemblance to mine. The title, "Lilith," was written unobtrusively across the bottom, and beneath that the name of the artist, John Waterhouse.

"Is it the hair?" I asked.

"Is what the hair?" Ethan lowered me onto the teddy-bear sofa, which was every bit as soft as it looked. Then he opened the antique trunk that served as a coffee table and pulled out a blanket.

"In the painting," I said, and I pointed. "Is it because our hair is alike that you called me by her name?"

"Partly that." He draped the blanket over me, then turned to gaze at the picture. "But there's a lot more to Lilith's story than her hair. Legend has it that she was the first woman, created by God alongside Adam. His equal. She refused to submit to him, was too independent to be tamed, much less

46

owned or commanded. And so she left him, and God was forced to make another companion for him. That time he made the woman from Adam's rib, so she would know her place."

"And that was Eve?"

"So the story goes. And even then, poor submissive Eve got blamed when things went to hell. Didn't do her much good to behave, did it?" He faced me again.

I frowned, unsure what he was getting at. "Why are you telling me this?"

"Because I sense you're a lot more like Lilith than Eve. Your spirit is like hers, indomitable."

"I don't feel very indomitable just now."

"You are. Trust me."

"How do you know?" I tried to see whatever was hiding behind his eyes, because I was sure something was. "Do you know me, Ethan?"

He lowered his head quickly. "How could I?" As he said it, he crossed the room, and then he left entirely.

I rested my head on a russet pillow, listening as he rummaged around in the next room. When he returned, only moments later, he brought with him a huge ceramic stein. He pressed it into my hands. It was warm.

I smiled, thinking of hot cocoa, and immediately brought it to my mouth for a long drink. And yet the moment it hit my tongue, I knew it wasn't cocoa. But it *was* exactly what my body needed. What I craved. It was rich, thick, tasting slightly of sulphur and salt, and yet I found it irresistible.

He stood watching me as I tipped the stein upward, drinking and drinking and drinking, until I'd drained it all. I lowered the stein and wiped the back of my hand over my lips.

It came away red.

Blinking down at my hand and then up at him, I asked, "What was that?"

"Just a favorite of mine. Call it a — protein shake."

"*What* did I just *drink,* Ethan?"

"Close your eyes and relax, Lilith. There are things I have to tell you, and you're going to need that inner strength you don't know you have — you're going to need all of it."

I didn't close my eyes, and I didn't relax. Instead, I sat up straighter on the sofa, planted my feet on the floor and held the blanket around me like a cloak, watching Ethan as he paced away from me.

"You said you'd tell me," he said. "Everything you remember."

"I hope you don't expect that to fill the evening." My attempt at levity fell flat, and I drew a breath, wished to hell he would stop pacing and lifted my head.

To my surprise, he *did* stop pacing — just when I thought it. He met my eyes and moved to the overstuffed chair beside the sofa. As he sat, I organized my thoughts, going back as far as I could remember.

"I woke up on a hillside underneath a bridge. It was raining. I didn't know who I was or what I was doing there. I still don't. A car came along, and I ignored my instinct to run and instead stood there waiting, hoping they would stop and help me. They did stop. And then the window went down a little, and someone poked a gun out of it and ordered me to get in."

His expression grew tighter, more troubled, with every word I uttered.

"A man's voice? Or a woman's?" he asked.

"Man's."

"Would you recognize it if you heard it again?"

I lifted my brows. "I don't know. Maybe."

"What about the car? Would you recognize that?"

I swallowed, closed my eyes, tried to remember. "It was a big, black SUV. The windows were tinted so dark that I couldn't

49

see who was inside. But I know it was a Cadillac. A black Cadillac Escalade."

"That's very good."

I smiled slightly in response to the praise and opened my eyes. He still looked troubled. "I want you to close your eyes and relax, and just think about when you first woke up under the bridge."

I leaned back on the sofa, letting my eyes fall closed again, relaxing my body. "I remember waking up."

"Do you remember sleeping?"

My brows drew closer. "I was exhausted. I'd been running and running and — it was almost dawn, and I remember thinking I had to find a place before then." I frowned and squeezed my eyes tighter. "What an odd thing."

"It's not so odd," he said. "Do you remember anything before you started running? Do you remember what you were running from?"

I tipped my head to one side as images assaulted me in tiny, insignificant bits that told me nothing. "I remember a tall fence. I remember thinking, 'Don't touch.' I remember jumping it." I smiled a little and shook my head. "That part had to be a dream."

"Maybe. Go on. What about before the fence?"

I saw another flash, but it was brief. "A white room. Like a hospital room. And I . . . I have a blade. I'm . . ." My eyes flew open as shock jolted through me at what I had seen. The blade. My flesh. A spurting stream of blood.

"I cut my wrist!" And even as I said it, I turned my palms upward and stared at my wrists in search of the scars. "I must have been in some sort of . . . of asylum! I tried to kill myself. And then I ran away." I searched his face. "I'm an escaped lunatic, Ethan. And where are the scars? There should be scars on my wrists, where are the —"

"You didn't escape from an asylum. And you didn't try to kill yourself, Lilith."

"I didn't?" I shook my head, looking again at my wrists. "But . . . why would I cut myself like that? And where are the marks?" Meeting his gaze again, I said, "I'm not an ordinary person, am I, Ethan?"

"No. You're . . . like me."

"I'm not like you. I'm not like anyone. I can outrun a deer. I did, when I ran away. I can see perfectly in the dark, and over vast distances. I can hear so well I think I can hear the grass growing. Seriously, sometimes I hear things . . . that aren't . . . audible."

"Like . . . thoughts?" he asked.

51

I nodded. Then I blinked. "How do you know that?"

"Because you and I are the same, Lilith. We're not . . . exactly human." He came to me, sat beside me on the sofa and took both my hands in his.

"And there's more about your new nature that you don't yet know. Bigger things than you've had a chance to figure out yet. It's going to be hard to understand, but I want you to hear me out and just try to keep an open mind."

"All right."

He nodded, licked his lips and held my hands more tightly. "We don't — well, we don't age, Lilith."

I frowned as that statement sank into my brain and I tried to understand what it meant. A simple phrase. *We don't age.* And yet it couldn't mean what it seemed, on the surface, to mean.

"We only die if we bleed out, or if we're burned. Our bodies are extremely flammable. Open flame is dangerous to us. The sun, too, will roast us to death."

"The *sun?*" I sat up straighter, pulling my hands free of his and letting the blanket fall from my shoulders. "That's ludicrous."

"Any wounds we may suffer heal during the daytime. That's when we sleep. It's not by choice, mind you. We just lose consciousness when the sun comes up. We have to sleep where we're protected from it."

I blew air through my teeth, relieved as I realized he was joking. It wasn't very funny, but maybe he just had a twisted sense of humor. I shook my head and smiled. "Next you'll tell me we subsist on human bloo—" I broke off there, as my eyes shot to the empty stein on the table. And I knew. I *knew*. I gagged and clapped my palm over my mouth.

"Don't," he said. "You won't throw it up. There's some part of your mind that's repulsed by the notion, Lilith, but it's the part you let go of when your mortal life ended, the night you slit your wrists and let yourself bleed nearly to death before ingesting the blood of one of us to replenish you. To transform you."

"That's insane. Where would I get the . . . the blood of one of you?"

"Some sort of lab — not from a living being, or you wouldn't have had to cut your own wrists or go on the run on your own. Of course, I'm only guessing. How you got this way, I can't be sure. But I know what you are, Lilith. You, the woman you are now, are not sickened at the thought of drinking blood. You need it. You crave it.

You relish it.

"You're a vampire, Lilith. And so am I."

A vampire. It was insane. It couldn't be real.

But even as he said it, he pulled something from one of his pockets and held it out to me. It was a small round mirror, with a little wire hanger on it. He must have gotten it when he'd been in the kitchen getting me my . . . beverage.

I didn't move as he offered it to me.

"Go ahead. You're not going to believe me until you see proof. So take a look, Lilith. You cast no reflection. And while you're at it, feel your incisors. Or just take a look at mine."

He bared his teeth, and I sucked in a sharp breath and jerked backward. But even as I did, my tongue was exploring my own teeth and finding the same thing I'd seen in him. My eyeteeth were slightly elongated, pointed — and razor sharp. I met his eyes and had the feeling he knew what I had just discovered, and then I stood and reached for the mirror with a trembling hand.

I held it away from me and looked into it to be sure it reflected other things. The throw pillows, the dancing flames, the painting of Lilith above the hearth. It did.

Swallowing hard, I tipped the mirror

slowly toward my face. And then I blinked, because I wasn't there. The mirror reflected the wall behind me, but not me. I lifted a forefinger and moved it back and forth in front of the mirror. But there was no image reflected there.

My hands went numb, and the mirror fell to the floor and shattered.

4

Ethan had watched the reactions cross Lilith's beautiful face as he'd revealed, bit by bit, the truth to her. First there had been confusion, followed quickly by amusement when she finally got the gist of what he was trying to tell her — but thought he was making a joke.

But even then, there had been something more, something lying beneath it all. Some instinctive, living part of her being that recognized the truth when she heard it. And as he went on, slowly, ruthlessly, convincing her, *showing* her, her expression had turned to one of disbelief and then, as she gaped at the glass, to one of horror.

As the mirror fell, her body sank heavily, all at once, onto the sofa. She didn't fall, but she didn't sit down, either. She just . . . let go, landing hard on the cushions, her head hanging, eyes unfocused, gazing at nothing.

"Lilith . . ." he began as he moved closer, knelt in front of her, wished he could have found an easier way to tell her what she was.

"I knew," she whispered. "I mean, part of me knew. It didn't even sound untrue when you said it." Then she snapped her gaze up to his, focusing at last. "How did you know? Do you know me, Ethan?"

He averted his eyes. "Vampires can sense other vampires. I knew what you were before I ever set eyes on you in the stable. What I didn't know was whether you had come here to kill me."

"You keep saying that. Why?" she asked.

He sat in the chair again and let his own head fall forward as he rubbed the back of his neck and wrestled with his conscience. How much should he tell her? Because the thing was, he *did* know her. Though they'd had almost no interaction at The Farm, he knew her. He'd watched her, seen her, learned her nature. Her reaction, once she remembered, would be as predictable as her need for blood, her aversion to sunlight.

She would go back. He *knew* she would.

"I need to know," Lilith said softly. "If there are vampires out there hunting down and killing other vampires, then don't you think I need to know?"

"You'll be safe as long as you stay here."

57

His head came up then, and he plumbed her eyes and her mind at once. "And as long as you aren't lying to me."

"I've told you everything that's happened since I woke up beneath that bridge. It feels to me as if I were born in that moment."

He tipped his head to one side, ran a hand over his chin. "I suspect you were."

"What do you mean?"

"I believe, Lilith, that you were made over into a vampire, just prior to this . . . sleep. I think it likely that you awoke to your new life tonight for the very first time."

"Do vampires normally forget everything that came before?"

He shrugged. "I didn't. And I've never exactly . . . known any other vampires."

She flinched when he said that, her head jerking slightly to the left as her eyes squeezed tight.

"What? What is it?"

Brows furrowed, she pinched the bridge of her nose with thumb and forefinger. "A flash, maybe. I don't know."

"A memory?"

She opened her eyes and speared him with her steady gaze. "I saw a person — at least I think it was a person, though it looked more like a decomposing corpse. It was bound in chains, and I felt its agony. And that was all."

He tipped his head to one side, studying her and wondering what horrors she had seen at The Farm that he had not.

"Do you know what it could mean?" she asked.

He shook his head slowly. "No, I don't."

"What *do* you know about our kind?"

How could he answer that? He only knew the Chosen — the captives who, like the two of them, had been raised at The Farm. Everything he knew of vampires had been taught to him by the keepers. And he didn't trust them — he never had. But as he thought it over, he wondered. If amnesia *was* a common aftereffect of being made over, that would explain why he'd never heard from James in all this time. Maybe his brother didn't remember him.

"But then, why all the training and education? Why teach us things we're only going to forget?" he muttered.

"What are you talking about?"

He snapped his gaze back to hers, aware he'd journeyed deeply into his own mind. "Nothing," he said. "Just . . . thinking aloud."

"Oh." She stiffened her spine. "That's not the only . . . flash of memory I've had," she told him.

He looked at her and tried not to show her that the revelation startled him a bit. Hell, it wasn't as if he honestly wished her memory were gone forever. He just needed some time — to figure things out.

"I . . . remember kissing — or being kissed by — a man." She blinked, but didn't avert her eyes from his. "It felt like you."

"But we've only just met," he told her.

"Have we?"

Clearing his throat, he got to his feet, feeling fidgety. "I need to go back to the stable. I was on my way to tend the horses when I found you."

She nodded, then turned her back to him and walked toward the fireplace, leaning one hand on the mantel, lowering her head so that her hair fell as suddenly as a curtain falling across a stage. It was as if she were already alone in the room.

"You can come with me, if you like."

Without moving at all, she said, "I'll stay, if you don't mind. I have a lot to . . . process."

"All right." He started for the door, then paused, because he hadn't covered half what he needed to. And he wasn't certain how he could, not without revealing everything, something he wasn't confident enough of her motives to do yet. "Lilith, that car you encountered — the Escalade. Are you sure it didn't follow you here?"

"I'm sure."

Two words. He hoped she meant them. "If you need me . . ." he began.

"I'll open the door and shout."

No need. Just . . . shout at me with your mind. I'll hear you.

Her head rose slowly, and she turned toward him, blinking in surprise. "You will?"

Now that she was looking at him, she would know for sure he wasn't speaking aloud. This was a skill she needed, and one of the easiest to master — over short distances, at least, and with a willing partner.

It's one of the benefits of being . . . what we are, Lilith. He spoke to her clearly, without saying a word, and as she watched, her eyes sharpened with interest. *One of many,* he added. *It's not a bad thing, being immortal. Not at all.*

As he watched her closely, she closed her eyes, and then he heard her thinking, *But we aren't really immortal, are we?*

He smiled. "It depends on how we define the word, I suppose," he said aloud. "Take care around the fire."

She smiled, apparently pleased that he'd heard and answered her question. That she could speak to him with no more than a thought. He actually thought there might have a been a glimmer of the old light in her eyes.

"Thank you for taking me in, Ethan."

"You're very welcome," he said. And he meant it.

Because, after all, Lilith was the only thing about The Farm that he'd regretted leaving behind. He'd thought of her so much that he'd been unable to keep himself from buying the Waterhouse print when he'd seen it. Because it reminded him of her. Of Lilith. She'd been nineteen when he'd left, and already notorious. Everyone knew who she was.

She was the one they couldn't break. She was the one who would rather die than submit. She was the voice of his conscience whenever he closed his eyes long enough to listen. She was the face he couldn't stop seeing in his mind, the name he heard on the wind.

She was the one kiss he had never been able to forget.

He hadn't named her Lilith because *she* reminded him of the print. He'd bought the print because *it* reminded him of *her,* right down to her name.

She *was* Lilith.

And somehow, she had found him.

He was going to have to make her tell him how.

The taxi dropped Serena off in front of a cracker-box house in a neighborhood full of cracker-box houses and pulled away. She'd never felt more alone.

It wasn't a new sensation, of course. Serena had always been alone. She'd been orphaned at nineteen and had been making her own way ever since, waiting tables at the Broadway Grill, living in her tiny apartment in the low-rent district. On her own. That was how it had always been. The one-night stand that had resulted in the pregnancy had been just that. A one-night stand. A stranger in a bar on a particularly bad night when she'd been too depressed to want to go to bed alone. She didn't even know his name.

But for the last nine months, she hadn't felt lonely at all. She'd had her baby daughter growing inside her. She'd talked to her. She'd laughed with her. She'd sung to her and read her stories. Then she'd given birth to her — and someone had stolen her away.

It wasn't fair.

She'd briefly considered going back to her own apartment. Her own job. Her own life.

63

Until she'd seen the one person who had tried to help her blown to bits in her own car.

Now Serena was scared. She was angry, and she was grieving the loss of her baby, but fear had layered itself over both those emotions. She'd given her name and address, her employer and insurance information, when she'd checked into the hospital. She wasn't going back home, not until she knew exactly what was going on. It might not be safe.

So she stood in front of the little house staring down at the key chain from the knapsack and wondered briefly if this had been Maureen Keenan's home. If it was, and if Maureen had been killed because she'd tried to help her, then wouldn't those dark killers know where she lived? Wouldn't they be watching?

Serena turned and looked around. There were other houses just like this one lining both sides of the smooth, narrow, perfectly paved road. There were little maple trees spaced at regular intervals along both sides. There was a sidewalk unrolling in front of the houses, not a chip or a crack in it.

A few cars were parked in a few driveways. None along the curb. None with anyone lurking inside. There were swing sets and tricycles in several yards. The place looked for all the world like a cozy, friendly, safe little neighborhood. No faces peered out through parted curtains as far as she could see. Maybe it would be safe to go inside.

Drawing a breath, she went up the perfect little sidewalk to the front door, knocked and awaited an answer that never came. So, with hands that trembled, she slipped the key into the lock, turned it and opened the door.

The house was dark, but it wasn't empty. She didn't know why no one had answered the door, but she could feel another's presence. And along with that feeling, there were the aromas. She smelled something hot and rich, and her stomach growled.

She looked through the darkened room she had entered to the rectangle of light that was an open doorway at the far end. A woman's form stepped into that opening, no more than a dark silhouette.

"Serena?" the shadow asked softly, but the tone of her voice said she already knew.

"Yes."

"And where is Maureen?"

Serena got the feeling that the faceless woman already knew what her response to that question would be, as well. "I . . . got off the bus where she told me. And she was

there, in her car, and she waved to me. . . ."
She spoke faster than she should have, her tempo increasing as she went on. "I started to cross the street, and then her car, it just — it just — exploded. And she was . . . she was gone. She was just gone, and I couldn't —"

Her throat closed too tightly to let her go on, and she tipped her head back, eyes focused on the ceiling as she tried to swallow, tried not to just burst into the hysterical tears she felt pushing at the gates to get through.

She heard the woman's footsteps coming closer. Felt a hand on her shoulder and lowered her head to see a pair of kind eyes brimming with tears, an attractive face with full lips that trembled and high cheekbones that seemed pale in the insufficient light.

"I'm so sorry," Serena said, and sniffled hard. "She was your friend, wasn't she?"

"She was . . . more than a friend. She was a sister. Not by blood, but . . . well, hell, you'll understand soon enough."

"Why was she killed?" Serena's stomach clenched, and she tried to quell the sickness writhing inside her. "Was it because she tried to help me?"

"She knew exactly what she was risking, Serena." The stranger squeezed Serena's shoulder and spoke these words firmly, as if they were very important. "This . . . this situation is way bigger than just you or your baby. You bear no responsibility for what happened to Maureen. Even if she had known what the outcome would be, she would have done exactly the same thing."

Serena lowered her head and let the tears flow. "I'm so confused. I don't know what's going on. Where's my baby? Why would someone take her? Why would they kill an innocent nurse?"

"I know all this is overwhelming to you right now. But I'm going to explain everything, I promise. Just . . . not here."

"We have to go?" Serena knew her tone was whiney, and yet she couldn't help herself. "But I'm so tired."

"I know. I've made you soup and a sandwich to eat on the way. This is a safe house, but we can't risk that you might have been followed. My car's in the garage. This way."

The woman took Serena's arm and led her to the kitchen, where the stranger picked up a Thermos and a zipper bag with a sandwich and a spoon tucked inside.

"Grab something to drink from the fridge, and then we'll get out of here," she instructed.

Serena opened the refrigerator, which was

well-stocked, as if someone lived here.
Maybe someone did. Or had. She pulled
out two bottles of diet cola and closed the
fridge again. The woman was opening a
door, and beyond it Serena saw the garage
and a blue compact car.

"Come on."

"No." Serena stood where she was, finding her spine and her courage at last. "No,
not until you tell me."

Nodding, the woman asked, "What would
you like to know?"

Serena frowned as her mind raced. "Something. Anything. Where we're going. Who's
after us. Where my baby is. Even . . . your
freaking name. Tell me something, for God's
sake."

The woman's face softened. She was
perhaps thirty, Serena thought. Brunette
hair in a silky, minklike ponytail. Brown
doe's eyes beneath perfectly arched brows,
and skin like a fresh peach, devoid of
makeup.

"Terry. My name's Terry. I'm part of a . . .
a secret society, I guess you'd call it. The
Sisterhood of Athena. We . . . we watch, and
almost never interfere. But when things go
wrong, we step in to set them right again.
Maureen was one of us."

"You . . . watch . . . ?"

"Yes."

"You watch . . . what?" Serena asked.

Terry pressed her lips tight, as if deciding which words to allow passage. "Your baby was — is — special, Serena. She was born with a very rare antigen in her blood."

Serena remembered the file she had read. There had been something about an antigen. "Belladonna," she said, trying out the word for the first time.

"Yes. Belladonna. People who are born with the Belladonna antigen have . . . special qualities. It's complicated, and it's something you need to hear about, but later, when we have more time, and when we're sure we're safe. But for now, all you need to know is that babies and young children with the antigen have been disappearing at an alarming rate for the past five years. And in most cases, their parents have been killed."

Serena felt her eyes widen, her heart skip. "Murdered?"

Terry nodded once. "Usually it looks like an accident. Car wrecks. Plane crashes. Carbon monoxide leaks. House fires. Deadly falls from dangerous cliffs. Drownings. But it's happened too many times for it to be coincidence. So we've placed some of our members in various places — hospitals, doctor's offices, child protective agencies —

undercover, just to watch and wait. And when someone mentions the antigen, we try to get to the mother and the baby before it's too late. Maureen wanted to get to you before they took your baby, but the best she could do was get to you before they arranged some accident that would take your life."

Serena watched Terry's face while she spoke. The things the woman was saying didn't make a lot of sense, but she believed them. Maureen had believed them. She'd died because of them. How could Serena doubt?

"So where are you taking me?"

Terry put her hand on Serena's shoulder. "Someplace safe."

"Is it far? I mean, I can't go far. I need to find my baby."

Terry lowered her eyes, and her voice softened by degrees. "If you choose to stay with us, we'll help you search for your baby, Serena. We have more resources, more connections — a much better chance than you would ever have alone. But it would mean giving up everything you've known before. Joining the Sisterhood means being reborn. You'll have a new family, a new life. Your past will be lost to you forever."

Serena pondered briefly before asking,

"Have you found any of the other children who've been taken?"

"No. Not yet. But we're getting closer all the time."

"Oh." A wave of disappointment nearly drowned her, but she managed to push it aside. "Then . . . I don't know."

"You don't have to make a decision now. You can spend a few days with us, learn a little bit more about what we do and why, and then you can decide. If you want to leave, you can. But the truth is, you're not safe here. And we have to go. Now."

Serena nodded. "All right."

She followed Terry to the little blue car. Terry started the engine, thumbed a button to open the garage door and then backed out, looking both ways. As she drove, she checked the rearview mirror almost constantly.

"Go ahead and eat," Terry said at length. "You need your strength, and besides, it'll settle your nerves." She nodded at the Thermos and sandwich she had placed in the console between them. Their drinks were in the cup holders.

Serena twisted open the Thermos and poured some of the steaming-hot chicken soup into the cup. Then she sipped, and it soothed her stomach, eased the tension in her spine and even the ache in her heart a little bit, so she sipped some more. When she finished the first cup, she filled it a second time and downed that, as well.

And with every sip her anxiety eased a bit. She sank into her seat, let her head rest against the back as she swallowed the last of the soup and replaced the cup.

Her eyes felt heavy. She let them fall closed, then opened them abruptly as a wave of gentle relaxation washed through her brain.

Frowning, she looked toward Terry. "Was there . . . Did you put something in the soup?"

"Yes. Nothing harmful. But we're going to the Sisterhood's headquarters, and it's not permitted for outsiders to know where that is. No matter what. So you're going to sleep now. You need to anyway, Serena. And when you wake, you'll be in a beautiful, safe haven, surrounded by women who would give their lives for each other — and who would give their lives to help you find your baby, as well."

There couldn't be any such place or any such people, Serena thought. No one could possibly care that much about someone they didn't even know.

Could they?

She let her heavy lids fall closed and prayed that they could.

5

When Ethan left, I hurried to the front door to watch. Just to be sure he really was going and not playing some trick to catch me in the act. But he kept walking right along the meandering path and on to the stable.

I let the heavy curtain fall and turned, sweeping the living room with my sharper-than-human gaze. He was lying to me. I didn't know how I knew it, but I did. I wasn't sure what he was lying about — but there was something.

He was familiar to me somehow. Despite my amnesia, I was sure of it. It wasn't a memory, it was a sense. A feeling.

My senses were sharper than before. He'd told me as much. And there were new ones. I could speak without speaking, sense another's essence, almost like a scent, without smelling. I could feel the approach of danger. I could tell whether another be-ing was human — or a vampire, like me.

With all that knowledge slowly making itself at home in my mind, how could I doubt this feeling of recognition when it came to him?

Or worse, the feeling of longing that had plagued me from the moment I set eyes on him. The longing to be closer. To touch. To feel those hands on my body, those lips on . . .

No. I wouldn't let those thoughts linger. He was lying to me. There was something more to all of this than he was telling me. And if I had to search this entire place, I would find out what it was.

I looked around the living room and whispered, "It's always best to begin where you are." I vaguely remembered someone saying that phrase often, and how wise I thought it was.

A woman. A kind woman. A mortal.

I got a flash of short butterscotch hair that curled inward, just below the ear, and blue, twinkling eyes. The life in those eyes had always seemed out of place amid all the dull-eyed others.

What others?

I didn't know, but in my mind, I saw her lips move and heard her voice saying, "It's always best to start where you are."

Callista.

The name floated into my mind as if from nowhere. Her name was Callista, and she wasn't like the others.

And that was all. Though I fought to grab hold of the memory and wrestle more from it, it was like trying to grab a handful of mist. And yet I was reassured even by that slightest touch of the familiar when all the world was foreign.

It emboldened me.

My memory wasn't gone forever. It was returning, albeit in pieces. And so I began searching Ethan's haven, hoping to find some clue to my past, to how I knew him, that might tease my wounded mind into telling me more about who and what I was. But even as I did, a niggling worry crept into my brain, and I found myself moving to the window, parting the curtain and gazing out toward the stable. What if he didn't come back? What if he had abandoned me?

Just like before.

I frowned at the odd thought that had crept, unbidden, into my mind. And I was more certain than ever that I knew him. We had a history. God, why couldn't I remember?

Serena woke to find herself lying on a fainting couch in a large room that had to be part of a mansion. That was her first impression as she blinked, pressed a hand to her head and sat up slowly. She looked around and saw women standing in small groups of two or three in different parts of the room, all speaking softly, nodding sadly, sipping from china cups and nibbling on pastries. Terry was there.

One of the women noticed her and, meeting her eyes, said, "You're awake."

And then, one by one, the others turned their attention to her. Serena noticed that some sets of eyes were damp and remembered Maureen being blown to bits, all because she'd tried to help.

"Hello, Serena," one of the women said. She set down her teacup and made her way over, taking a seat beside Serena. She was beautiful, probably in her thirties, though she had an ageless look that could be very deceiving. All the women did. There was a wisdom in their eyes that suggested the toned bodies and unlined faces were less than the entire story.

The woman indicated the tea service that sat on a table across the room. China, a pink pattern that looked Asian. Another woman quickly poured a cup of tea.

"My name is Ginger. I'm the leader here. And I'm very sorry about your baby."

Serena nodded, tried to speak, but her voice caught in her throat. Kind hands pressed a warm cup into her own, and she took it and sipped. It was hot and sweet and creamy. That other woman had also brought over a plate of pastries.

"Didn't know if you take cream and sugar, but I figured you could use them after what you've been through."

Serena sipped some more. "Thank you." And then she looked at Ginger again. "I'm sorry about your . . . about Maureen."

"Maureen wouldn't have a single regret, other than maybe not finding the bomb before it went off. I can promise you that. She lived for this work."

Serena blinked and looked around the room. "This work . . . Which is . . . ?" Then she licked her lips. "Do you know who took my baby? Or why?" And then, frowning, she added, "Terry said something about a rare antigen in her blood."

"Yes," Ginger said. "I suspect a government agency is behind this. One most people believe ceased to exist several years ago. It was known as the DPI, and it was a highly classified, top-secret subdivision of the CIA."

Serena felt her eyes widen, and a million questions swirled in her mind. "What does it stand for? DPI?"

"The Division of Paranormal Investigations," Ginger said.

Ginger was watching her closely, gauging her reactions, Serena thought. She clearly didn't want to upset her, but she wasn't coddling her, either. Not telling her she'd been through enough for one day or asking her to wait, but giving her direct answers to her questions.

"It's a bit of a misnomer, though," Ginger went on. "Their interest in most areas of the paranormal is shallow, at best. Their real focus is on the Undead. Vampires."

Serena blinked, and her gaze shifted from one woman to another, looking for the giveaway. This had to be a joke. But no one was smiling.

"Are you trying to tell me that my baby was a —"

"Oh, God, no," Ginger said with a wave of her hand. "No, but as her mother, you do need to know about them. No, your baby was human through and through. But she's related to them, in a way. You see, every vampire in existence was born human, and every one of them was born with the Belladonna antigen. It's the thing that allows them to become vampires."

Serena sat there, taking in this outrageous, impossible information.

"I know it's hard to believe, much less understand. But if you stay with us, you'll see proof soon enough. And I want you to know that even if you don't choose to join us, we'll try to find your baby for you. And we'll trust you to leave with information few outsiders have ever been allowed to possess. As the mother of one of the Chosen, you have a right to know."

"The Chosen?"

"That's what those with the antigen are called. Vampires, by nature, sense them, and they're compelled to protect and watch over them. But lately, the Chosen have been vanishing. The vampire community is aware of it, too. But so far, no one knows where the children are being taken or why."

"But . . . you have your suspicions?" Serena asked.

"Yes, but we have no real information."

"What did the DPI do before they were supposedly shut down or whatever?"

Ginger looked away, met Terry's eyes and licked her lips nervously. Serena knew that whatever was coming wasn't good.

"They were mostly interested in . . . research. Learning how vampires' bodies work, how to control them, how to eliminate them."

A small cry flew from Serena's lips before she could bite it back. "You think my baby is a lab rat for some government experiment?"

"We have absolutely no evidence of that."

"Oh God." Serena lowered her face to her hands, sobbing so hard she thought her chest would tear in two.

The rest of the women left the room one by one. She heard them leaving, felt the emptiness when they had gone, then lifted her head and wiped her eyes. Terry and Ginger now sat on either side of her.

"I don't understand what it is you do here."

"We're the Sisterhood of Athena, and we've existed for centuries. What we do — well, we watch. We observe. We try not to interfere unless it's absolutely necessary. Our stated mission is to protect the supernatural order. Which is really the natural order, simply the parts of it that few people know about."

"You . . . protect the vampires?"

"They have a right to exist. They're a part of creation, just as we are, and their elimination would send things out of balance, just as the extinction of any species would. We want to see them allowed to live naturally, evolving in whatever way they're supposed to, without interference from humans."

"But . . . don't they . . . you know, feed on humans?"

"They're just like us, Serena," Ginger said. "There are good ones and bad ones. When there is a bad one, though, the good ones tend to get rid of him. They feed on blood from blood banks or occasionally take criminals. Few ever kill a human being except in self-defense. They're just people.

"So we observe," she went on. "And yes, when necessary, we protect. Even the vampires aren't supposed to know of our existence — that's how discreet we are."

"What we do here is dangerous," Terry said. "Working against government agencies, undercover assassins, vampire hunters who want to exterminate them all."

"Not to mention," Ginger added, "the vampires themselves. Sometimes when they catch on to our knowledge of them, catch one of us snooping around their secrets, they see us as a threat. It's not always possible to explain in time."

Serena closed her eyes slowly. "This is a lot. It's just . . . a lot."

"We know," Ginger told her. "But that's about all the information I'm willing to give you for now. If you decide to stay, to join us, you'll be entrusted with more. A great deal more. Our history, case files from which you will study and learn, physical training, and mental training, as well. But all of that is for later. And you don't have to make any decisions right now. Stay with us for a few days. Recover your strength. We'll begin searching for clues about your baby. Maybe she'll be the one who leads us to the rest of the missing Chosen."

"Yes," Terry said. "Just be our guest and relax. If you want to go back to your old life in a few days, that's fine. We'll trust you to keep your knowledge of us secret. We know you will, because we're the only hope you have of finding her."

Serena nodded. "You're right about that. I wouldn't betray your secrets. But I don't need a few days to think about it."

"Careful, Serena," Ginger said. "This is not a decision that can be undone. If you join this sisterhood, you join for good. There's no going back to your old life."

"I have no life to go back to. All I had was my baby. And I'll devote the rest of my life to searching for her and making those who took her pay — and making sure they can't keep doing this to women like me, to babies like mine."

Ginger slid a look at Terry, who shrugged.

"I'm sure," Serena said, looking from one to the other. "I want to join the Sisterhood of Athena."

Ginger nodded. "So be it, then. I'll make arrangements for the dedication ceremony. But you'll still need a few days to recover, and to prepare. There are lessons, meditations. But tomorrow is soon enough to begin." She turned to the other woman.

"Terry, why don't you show our new sister to her rooms now?"

The Present

Ethan opened the rear door of the stable, and it swung wide onto a grassy moonlit meadow, five acres, enclosed by a white wooden fence that seemed to rise and fall with every curve of the ground. A bubbling stream bisected the meadow, providing a supply of fresh water. And beyond the meadow, the trees began, then thickened into a full-blown forest that stretched all the way to the mountains that formed a backdrop to the view.

He loved it here.

He went back inside and opened first one stall, then the other. His companions knew without being told that it was their time to romp, and they trotted out of their stalls and straight through the open back door, barely pausing long enough to accept Ethan's strokes as they went.

Ethan watched them as they moved. The second they emerged from the building, they tossed their manes and cut loose into a full gallop, whinnying in joy as they raced into the night.

No one liked being shut in. Being captive. Even knowing they would be released each night, the horses always reacted as if they'd been locked up for years and were just catching their first taste of freedom.

They felt, he thought, the way he'd felt when he'd escaped from The Farm. The way he still felt, every single evening, when the sun set and he awoke to freedom.

He took a fork and shovel and moved into the first stall to begin the usual soothing tasks of cleaning the stall and putting down fresh bedding.

He wouldn't risk his freedom for anything. Not even for Lilith. God, he wished his brother were here to tell him what the hell to do about her. She could be lying. She could be faking the amnesia. She could have been sent to kill him. It was, after all, inevitable that they would send someone sooner or later. And even if she wasn't the one, she could have been followed, all the while being totally unaware of it.

She was a risk. A threat to his freedom. So why the hell hadn't he sent her packing?

Lowering his head, he realized why. Because it would do no good. To send her away would risk her telling others where he was. The only way to ensure that never happened would be to keep her here — or kill her.

He paused in his work, leaning on the shovel's long handle and closing his eyes. He knew damned good and well that he couldn't kill her. He'd wronged the woman. He'd been racked with guilt ever since he'd been forced to leave her behind. And he'd wanted to go back for her — but he hadn't.

Because he would have had no chance of surviving. Because he hadn't even known if she was still alive. Because he'd thought if he could only find his brother first, maybe the two of them could save her. And most of all, because he'd known she would refuse to leave that place without taking every other captive along with her. And that would have been impossible.

So he hadn't gone back for her. And he knew damn well that part of the reason he wasn't telling her the truth about how they

86

knew one another was because it would mean admitting what he had done. That he'd saved himself and left her behind, and that had been eating his soul bit by bit ever since.

Finishing the stall-cleaning in record time — because leaving her alone in his haven made him nervous as hell — he returned the tools to their places, closed the rear door and headed out the front, then along the winding pathway back toward the house.

Through the window, he saw her, a silhouette backlit by the fire's amber glow, and the sight of her stopped him in his tracks. She was beautiful.

For years at The Farm, he'd watched her from a distance, and early on, he'd feared for her. Almost weekly, she would be punished for refusing to submit to the rules or learn the lessons or vow obedience to the DPI. More recently, she'd been in trouble for trying to stir revolt in the others. The two of them had barely even talked. But eventually she'd noticed him looking at her when they passed on the compound. The DPI kept their captive males separate from the females. They were closely guarded, their every moment scheduled for them, from lessons and training to limited recreation. They were told when it was time to take to their cots in their barracks, and told when it was time to rise and begin another day. Even their bathroom and shower usage was rigidly scheduled. There was little time to form friendships or have casual conversations.

He always saw her among a line of girls as they walked from their barracks to the classroom. He would be in a line of young men, walking the opposite way, after combat training.

When she noticed him, she looked back. And she kept looking. Day in and day out, that was their only communication. Until that last night, the night he'd left.

That night, he had crept into her barracks, hoping against hope that there would be some way to take her with him, avoiding the guard, risking everything for this one moment. And as the others slept, he'd slipped silently between the two rows of cots, straining his still-mortal eyes to see each sleeping face, until he found her.

She lay awake, eyes open, but not truly seeing. She'd been in isolation for the past week, drugged, punished for her ongoing disobedience. He couldn't imagine what had been done to her. And he didn't want to.

He thought she'd been aware of him, even

in her stupor, ever since he'd climbed, awkwardly, through the open window, and he'd paused momentarily when he met her curious, unfocused eyes. Then, when she opened her mouth to speak, he quickly put a finger to his lips to silence her.

At last he moved closer and knelt beside the cot. She rolled onto her side, propped her head on her hand, too weak even to hold it up otherwise, and stared at him, a thousand emotions in her eyes. A thousand questions. And a yearning that could not be concealed, even by the drugs still coursing through her veins.

Without a word, he cupped her face between his palms, leaned closer and pressed his lips to hers. He felt them part, felt them tremble, and then felt the warmth of her breath as she released it all at once. At last her arms slid around him, and his body caught fire. He kissed her more deeply, more passionately, and she responded with an eagerness that thrilled him. On and on they kissed, until someone in another bed stirred, and the sound made them jerk apart all at once.

She was breathing hard. So was he, and nearly too aroused to force himself to stop. He'd never kissed a woman before that night. He was certain that she was every bit as innocent as him.

Leaning closer, his lips against her ear, he whispered, "I'm sorry." And then, calling up every ounce of willpower he possessed, he rose. It was almost physically painful to turn away from those wide, passion-glazed eyes. But he did. He walked away from her, slipped out the window and put his plan for escape into motion.

And for that, even though it had meant his very survival, he would never forgive himself.

I had opened every drawer, fanned the pages of each book on Ethan's bookshelves, explored every cabinet and closet, and still I had found no clue as to his past. Or mine.

Maybe I was imagining the familiarity. Maybe it didn't mean anything at all. Maybe . . .

I sensed that he was near and turned my head slightly to see him standing a few yards from the house, staring through the window at me. I couldn't help but smile a little bit at the sight of him, so great was my relief that he had actually come back. And in spite of my fear that I would seem silly and needy, I hurried to the door and flung it open.

He remained still for only a moment, as

his eyes met mine, and I felt the oddest familiarity about the intense gaze we shared. Everything inside me seemed to quiver with an unnamed anticipation. My stomach clenched tight when he started walking toward me. It was only a few steps, and yet they were powerful, deliberate strides, and I shivered in delicious longing.

I only moved away when he reached the doorway, and then only enough to let him pass through. As soon as he stepped across the threshold, his arms snapped around my waist and pulled me hard against him. He lowered his head and took my mouth in a way that told me he was eager, that he was hungry for me. I felt an answering hunger burning inside me as I opened to him, threaded my fingers through his hair and kissed him back as my body seemed to burst into flame.

I had been taught about the workings of the human body — how, when, by whom, I did not know. The knowledge, though, remained. I knew about mating and repro-duction — at least as such things pertained to mortals. I had no idea what, if anything, was different among our kind. The Undead. And yet I had never, I thought, understood or expected this feeling that engulfed me in that moment in his arms. I had never, I thought, realized that there would be this fire.

Or had I? Because his kiss was . . . familiar.

When he finally lifted his head, I opened my eyes and then gasped, because his were glowing, as if this fire I felt was burning in him, too, and had made itself real, visible there in his eyes.

I couldn't look away. "Are my eyes glowing, too?" I asked him.

He nodded, searching my face.

A wave of tiredness washed over me then, suddenly and without warning. My knees felt weak, but I stiffened them — and my slowly relaxing spine, as well.

"You've kissed me before, Ethan," I told him. "I know you have."

Again he nodded.

"You have to tell me. Please, Ethan, I want to know. I want it as badly as I want — as I want . . . you."

He almost smiled. But only with his lips. A brief tug at the corners of his delicious mouth, and then it was gone. His eyes, as the fiery glow faded, seemed to convey worry — a worry I didn't understand. At last he nodded. "I'll tell you. I'll tell you all of it. But there's a lot, and we're out of time."

"Out of time?" I frowned, not understanding, but my eyes felt inexplicably heavy, and my neck seemed too weak, suddenly, to support the weight of my head.

"You feel it. I can see you do. The sun's about to rise, Lilith. We need to rest now. I wish to God we had a choice in the matter." And even as he said it, he turned me slightly, keeping one arm around my waist, propelling me forward at his side. He paused only long enough to close and lock the door, never letting go of his hold on me, and then he guided me toward the stairs.

My head fell sideways against his powerful shoulder as we climbed, and my body slumped once more. Instantly Ethan scooped me up in his strong arms. I curled my own arms around his neck and was asleep before we reached the top of the stairway.

6

Present Day

Ginger Walters, head of the Appalachian Regional Branch of the Sisterhood of Athena, frowned at the telephone as it rang.

Serena looked over at her with curiosity, but nothing more than that. She'd been living with the sisters for more than twenty years now, and she knew how things worked. You knew what you needed to know, nothing more. Hell, aside from herself, Terry — who'd brought her here — Ginger and a handful of others, no one in the entire organization knew that she was the mother of one of the Chosen, one of those rare humans who had the potential to become a vampire. One of the people they watched. Ginger said they never would have let her in, if they'd known. "They" being the higher-ups in the organization. To say they were strict was an understatement. In her time there, Serena had picked up on the unspoken knowledge that once a woman joined the Sisterhood, she was never allowed to leave.

Never.

As they grew older, members were transferred to other branches, where research, record-keeping and the like became their jobs, while younger recruits replaced them in the ranks.

That no one left was extreme, perhaps. But she could see the need for such measures. And the need for secrecy, the need for all of it. She had become as loyal and as devoted to the cause as any of them.

They were just returning from the wide, fenced-in and ultraprivate lawn in back, where they gathered morning and evening for chi kung and kung fu practice. She had a towel around her neck, was wearing a sweat-damp *gi* with a black belt around her waist and was barefoot. So were the others who trooped through the house ahead of her, all of them heading to their rooms for a shower.

They'd come in through the rear door, so it was the kitchen telephone that had sidetracked the honcha, as Serena liked to call their leader. But when Ginger brought the phone to her ear and said, "This is Ginger Walters. Who is calling?" there was something off about her tone. Something that brought Serena up short.

And when she saw the look on the other woman's face, she knew something big was going on.

Ginger's eyes shot to hers. "Get Terry back here, and close the door. Hurry."

Serena nodded and ran out of the room. The others had gone their various ways, but her shout brought Terry in a hurry. Maybe her own voice was giving things away, too. But even if it did, the others wouldn't snoop or pry or try to listen in. It just wasn't how they operated. They trusted each other — they had to. Their lives too often depended on it.

Terry joined her, and together they rushed back into the kitchen. Serena closed the door behind them, and Ginger said, "All right, Callista. Go ahead." And then she pressed the speaker button and set the receiver down.

"Callista?" Serena whispered in disbelief, sending a quick stunned look at Terry. It had been twenty-eight months since anyone had heard a word from her. She was a sister who had begun a passionate affair with a suspected DPI operative, pretending to know nothing about his work the entire time. Eventually she'd become close enough to him to win his trust, and he had helped her get a job as a "keeper" at some mysterious place they called "The Farm."

She'd planned to work undercover, to send back information on The Farm's location and find out whether the place had anything to do with the missing children they'd been trying for so long to find, including Serena's own missing baby girl — who would be twenty-one years old by now. But it had been as if Callista had fallen off the planet. And no amount of searching or digging had turned up any sign that she was still alive.

All of that whirled through Serena's mind like a twister, and then she was focused again on the call.

"Go ahead, Callista," Ginger said. "Where are you?"

"I'm at The Farm." The words were whispered. Frowning, Ginger hit the volume button. "I've been here the entire time, but what they don't tell you 'til you're here is that once you're hired, there's no contact with the outside world. You're not allowed to leave until your contract is up. And even then . . ."

"So how are you making this call?"

"They'll kill me if they find out. I stole a cell phone from a guard who smuggled it in. If he reports it, they'll shoot him, though, so I might be safe. And I *had* to get in touch."

"Why?"

"Serena's daughter —"

"She's *there?*" Serena lurched closer to the phone, as if she could grab hold of it, and her child through it.

"She was," Callista said. "A prisoner — one of many. But she escaped. I'm fairly certain she . . . she changed over first."

Serena felt her body turn to stone. She couldn't move. She couldn't feel. She was devoid of warmth. "She's . . . she's a . . ." God, she couldn't even *say* it.

"I think so, Serena. She goes by the name of Lilith. But after an earlier escape, the keepers instituted a new tagging program. The residents have all been implanted with a tracking device that can be remotely activated if they get away. All without their knowledge. They'll find her in short order, and when they do, she'll be executed. That's why I had to risk everything to call you. You have to get to her before they do."

Serena nodded dumbly. Terry's arm came around her shoulders, as if to comfort her or soothe her tears. But there were none. She couldn't cry. She'd lost her daughter. She'd *lost* her. Lilith wasn't even human anymore.

"Callista, can you get out of there?" Ginger asked.

"I couldn't before, and now that Lilith has gotten away, security has gone through the roof. I'll look for an opportunity, but I have a feeling I'm going to have to stay another eight months, until my contract is up."

"They let people leave after that?" Ginger asked. "They trust them to keep quiet?"

"Anyone who talks is tracked down and executed. They make very sure we all know that."

Ginger nodded. "So tell me all you can now, then, if it's safe."

"It's not. But I might never get another chance. I can't tell you where The Farm is. They blindfold us when they bring us in, and we never leave until our time is up. I have no idea where I am. But I do know it's about two hours from Athena House, maybe less. They could have driven me around in circles for a while to throw me off, for all I know."

"Okay. What else do you know, Callista? What do they *do* there?"

"Program children. Brainwash them. Train them to . . . to kill on command. To obey without question. They're taking any kids with the antigen that they can get their hands on and raising them here. When they're grown, they transform them and take them elsewhere. They are . . . they're creating a vampire army, Ginger. Loyal to the point of death to the United States' government's most ultrasecret agency."

Ginger's eyes went wide with horror, and she gazed at the other two. Serena felt her heart breaking.

"They couldn't break your daughter's spirit, Serena," Callista went on. "You should know that. She never lost her will. She was a rebel to the core."

A little frown bent Serena's brows.

"She's an incredible woman," Callista continued. "Vampire or not. I . . . I loved her. You will, too. If you can get to her in time." She paused, then added, "I'm sending you an e-mail from this phone with her picture. It should help."

Ginger nodded slowly, then began to pace. "I don't suppose you have any idea where she would have gone, do you?"

"Only one clue," Callista said. "A month after I arrived here, there was another escape. A young man called Ethan. No last name, as far as I know. I sort of . . . helped him. But I had no choice."

"We know about a vampire called Ethan!"

100

Terry said. "He has a place in Mesina. We've had him on the radar for a year now."

"He's a legend here. So will Lilith be, before week's end. But . . . she used to talk about him. And there was something in her eyes and her voice when she did . . . I don't think I'm imagining it. And I know he had feelings for her. So maybe . . ."

"Good work, Callista."

"Thank you. Thank you so, so much," Serena said. "Please be safe."

"I'll do my best. I want to get out of here as badly as — I've gotta go."

And that was it. The connection was broken.

Ginger hung up the phone and turned to look at Terry and Serena. "It's time we notified the powers that be of what we've been up to. It's going to take more than just the three of us to protect Lilith and rescue Callista."

"It's going to take more than the powers that be," Terry said. "More than the entire sisterhood."

Serena nodded. "If they have a vampire army, the only way we're going to fight them is if we get one of our own."

"Absolutely not." Ginger shook her head firmly. "We do not interact with them. We try not to so much as reveal our *existence* to the Undead. That's policy, and it's one I agree with — one that's essential to our continued ability to operate. Do not even think about breaking it. Is that understood?"

Serena nodded and lowered her head.

"Good. Now, let's get out to that vampire's ranch shortly after nightfall and see if we can find your daughter. If nothing more, maybe we can at least warn her."

Lifting her head, Serena felt lighter. "My God," she whispered. "I might actually see her . . . tonight."

"You can see her now," Ginger said, and, smiling, she led the way through the kitchen and the huge formal dining room, then into the library. She closed the door and quickly moved behind the desk, where, without even sitting down, she began tapping on the keyboard. After a moment, she straightened and smiled slowly. "She looks like you."

Her heart in her throat, Serena moved around the desk and blinked away the tears that blurred her vision. There on the monitor screen was a photo of a beautiful young woman with spiraling auburn curls and vivid green eyes.

At her shoulder, Terry whispered, "She's beautiful."

Serena nodded but found herself too overcome with emotion to speak. All she could manage was to raise one trembling hand and press her fingertips to her daughter's cheek as tears finally spilled down her own.

Ethan woke at sundown with Lilith curled in his arms — just the way he'd gone to sleep. Maybe he shouldn't have done it, but he'd carried her into his room that morning. He'd changed his own clothes and left hers in place — though that still consisted of only his button-down shirt, which was far too big. Then he'd crawled into the bed and curved his body to fit hers, wrapping her in his arms, and he relished both his relief that she was okay and his admiration for her strength.

As he'd drifted into sleep, he'd traveled backward in his mind to his final night in captivity.

He'd kissed her that night, which had done nothing but leave him wanting more and aching at the impossibility of what he had to do: to leave there — to leave *her* . . .

"You *have to. Now,* Ethan."

He nodded, hearing the soft whisper from beyond the window. Callista, one of the keepers — but one who was so different from the others that he wondered who she really was.

He stood by the barracks window, but for the life of him, he couldn't move any farther. He stood as if rooted to the spot, relishing what he was certain would be his last sight of Lilith.

"Ethan, it's for her sake, as well."

He shook his head, but he somehow tore his eyes from her and moved away, careful not to make a sound as he slipped outside, watching and listening with everything in him.

Callista moved at his side. It had been a warm autumn night, that first night of his new life. And it had been . . . almost anticlimactic, the way it had all taken place.

She took him to the most remote area within the compound: a stand of brush and a handful of scrub-apple trees, between the southernmost outbuildings and the electrified fence. She led the way, hurrying, and nervous as hell.

Finally she pointed to a blanket on the weedy ground. "Lie down."

He frowned at her. "I thought you were going to help me escape."

"You can only escape if you can jump the fence, and you can only jump the fence if you're a vampire. So I'm going to help you change over. Lie down."

He went still and stiff, suddenly wary. "Is

this some kind of a trick, Callista? Are you testing me, so that the minute I agree, the other keepers will jump out and punish me? Is this the challenge you said they were about to give me? The one you said I was certain to fail?"

"No, Ethan." She knelt beside the blanket, opened a pack and began removing bags of blood and tubing from it. "The challenge they would have given you would have proven to them whether you could be trusted once you'd been transformed."

He sat on the ground, but he didn't lie down. Overhead, the stars gleamed bright, flickering like fireflies on the velvet blanket of the night. In the distance, a night bird mourned.

"And if I failed, they wouldn't change me. I would stay as I am. I don't see that as such a bad thing."

"If you fail, Ethan, your fate will be far worse than death."

"What could be worse than death?" he asked, arrogant laughter in his tone. But when Callista met his eyes, the look in hers made his blood turn cold.

"They would transform you anyway. And then they would drug and starve you to keep you weak, and drain your blood when-ever they needed it to create another vampire. You would be nothing more than a machine to dispense blood, your entire existence lived in a tiny cell with no light, no heat, no human contact."

He blinked and gave his head a shake. "Is that . . . is that how they do it? They have a captive vampire somewhere?"

"Mmm," she said with a nod. "But he's not going to live much longer. They need . . . new blood, if you'll pardon the pun."

He swallowed, his eye drawn to the bags. "This came from him?"

"With his blessing," she said. "He wants you to get out as badly as I do."

He licked his lips, then looked away from her very quickly. "I can't go. I can't leave her behind."

"I told you, she's too weak tonight."

"Then I'll just have to pass this challenge of theirs and stay in their good graces."

"Pass the test and they'll send you away all the same, but in their employ, not as a free being. But you won't pass the test Ethan. You won't."

"How can you be so sure?"

She met his eyes, at the same time pressing against his chest to get him to lie down. He resisted, and she whispered, "Their plan is to order you to kill Lilith. They make every test fit the person, and they know you feel something for her, so asking you to kill her will test you in a way nothing else can."

The strength went out of him, along with his breath, allowing Callista to push him flat on his back. Before he could even blink, she was rolling up his sleeve and sinking a needle into his arm. It led to a tube, which led to a pit he hadn't noticed before, dug in the sandy soil. And even as he watched, his own blood began to seep along the tube until, within seconds, it was trickling out the other end into the two-foot-deep hole.

"And if you refuse to kill her, they'll do it for you. She'll be dead either way, and you'll either be expelled from here to do their bidding or held captive until you die. It's better this way, Ethan. I change you, and you escape."

"What about Lilith?" he demanded, lifting his head. Dizziness hit him, and he quickly let it drop again.

"I'll watch over her as best I can. I'll try to keep her safe until the opportunity arises to get her out, as well."

"You're risking your life by doing this," he told her. His words were becoming slurred with weakness.

"Yes, I know. That's my choice."

"But why? You're not even . . . one of us."

"A so-called Bloodliner? No, that's true

enough, I'm not. But there's right and there's wrong, Ethan. And what's happening here is wrong."

He nodded.

"You've no idea how wrong," she added.

He tried to nod again, but nothing happened.

"Listen to me," she told him. "You're going to want to sleep right after this is finished, but there's a burst of strength, and you have to use it. You have to jump that fence. You have to be brave and take a leap of faith, believe you can clear it — because you can. You will."

He looked up at the looming fence and doubted.

"Once you get over, run as fast and as far as you can, fight the sleep hard. And then rest only when you've found a place where you will be sheltered from the sun. Do you understand?"

"I . . . under . . ." His lips went numb, then, and he gave up trying to reply. Soon he felt her sliding a fresh bit of tubing between his lips and heard her telling him to drink. He did, sucking until he tasted fluid that made him want to retch — because his mind knew what it was — but also to guzzle it all at once — because his body craved it.

He drank. Callista withdrew the needle from his arm and taped the pinprick hole with as much care as if it were a terrible gaping cut. All the while he drank until the fluid was gone, and he was still trying to extract more when she took the tube away.

"You have to go now. I promise I'll do what I can for her. But you must never come back, Ethan. Never. They wouldn't let you leave a second time. And I tell you truly, that if I *can* protect her, she'll be safe, and if I can't, she'll be dead long before you can make your way back here. So don't try."

"I can't believe I'll never see her again."

"Then don't believe it. Maybe you will. This place won't stand forever."

He frowned at her then, shocked to realize he could suddenly sense her thoughts, though he was having trouble deciphering the specifics. "Who do you really work for? Does anyone else know where you are? I could contact them, tell them —"

"I can't tell you that. Now go. *Go.*"

He tried to probe her mind, but he could feel her blocking him and, already overwhelmed and distracted by all he could feel and see and hear now, he stood, took a deep breath and bent his knees. He focused on clearing the fence and pushed off. And then he was sailing straight over top, through the night, hearing the wind whistling past his ears as he landed hard on the freedom-scented grass on the other side.

Then he got up, ran — and left Lilith.

Now, more than anything else, he wished he could keep her from ever knowing any of that. And yet, sooner or later, she was going to have to know.

Leaning close as she stirred awake, he pressed his lips to hers and whispered. "I'm going out to put the horses in. We'll talk when I get back."

She nodded, and closed her eyes again.

Gone. He was gone, and I couldn't believe I'd let him go. Last night he'd seemed on the verge of telling me why he seemed familiar to me, why he —

Wait!

I frowned, hard, because there was new knowledge inside my brain. I felt as if it had been told to me — no, *shown* to me, like the film reels they'd shown us during our lessons . . . I *remembered* those films. The classroom.

Ethan.

But this new bit, this was not a memory. Or . . . not *my* memory. It was Ethan's. And I realized that he must have been lying there, holding me in his arms and thinking or dreaming or remembering, and that I, being a vampire like him and no longer truly asleep but only enjoying being held in his arms, feeling safe enough to linger there, had been reading his thoughts without even intending to.

I saw what had flickered through his mind. I felt him staring at me as I slept. I saw the woman — Callista, her name was Callista! — leading him away. I saw her take him into the brush and drain his blood, then feed him more. I saw her talking to him. What she said, though . . . *that* I did not know. I could *feel* its essence, though. He had no choice. He had to go.

And then I felt him leaping the fence and running away into the night.

I felt him abandoning me to my prison — or whatever that place had been.

How could he? And how could he lie to me *now,* when I had no clue who I was, and he knew? He'd known the entire time and let me suffer. How dare he?

Furious, I flung back the covers and stalked to the closet. There were no clothes that would come anywhere close to fitting me, but I yanked down a T-shirt, a sweatshirt with a hood, a pair of jeans that would be far too long and a belt I could use to hold them up. I located a pair of socks and wished for women's underwear. I took it, all of it, with me into the attached bathroom.

And then I paused and stood staring in wonder. My God! The bathtub was huge and square, the shower stall small and private, with frosted glass doors. I dropped the clothing I'd pilfered and opened those doors. Though the thought of a long soak in the oversize tub tempted me, I was in too much of a hurry to take the time. Cranking on the shower's taps, I stepped under the deliciously hot spray. All my anger melted as I relished a shower all to myself, the fruity smell of his shampoo and the herbal smell of the soap. Oh, it was heaven, all of it, right down to the thick, fluffy towels I wrapped myself in when I emerged.

Smiling, I decided that I'd never had it this good before — at The Farm. The place from whence I — and he — had escaped. I didn't know what it was, or what went on there or how we'd come to be there, but I knew more now than I had before. And I would make him tell me the rest of it before this night was done.

I dressed quickly, brushed my hair more slowly, and then decided to bundle up a bit and walk down to the stable, rather than putting our conversation off until he returned. I would need footwear, and some sort of a coat.

I found a pair of hiking shoes, which I laced up as tightly as I could, and then I clomped down the stairs and went to peer out the window.

And then I froze, because I saw what I should have sensed far sooner. Ethan was standing beside a car I'd never seen before, talking to the stranger behind the wheel.

Every nerve in my body began to tingle with warnings. The car was small and blue — nothing like the one that had accosted me under the bridge. I narrowed my unnaturally keen eyes as its window lowered, and I saw the woman who occupied the driver's seat.

Maybe it had been a woman in that other car, too. A deep-voiced female, or someone disguising the sound of her voice by trying to sound like a man. How could I know? I never saw the face, only the black barrel of a gun.

She had auburn hair, with strands of gray here and there, which I shouldn't have been able to detect from this distance. She had a gentle face, and kind eyes with crow's-feet at the corners. She also had a dire, desperate feeling about her that belied the smile she wore.

As I watched, the woman spoke to Ethan

and held something up for him to look at.

Pressing still closer, I honed my senses and found that, if I tried, I could hear her voice. I could feel his thoughts. I could . . .

"I'm looking for this young woman," the stranger in the car told him. "She could be in danger if she's not found. Have you seen her?"

Snapping my vision to the object in the woman's hand, I saw that it was a photograph. And it was of a face that was familiar to me in a way no other face could be. There had been no reflection in that cursed mirror of Ethan's, but the photograph in the woman's hand was of me. I knew it. I'd seen my face before I'd been . . . made over. I knew it well. Knew it deep in my gut.

And even as I stared at it, the memory of *me,* of how I looked and, more, how I thought and felt about things, came surging back to me, almost as if it had never been gone.

"No, I haven't seen her," Ethan said. I heard his voice, but I heard his thoughts, as well. *This is exactly what I was afraid of.* And then, aloud again, "What makes you think she's in this area? It's pretty remote."

"She was spotted by some locals who said she was headed this way."

"Well, she must have veered off, or else

your witnesses were mistaken. You say she might be in danger. From what?"

"I'm afraid I can't go into any detail on that."

"I see."

"But she *is* in danger. Dire danger. And so is anyone who might be with her. Please take my warning very seriously. I want nothing but to help. There are people after her. People who — are going to find her quite easily."

I felt Ethan frown as his suspicions rose. "How?"

The woman twisted her car key. "If you see her, *please,* give me a call." She lowered the photograph and handed him a card instead. "It's important."

Yeah, I'll just bet it is. Aloud, Ethan said, "May I keep the photo?" The woman frowned at him. "Just in case," he added.

The woman handed it to him with a nod, then put her car into gear. "Don't try to help her on your own, or you could both end up dead. Call me. I can protect her. Both of you, if need be."

"Thanks for the advice." *But I can protect her just fine all by myself.*

Yes, I thought furiously. *Like you did when you ran away and left me in that prison? Was that your idea of protection, Ethan? And then* other thoughts rushed in. Since when had I ever needed anyone to protect me? I still didn't remember everything, but I *did* know myself, at long last. And as I watched the woman drive away, I knew I wouldn't want anyone's protection but my own.

By the time I realized that my angry thoughts had reached Ethan's mind, projected by my rage, I was already in flight. I'd yanked the plush white blanket, lined in thick buff-tinted fur, from the sofa, and pulled it around my shoulders and over my head, like a hooded cloak, to hide my face and my long hair from that woman or anyone else who might be looking. Then I headed out the back door, racing through the night at the speed I'd discovered was a common thing among my kind.

The Undead.

Vampires.

Were they — were *we* — all hunted, as Ethan seemed to believe *he* was? As I apparently was? Were we all in danger? Or was there something special about the two of us that made us targets? Maybe he was lying about that, as well, telling me he was a target for reasons of his own. He'd certainly shown no compunction about lying to me about plenty of other things. Like the fact that he'd known me before. And left me behind to save himself.

To save us both, a small voice in my mind argued. But I was too angry to listen.

7

I raced around the perimeter of the yard, keeping to the shadows, moving too fast to be seen — except by him. He would have seen me, had he looked. I tried to imagine that the cloak covered any sense of my presence, tried to keep him from feeling me as I dashed from the house to the stable, giving him a wide berth.

And then I kept going, to the back of the stable. A fence blocked the meadow, but I leapt it with barely a thought or an effort. He saw me then, just before I moved beyond his line of sight. He saw me, and he shouted my name.

"Lilith! Wait!"

But he'd lied to me. And that meant I couldn't trust him.

I came to a stop in the meadow, looking left and right and ahead of me at the forest and mountains beyond. And then my eyes met those of the mare. Buff and huge, she shook her shaggy cream-colored mane at me. Ethan hadn't yet put the horses inside for the night.

"Please," I whispered. "Help me?"

I *know* it makes no sense to believe that the animal heard me, much less understood my words and the emotion behind them. But she responded. She trotted eagerly right up to me. I gripped a handful of her mane and launched myself onto her back, swung a leg over, clutched my fur-trimmed cloak around me and held on. I kicked her sides lightly, and she responded as if reading my mind, twirling fully around and then exploding into a gallop even as Ethan came running toward us, shouting at me to wait.

I didn't wait.

The mare didn't, either. She never even slowed her pace as she approached the pristine white fence. If anything, she ran faster, stretching her long neck, giant hooves pounding the ground beneath us. And then we were airborne, sailing over the fence as if the big draft mare had sprouted wings. As if she were Pegasus. I held on, leaned forward, braced for the landing, and then we kept right on going.

He couldn't believe she'd fled like that. Obviously, she'd seen the car, overheard at least some of his conversation with the stranger. God, if she had no memory, what the hell had her so afraid? Or maybe that was just it. She didn't know who she was, who she could trust or who was after her. But she knew someone was.

And she knew something else, too. She knew that he had been with her at The Farm, and that he had escaped and left her behind. He should have told her, but his guilt had suffocated his ability to do so. But there was no point in keeping the truth from her any longer.

He hesitated only briefly, because something caught in his chest at the sight of her. She'd wrapped the fur-lined blanket from his sofa around her head and shoulders, but it had blown back, and her hair flew behind her as Scylla ran full out. Lilith's body moved with the mare's, instinctively, as if they were one being. And then they leapt, like a pair of goddesses, and were gone.

Her thrall over him broken, he shook himself and whistled for Charybdis. The stallion trotted to him, and Ethan gripped his halter and led him back into the stable for a saddle, blanket and bridle. He added extra blankets to a pack, and took time to fill a Thermos from the house, because God only knew what kind of a chase she would lead him on. And if the woman in the car had been telling the truth . . . Hell, it might be a while before either of them could return.

His home, his haven, was no longer a safe place. And yet, he had no desire to return to it without her. For so long, he'd believed he would never see her again. To have her show up here, of all places, even without her memory — it had to be fate. It *had* to be.

With the saddlebags packed, he rode out after her, knowing he would catch up. It was inevitable. She'd been led to him. He was meant to be with her, to help her survive, if he could. And though he felt the weight of the odds against them like leaden blocks on his shoulders, he knew he had to try.

For both their sakes.

He scanned for her with his senses, tried to pick up her essence on the night's very breath. He hadn't taught her to block her thoughts or to shield her presence from another of their kind. Hell, he hadn't taught her anything yet. She couldn't possibly survive on her own, even without the dark forces hunting her down.

That thought skidded to a halt in his brain as he asked himself just who he was kidding? He'd made it on his own since leaving the compound. She was ten times as strong, as resilient, as clever.

He and Charybdis picked their way over trails and around pines, deeper and deeper into the woods. There was no point in driving the stallion into a full gallop. They were huge horses, bred for working, for battle, not for racing. Scylla would tire before long and slow to a walk herself. He would catch up.

Eventually he did. All at once, Ethan *felt* Lilith. He felt her essence wrapping around him and drawing him in like a siren's call. He didn't speed up. He didn't call out to her mentally. He blocked his essence and thoughts so she wouldn't feel him coming, and he kept Charybdis to his slow, steady gait as they moved, patiently, ever closer.

For the better part of two hours, he rode, and then, finally, he saw Scylla a dozen yards ahead, among the trees. She was riderless and leaning down, stretching her long neck to sip cool water from a bubbling stream.

He scanned the area around her, and in moments he spotted Lilith. She was seated on a flat rock, staring contemplatively at the rushing water, deep in thought, waiting for the horse to drink, compassionate and wise enough, he thought, to know Scylla needed a rest.

He smoothed a hand over Charybdis's warm neck and patted him gently. Then he eased down to the ground and walked silently to where Lilith sat.

"You didn't need to —"

She sprang to her feet and spun all in one fluid motion, one leg rising and sweeping his own legs out from under him before he finished the sentence. He hit the ground hard, and the impact knocked him nearly senseless. Shaking himself, he blinked his vision back into focus, holding up one hand in defense. She stood over him, fists clenched, ready to pummel him if he tried to get back up.

"It's only me."

Her eyes boiled with agitation and fear, and the flight-or-fight — or, perhaps more accurately, just plain fight — reaction held her rigid. But then recognition eased the fear from her eyes. She relaxed her stance and stood just watching him, still wary, cautious. The mistrust in her expression and in her aura made his stomach ache.

"You didn't have to run."

"That woman was looking for me."

"Yes, but I meant you didn't have to run from *me.*"

"She had a photo of me. I saw it."

"I know. But I don't think she was DPI."

"What's DPI?"

He licked his lips. "It's . . . it's some kind of government agency. They operate the place I'm pretty sure you ran away from." The lie came automatically, before he could remind himself that she already knew the truth.

She lifted her brows. "You're *pretty* sure? You know damn well where I ran from, Ethan, since you ran away before me."

He hesitated, looked away. "You do remember," he whispered.

"I barely remember a thing. But I remember *me,* Ethan. I remember who I am — and *how* I am. And I remember you. The rest, you're going to tell me. All of it."

He nodded. "Can I get up without you kicking my ass again?"

She glared at him for a moment longer, then sighed and nodded. "I didn't even know I could do that. It was automatic. As if I've had . . . training."

He got to his feet, brushed off his jeans, said nothing.

"I have, haven't I?" she asked.

Lifting his gaze slowly, he met her eyes. Green fire danced in them, reminding him that he'd decided to tell her the truth. Also

124

reminding him that she wouldn't accept anything less. "Yes, you've had training. In martial arts, in weapons, in hand-to-hand combat. We both have. It was part of the program at the place where we were raised."

"The Farm, right? What is it, Ethan?"

He took hold of her forearm, intending to lead her back to that flat stone so they could both sit down. But she jerked away as soon as he touched her, and that stung. "The Farm is . . . well, it's sort of like an orphanage and a military school all rolled into one."

She crossed her arms over her chest, possibly so he wouldn't touch her again. "Why would people who run an orphanage want to chase after the orphans who leave?"

"We're not ordinary orphans, Lilith. We were born with a very rare antigen in our blood, called Belladonna. And it makes us special. It makes us . . . the only humans who can become vampires. And you and I, and the other Chosen at The Farm, we're members of a very special bloodline. That's what they call us there — Bloodliners."

She frowned. "I remember there being a lot of us there. How is it so many of us become orphans?"

"I'm not so sure we do. It's just as likely we're taken, kidnapped, our families murdered. I do know that we're never supposed to leave, at least not on our own. We're prisoners. We're expected to grow up there, get our training there, become utterly devoted, unquestionably loyal there, and then, when we reach adulthood, they turn us into vampires and we work for them."

"Doing what?" she asked.

"I don't know. I do know that when someone runs away, vampire assassins, graduates of The Farm, are sent to hunt them down and kill them. So that would be one job."

She frowned. "How many . . . how many vampires do you suppose have been made there?"

"I don't know."

"Why not?" she asked. Her tone was impatient. "You have *your* memory. You grew up there. So how many children, older than you, were there and then . . . weren't there anymore?"

He thought hard, never having considered the question that way before. "Perhaps . . . fifty. In the early days there weren't nearly as many there as there were more recently. Now there are far more in training."

"In captivity, you mean."

Nodding, he held out a hand. "I know I should have told you all of it from the beginning, Lilith, but I just didn't know if I could trust you or not. I thought you might have been sent to kill me."

Sighing, she took his hand, and he pulled her closer. She never took her eyes from his as she came to him and said, "I can see that's not the only reason you lied to me. There's more."

"Yes."

"Will you tell me?"

They walked along the edge of the stream, with him still holding her hand. It was small inside his, but strong.

"What were we, before they 'turned' us? I mean, did we have any special powers or abilities?" she asked.

"We were just humans, but special ones. The keepers tell us that they take children like us to live at The Farm for our own protection."

"Protection?" She tipped her head sideways, staring up at him with her green eyes wide and curious. "From what?"

"From other vampires. The Wildborns. Vampires who make each other. But the keepers say if they find one of the Chosen — that's us, before we're made over — they'll kill us on sight. And that if they knew the Bloodliners existed, they would kill us even more eagerly — even those of us who are already undead — because we're *so* different from them."

She blinked and stopped walking, sinking instead to the grassy ground beneath her. "If only the Chosen can become vampires, and if the Wildborns still make new vampires, then they must not kill *all* the Chosen."

He smiled, because he remembered her making that exact same argument in class — during their indoctrination. "I agree. It makes no sense. There must be some system they use to decide who to kill and who to bring over to the dark side."

"So you don't really know if they kill *any* of them."

He lowered his head. "They're savage, the Wildborns. It's their nature. They're hunters, predators. They feed off innocent humans, kill people. They have no rules, no inhibitions, no restraint. While we Bloodliners are civilized, educated, more evolved. They would see us as a threat to them and hunt us down if they knew about us."

Studying him, she waited a long moment and then said, "And who told you all that?"

"Everybody knows these things."

"*Do* they? And who told *them?*"

Shaking his head slowly, he said, "You have a point. It could all be lies, but it's not something I'm willing to risk my life to find out for sure."

"So you knew me there? At The Farm?"

"We never spoke. But I knew you."

"How?"

He smiled a little. "Everyone knew who you were. You were the rebel. You argued, refused to obey, disagreed with every lesson you were taught, questioned authority at every juncture. You couldn't be tamed."

"Like the other Lilith. My namesake." She frowned, studying his face and knowing something she hadn't before. "You bought the print in memory of me."

He admitted it with a nod, averting his eyes. "I . . . admired you. I never forgot you, Lilith."

She nodded and whispered, "You kissed me once."

"Yes. The night I had to go."

"And yet you still ran away and left me there. A prisoner. Along with . . . how many others, Ethan?"

"A hundred and fifty. Maybe two hundred."

"What did you think was going to happen to me there? The rebel who couldn't be broken?"

Meeting her eyes, holding them steady, he said, "I had to leave you. I was due to be

129

turned. Callista said —"

"I remember her," she said softly.

"She helped me. She was the one who told me what they were planning. Lilith, my final exam was to murder you. And if I refused, they would have killed you anyway. My leaving was the only way to keep you alive."

She tipped her head to one side. "Taking me with you would have accomplished the same thing."

"I had no time, no resources. I had to leave right then or not at all. I honestly thought it was for the best."

She blinked three times. "You could have come back for me." She got to her feet, walked toward the horse. "I'll see to it that she —"

"Scylla. Her name is Scylla. And the stallion is Charybdis."

"I'll see to it that *Scylla* is returned to you when I get to where I'm going."

"No, Lilith. You don't need to run away from me. I've told you the truth. There's more you need to know, to learn —"

"From *you?*" She shook her head. "No, I don't think there's anything I can learn from you, Ethan."

She walked to Scylla, stroked her. "I'll take good care of her, and I'll send word where you can pick her up."

"Dammit, Lilith, just where the hell do you think you're going? There are Wildborns out there who'll rip you to shreds like a wolf would a lamb if they find you. There are the Bloodliner assassins, trained vampires so loyal to the DPI that they'd kill us as soon as look at us. That woman, she said they would find you soon, though she wouldn't tell me how. And besides all that, there are mortals who don't even know we exist but would try to exterminate us if they ever found out. Just where in the hell do you think you can go where you'll be safe from all of that?"

"If you were so concerned about my safety, you'd have come back for me. You'd have found a way."

"I intended to, Lilith. I did. As soon as —"

"We've wasted enough time talking," she said, the words landing like a slap to his face. "That woman had a photo of me and she knew my name. She'll be back. She'll bring others."

"I told her I'd never seen you. I willed her to believe me." She frowned, and he went on. "It's one of our powers. She won't come back, I promise."

"Doesn't matter. I'm not going to run like you did." She leapt easily onto Scylla's back.

131

"Well, do you mind telling me just where you're going?"

"It should be obvious. I'm going back."

"Back?"

"To The Farm."

"What?" Even though it was precisely what he had expected her to do, she couldn't have angered him more if she'd tried. "Why the hell would you want to go *back?*"

Turning the mare to face him, she said, "To do the right thing. To rescue the others and put this obscenity to a stop, of course."

He shook his head. "Don't you think if that were possible, I'd have done it myself?"

"Obviously not — since you didn't."

"Lilith, you can't do this. Not if you want to live."

"I have to. How could I live with all those prisoners on my conscience?" She frowned at him, tipping her head to one side. "How have *you?*"

I sat there, astride the mare, watching him wrestle with his ego. His conscience, I thought, had long since been beaten into submission.

"Do you remember that place?" he asked me at length. "Do you remember what they did to you there?"

"No."

"Do you even remember where it is?"

"I'll find it."

"How?"

"The same way I found you, I imagine. I was drawn here, probably my . . . vampiric brain felt you, knew you were here. You said yourself, we can sense other vampires."

"There are other vampires everywhere. You'd have to be the luckiest person on the planet to just happen upon The Farm." He lowered his head, shaking it. "You'll never find it, Lilith."

"Then tell me where it is," I said.

"So you can go there and get yourself killed?" He shot his eyes to mine. "I couldn't live with myself if I did that."

"Yet you could live with your own escape, leaving me and the others behind. Believing I was probably dead by now. God, Ethan, you've thought I was dead this long without remorse. How is this different?"

He closed his eyes. "Not without remorse, Lilith. Never without remorse. Your face, your spirit, have haunted me ever since I left. Why do you think I bought that painting? It was to remind me, in case I should ever forget. I look at it to punish myself for saving my own life and claiming my own freedom."

"And yet you didn't come back for us."

133

He drew a deep breath, squared his shoulders. "I intended to. But not just yet."

"If not now, then when?"

"When I find my brother."

I frowned, searching his face. "Your . . . brother?"

"James. He was there with me, ever since we were kids. I think he was five and I was three when they took us to The Farm. Our parents had been killed. We both had the antigen."

I was interested. My common sense told me to just turn the horse and ride away, to go about my newfound mission. But I wanted to know. And there was something else. Something I hated to admit, even in the most hidden parts of my mind. But I didn't want to leave him. I didn't want to believe he was the kind of man who would save himself at the expense of others. I wanted him to convince me that he was . . . better than that.

Giving in to such useless feelings was likely counter-productive, and yet I slid down from the mare's back.

"One day, almost three years ago, James disappeared," he said, when he saw that I wanted to hear more. "No one would tell me where he'd gone. The keepers would only say that I had to obey without question — and that included questions about James."

"He was older. You said we were all intended to be transformed and sent out on missions for this . . . DPA."

"I. DPI," he corrected.

"What does it stand for?"

"I never knew." He shrugged. "There were rumors about James, of course. Some said he'd escaped and that they'd sent an assassin to kill him. That he was cold in the ground before his first night of freedom ended. Others believed he had been transformed and put to work."

"What did you believe?" I asked him.

He swung his head around, as if he had briefly forgotten I was there. "I *believe* he escaped and survived. That's why I ran away myself, eight months later. To find my brother, to ask him what was really going on."

"Why do you think he would know any more than you do?" I asked.

"He's my older brother. He's always known more than I do. Besides, he remembers more about when we first went there. And he's been on the outside longer than I have. Long enough to find things out, maybe."

I paced to the water's edge, gazed at the

paling sky, realized I'd been riding nearly all night. And he had been following me patiently all that time. "It will be daylight soon."

"Too soon for us to make it back to the house."

"We can't go back there, anyway," I reminded him. "That woman —"

"I felt no threat from her. Though I'm sure she had her own agenda and was keeping things from me — lying to me, perhaps — I didn't sense danger. More a sense of desperation, in fact."

"And she told you the . . . the DPI would find me soon."

"Yes."

He sighed, studying me. "We'll find shelter for the day. It's too close to dawn for you to make any progress on this insane suicide mission of yours, anyway." He met my eyes, let his linger there. "Stay with me, Lilith."

8

"I'll stay with you," I told him. "But only for the day. At sundown, I'm leaving."

He was quiet for a moment. Then he clicked his tongue at Charybdis, and the stallion trotted to his side. Ethan took hold of the horse's reins and began walking. I walked alongside him.

"There are guards at the compound. Dozens of them. And they're armed," he said.

I shrugged. "They're also ordinary. I'm a *vampire.*"

"That doesn't make you invincible — not to mention that they have vampires on *their* side, too."

I sighed. "I have to help the others."

"Hell, Lilith, most of them don't *want* to be helped." I frowned at him, but he went on. "Don't you think I tried? I had friends there, people who could have escaped with me. They flat-out refused. Hell, one of them decided to turn me in, and if I hadn't overheard him and moved my entire plan up, I'd never have escaped at all."

"Why would anyone *want* to stay in captivity?"

"Because they've been broken. Their minds are like oatmeal. They've been programmed, brainwashed, converted into obedient, loyal servants, too afraid to question anything. They have no will of their own anymore."

"I did."

He looked at me slowly, and I thought he knew my next question before I asked it. "Did you ask me to go with you?"

"You'd been put into isolation. They couldn't break you, Lilith, and they were determined to. I had no idea what they were doing to you, or what you would be like when you came out. But yes, I'd planned to wait for you to return to the general population and ask you to come with me."

"But then your friend decided to reveal your plan to the guards," I said slowly. "And you had to leave or give up the idea of escape entirely."

"Yes. Callista helped me get in to see you, that last night. And even then, I hoped. But you were weak, drugged, barely coherent. There was just no way." He pointed.

"There's a cave up there. See it?"

I nodded. "Perhaps . . . I misjudged you," I said. In my heart, I hoped against hope that I had. But it would take some doing for me to truly believe in him, much less trust him again. "If I did, then I'm sorry."

"*If* you did. You're not certain, then."

"Certainty will take time. And . . . effort."

He nodded slowly. "Lilith, if we can find James, learn what he's learned about the organization, about The Farm, about the Bloodliners who've graduated, where they are and what they do — don't you see? With all that knowledge, we'll have a much better chance of getting the others out — *if* they'll come."

"But you don't know where your brother is," I said. "Or *who* he is. What if you're wrong about him? What if he really *has* become one of the DPI's loyal vampires — a house pet willing to do whatever he's told? What will you do then?"

"I don't know." He shook his head. "I don't want to believe that's possible."

"Why do you think he hasn't tried to find you, then, Ethan? Wouldn't he have come back for you if he could?"

"Maybe he did go back and I was already gone. And since then, I've been staying very well concealed. Whenever I encounter another vampire, I venture close enough to learn whether it's James. It's dangerous, but I don't know what else to do."

"I found you on my first night," I said. "Maybe you're not as well concealed as you think."

"We don't know for sure it was your first night." He stared at me. "Besides, there's a connection between you and me. There always has been."

"Stronger than your connection with your brother?" I asked.

"Stronger than my connection with . . . *anyone*."

I hadn't considered that one.

We'd walked up the slight incline and stood at the cave's entrance. Facing his horse, Ethan removed the saddle, blanket and packs. He left the bridle on, though, looping the reins through the headstall and then knotting them to keep them out of the way, then patted the horse on the rump, and Charybdis trotted back down the slope to join Scylla, already grazing in the lush grass alongside the stream. Above them, the trees rustled, their dying leaves fragrant with the scent of their decay. And even higher, the stars had paled until they were barely visible, as the sky became purple with the approaching dawn.

"Should we tie them or anything?" I asked.
"They'll stay close."

I was impressed but didn't say so. He slung the packs over his shoulder and moved deeper into the cave. At the far end, I saw the charred remains of an old fire, a small stack of branches for firewood and, against the back wall, a rusty-hinged hurricane lantern hanging from a jutting rock formation. "You've been here before, I take it."

"I camped out here before I bought the place. In a few other places, too, always a bit closer. I wanted to watch — see who came and went — from a secure distance."

I lifted my brows. "You *are* cautious."

"You will be, too, when the rest of your memory comes back."

The words weren't meant to frighten me, but a chill raced up my spine all the same. "You think it's going to? Come back, I mean?"

"I think so. You remembered me, sort of. You knew that you'd known me, right from the start. Somewhere down deep, you recognized my energy, followed your sense of it right to my door, even though you didn't know that was what you were doing."

I nodded. "That's the way it works with

vampires, though, right? They sense each other?"

"Well . . ."

"But that can't be true. Or you'd be able to sense your brother and walk right up to *his* door, wouldn't you?" I frowned. "You're right. Our connection *is* stronger. Why is that, Ethan?"

"Sit. Here, why don't you unpack these while I build a fire?" He handed me the saddlebags as he spoke.

I took them and sat down on the cave floor, unbuckling the straps and listening to him as he began arranging twigs atop the blackened coals.

"I expected to be able to sense James. Maybe I'm just not close enough, though. Distance weakens the connection. But to answer your question, no, that's not exactly the way it works. I can sense another vampire who's near, but unless I knew him, had spent time with him, I probably wouldn't know who he was. Maybe not even then. I don't have enough experience with other vampires to be sure. But I think you must have been fonder of me than I ever knew, to have homed in on me immediately."

"Oh, you think so, do you?" I smiled a little as I tugged items from the packs. Blankets, a Thermos, a long-nosed lighter.

"Something inside you recognized and remembered me when you remembered nothing else, there's no denying that."

"I suppose not." I lowered my head. "What does it mean, do you think?"

"I don't know, but I feel it, too — this powerful link to you. As for your memories, I can only assume it means they aren't gone, exactly. They're only . . . sleeping. And even now, rousing. Night by night, they grow stronger. It won't be long before they all return, I suspect."

I felt myself relax at his interpretation, which was, if nothing more, some relief from my own. "I like that. They're sleeping. And beginning to rouse. That means they could wake up fully any time now."

"They could wake up at any moment. And for you to go back there before they have would be like going in with your arms missing. Your memory of that place might end up being the best weapon you could wield."

He was crouched in front of the fire, his back to me as he spoke, setting the twigs alight. I watched the flames lick higher, reaching the larger pieces of wood.

"That would make more sense if I knew for sure that my memory would return. Just waiting for it, without knowing, could mean leaving the others there indefinitely."

143

"If they really wanted to get away, they could. We did."

"Not everyone is as strong as you are, Ethan," I said. "Or as stubborn as I was."

"Was?"

He turned as he said it, amusement in his eyes, though the topic was a serious one. "You still are."

"So I've discovered."

"It's not just stubbornness, either. You're strong, too. Smart, short-tempered, willful, determined and fiercely independent."

I nodded. "I'm feeling more and more of that myself. But even now, I think you know more about me than I do," I said. "Which means you know I have to go back. With you or without you. I have to."

"I know. I think that's another part of the reason I didn't tell you everything from the start. Deep down, I was afraid you would react exactly the way you are."

A rush of something heavy seemed to flow into my head. It nodded before I was aware of it, suddenly feeling leaden, and then I snapped my chin up again as I fought to keep my eyes from falling closed.

"God, I'm so *tired* all of a sudden."

"It's the dawn. It's on its way. I feel it, too." He added larger logs to the fire, ensuring there would be a warm bed of coals still glowing at day's end. As he did, I quickly unrolled the blankets in what looked like a good spot. None of it was because we needed the warmth, because we didn't. We wouldn't be uncomfortable in the cold or even feel it once we fell asleep, nor would it kill us. But warmth was cozy, a creature comfort, and our kind apparently valued such things.

I stripped down to my T-shirt and slid in between the blankets, leaving room for him beside me.

Moments later, Ethan took off his shoes and jeans, and, wearing a T-shirt and boxers, got in beside me.

"It's been a long time — and it's extremely rare in any case — since I've slept with a woman," he said softly. "Literally *or* figuratively."

I felt myself smile. "It'll be literally this time, Ethan. But don't take it personally. I don't think I could stay awake if I tried."

"You couldn't. But there's always tonight."

I smiled weakly, already sliding into a sleep the depths of which I had only recently come to know.

And only once before that I could remember.

Ethan woke at sundown to find that he had

rolled onto his side, either just prior to falling fully into vampiric slumber or just before emerging from it, because once a vampire entered the day-sleep, he didn't move. He was lying with an arm draped protectively over Lilith's body, his hand resting near her hip. One of his legs was entangled with one of hers, and her head was resting against his shoulder.

He shouldn't be surprised, he supposed. He knew he wanted her, had always wanted her. But this was . . . different. It felt intimate, almost tender, holding her this way. It wasn't a feeling with which he was even vaguely familiar, much less comfortable. He found it more confusing than anything.

Gently, he began to change position, but even as he removed his arm from around her, she opened her eyes, turned her head slightly and met his gaze. Her sleepy smile filled his head with notions best ignored, but then it faltered as she took in the way they were embracing. She whispered, "Oh," but she didn't pull free.

"I suppose we were cold or something," he said.

"I'd bet more on the 'or something,'" she replied.

He took his arm from around her, rolled

onto his back, then sat up slowly. "Yeah. Well . . ."

"You said we barely knew each other back at The Farm, right?"

"Right."

"So we never — we never shared more than . . . that one kiss?"

"No," he said.

"And it was . . . well, what was it? Physical attraction between us?"

"The connection between us is . . . more. Deeper than that, I think. But then, I can't be sure. I mean, neither of us had any kind of experience with the opposite sex. No adolescent boyfriend-girlfriend drama, no dates, nothing."

"Didn't they teach us about sex? In the classes, I mean?"

"Sure they did." He cleared his throat, got to his feet. "Just the basic physical aspects of reproduction though. We knew how it worked, just nothing about . . . how it felt."

"I see."

He shrugged. "They kept us apart, kept the males and females as separate from one another as possible to prevent . . . problems. But you and I —"

He broke off there, and she sat up. Her smile was mischievous, as was the twinkle in her eyes. "There *was* something more

147

that happened between us, wasn't there, Ethan?"

"There were . . . looks. I was attracted to you, and the way you returned those looks . . . I got the feeling it was mutual. But we never got the chance to —"

"To do more than share one kiss," she said.

"No."

"I wish I remembered it more clearly. That first kiss."

"You might not have remembered it too well even if your mind were intact. You'd been drugged and God knows what else. You were still recovering."

"So you told me."

"Besides, we've kissed since then."

Her eyes flared so slightly that he might have imagined it, and she quickly averted them. "My memory isn't *that* bad, Ethan. I haven't forgotten." She shrugged, carefully moving her gaze back to meet his. Her eyes were beginning to gleam softly, a rose-tinted glow coming from somewhere beneath the surface. "We have the time now," she told him. "To do more than kiss, I mean."

He couldn't help that his gaze slid down to her breasts, even though they were hidden from him by the T-shirt she'd pilfered. "You want to?"

"I wouldn't have said it if I didn't." She got to her feet, sexy as hell in the oversize shirt, and moved closer to him. "Besides, it might help my memory."

She pressed her palms to his chest, and then her body was touching his as her hands slid higher and twined around his neck. She stood on tiptoe, tilted her head back, closed her eyes.

He had no earthly reason to resist the temptation she represented. None at all, and yet there was a tiny voice deep down inside him that told him there would be repercussions. He ignored that voice, barely even heard it above his body's own urgent demands. His heightened senses kicked into overdrive as she pressed herself against him and set his very soul on fire.

He locked his arms around her waist and bent his head until his lips touched hers. They met lightly at first, and then the pressure increased. He wasn't sure which of them was responsible for that — maybe both. And then she sighed a little, and her lips parted, and something sort of shot through him. It felt the way he was certain it would feel if he poked his finger into a live socket. The next thing he knew, he was holding her harder, bending over her and kissing the living hell out of her. He felt as if he could never get enough. And she was kissing him back just as eagerly, just as hungrily.

At last they pulled apart, took a step back, arms falling to their sides, and just stood there, equally stunned and, he thought, equally aroused, as well.

"Well," she said. "*That* was . . . even better than last time."

"Yeah."

"I guess you were right. I *was* returning your . . . looks."

He allowed himself a small, satisfied smile. "Yeah."

"And it worked, too."

He blinked and wasn't following. "It worked . . . ?"

"I remember. I remember . . . you." Her eyes narrowed on him, and he wondered exactly *what* she remembered. But before he could ask, he sensed a human presence. A heartbeat later, he realized he'd sensed it too late.

As his vision shifted beyond Lilith to the cave opening and the night beyond it, he saw female forms, silhouetted in the darkness. A dozen women, mortals, stood there just outside the cave. Then, moving as one, their flashlights came on, twelve — no, thirteen — glowing spots in the night, each one trained on his eyes.

He lifted a forearm to shield his face as Lilith suddenly became aware of the danger and spun around. He felt the ripple of fear move through her. He felt her wrestle with it, pin it and stand on its back.

"Just who the hell do you think you are?" she demanded. "Get those lights out of my face!"

"Relax," one of the women said. She moved in front of the others, making her all but invisible to him and, he knew, to Lilith, as well. "We just want to talk to you."

"I don't know who you are, woman, and it's clear you don't know who I am, either, or you wouldn't dare be here, in the dead of night, in the middle of nowhere, risking your life. Tell your minions to put the lights down and stop blinding me," Lilith snapped. *"Now."*

"I do know who you are . . . Lilith."

When the woman — and Ethan was fairly sure now that she was the same woman who'd visited earlier — said Lilith's name, she flinched backward. He wrapped an arm around her waist from behind, an instinctively protective gesture.

"I can't risk you getting away again," the woman said. "It's taken me a long time to find you."

Ethan saw the woman raising her arm, and he reacted instantly, whirling Lilith out of the way even as he heard the *pfft* of the weapon and saw the dart speeding toward them.

It missed its mark, just grazing Lilith's arm and flying harmlessly away. He pushed her behind him, clasped her hand in his, then turned and, with a low growl, lunged directly at the crowd of women. Their leader tried to take aim a second time, but he was too fast. Pulling Lilith along behind him, Ethan sped straight into their midst, knocking half of them to the ground with a single sweep of his arm, while still running at full speed. In another instant he and Lilith were emerging from the mob and racing through the forest.

Their feet pounded. Their speed was so great that it was difficult to avoid hitting branches, even with their heightened reflexes and preternatural night vision. At length he had to slow to a pace near that of a mortal, albeit a *fast* one.

"What the hell just happened, Ethan?" Lilith asked as they hurried along.

She kept stumbling, which worried him. At least the women, though his ears told him they were still in pursuit, had no hope of catching them. He'd put enough distance between them, and was increasing it all the time.

But deep in the forest, Lilith yanked her hand free of Ethan's and stopped. "I need to rest."

He frowned. "You're a vampire. You don't need —"

"Tell me what just happened. Who were those women?"

He shook his head, frowning at her. "The one doing the talking was the same one who came around asking about you. The one with the photo. I don't know about the rest of them."

"How the hell did they find us, Ethan?"

"I don't know."

"Well, don't you think we'd better find out?"

He put a finger to his lips and cut loose with a whistle that was too high for human ears to detect. Within a few minutes the pounding of distant hoofbeats whispered on the wind, drawing ever nearer, until they no longer whispered but thundered.

The beasts slowed to a trot as they reached him, tossing their great manes and blowing, excited by what they were sensing. Trouble. Danger. Impending flight.

"I say we go back there," Lilith said, gripping Scylla's mane and pulling herself up.

She only made it partway, then slid back down. "I say we grab one of those bitches and make her talk."

"And I say we get on these horses and leave here," Ethan replied as he peeled off his shirt. He moved beside her, laid the shirt over the mare's back, then cupped her buttocks and helped Lilith up onto Scylla.

"And go where?" she asked, wrapping her hands in the mare's thick mane and urging the horse forward.

"Somewhere safe. Somewhere we can hole up while I try to find my brother. James will know how they tracked us." He got up onto Charybdis, clicked his tongue and rode up beside Scylla, awaiting Lilith's reply.

"You've been on your own for how long now? Almost two years?" she asked. Even before he nodded, she was rushing on. "And they never found you. Now, within twenty-four hours of my arrival, you're being attacked by a pack of Amazons. So clearly it's me. Somehow, they're tracking me. Do you agree?"

He met her eyes and wanted to say no, but he knew it was senseless to lie. "Yes."

"I arrived stark naked, Ethan. So if there's anything on me leading them to us, it must be on the inside. We need to find it and get rid of it before we do anything else."

He urged Charybdis faster as they moved onto a narrow, winding trail that must have been some sort of deer path through the woods. He looked behind them. "They'll make it here soon. Come with me, Lilith, please. We'll figure out our next step once we've put more distance between us and them."

She thinned her lips and tapped Scylla's sides with her heels — already, Ethan imagined, missing the clothes she'd left behind. She was reduced again to nothing more than a shirt. He would have to find her something better.

"Is dawn near, Ethan?" she asked as they increased their pace. "I thought it only just got dark."

"It did." He looked back at her. "Are you all right, Lilith?"

She nodded, but she also blinked heavily, giving the lie to her response. "We could get me x-rayed. Maybe we could find something."

"Maybe."

"But once we know . . . then I have to go . . . to go back."

"Return to The Farm," he said. "Risk your freedom and your life to rescue people who might rather stay right where they are."

"That's ezakly what I've gotta do, an' you

155

know't."

Frowning, he turned, only to see Lilith slumping over Scylla's neck. He leapt to the ground and was already running back toward her when she fell from Scylla's back. She hit the ground hard, and he was kneeling beside her only an instant later. But she was stone-cold unconscious. Scylla turned and stretched her long neck, nuzzling Lilith's hair.

"Lilith!" Ethan shouted. He gripped her shoulders and shook her. "Lilith, what's wrong?"

"It was a tranquilizer dart," a voice said. "They must have gotten off another shot as you ran away."

Ethan went utterly still and then slowly looked up. But he knew that voice even before he saw the man who'd spoken.

"James," he whispered.

9

His brother rode a horse of his own, an Arabian, far sleeker and smaller than Ethan's powerful draft horses. He sat his mount well, wearing a long black coat that was split in the back. He was about ten yards ahead on the trail.

"How did you find me?" Ethan asked.

"There's no time. Take her north, Ethan. You'll emerge from the woods onto a road. Follow it west for fifteen miles. There you'll find a house you can use for shelter, something to . . . eat, and a shed for the horses."

"How did you know where to find us? And why now? Where have you *been,* James? I've been looking for you for —"

"If you don't hurry up, you're both going to end up back on The Farm. They're coming. Get her up, dammit!"

Ethan gathered Lilith up in his arms and held her against himself as he climbed onto Charybdis's powerful back once again. He placed her sideways in front of him, her legs dangling over one side of the horse, her body against his, his arm holding her hard around the shoulders. He took the reins in his free hand and clicked his tongue, then turned his head to look at his brother.

"Thank you, James. I —"

But James had vanished.

Ethan fell silent, scanning the woods around him. He could still hear the Arabian's hoofbeats fading in the distance as his brother galloped away. Urging Charybdis into a trot and holding Lilith tightly, Ethan sent out a mental call to James, but it went unanswered.

God, he hadn't seen his brother in over two years. For him to appear to him just this once — here and now — how could it be? How had James known? Ethan's mind was spinning with so many questions.

But James was long gone, and Lilith needed him. A tranquilizer. It had taken a while to work, and he suspected she'd received only a partial dose, possibly from that first dart that had grazed her.

He glanced back, glad to see Scylla following along behind them as he rode in the direction James had suggested — although the entire time part of him fought not to wheel his horse around and gallop after his brother instead.

Serena remembered it so vividly that it was as if it were still happening. She felt herself standing at the dark entrance to the cave, staring inside and wishing she could see the two who hid within its shadowy walls. But she didn't have a vampire's vision. Behind her, at her signal, a dozen of her sisters turned on their flashlights and aimed them into the cave's mouth, both to reveal whoever lurked inside and to blind them enough to prevent an attack.

Because they might attack. The vampires had no way of knowing that the Sisterhood of Athena was on their side. And they must know they were being hunted by those who wanted only to kill them.

For just one brief moment, Serena glimpsed the tall, proud beauty within, shielding her face against the light, her pale skin and endless copper hair all that were really visible. There was a man with her. Vampires, both. Serena had been with the Sisterhood long enough to easily tell mortal from immortal, even with no more than a glance. And no more than a glance was all she gave the male. The woman was her goal. Just as she had been for the past twenty-one years.

Lilith. Her daughter.

So beautiful. Ivory skin, smooth as silk. Long, wild curls that twisted and writhed all the way to her hips, gleaming bronze in the flashlight beams. She was tall and very slender, and her eyes — were they green like Serena's own? Was there a slight resemblance in the bone structure, the cheekbones, the stubborn chin? Could this really be her long-lost baby girl?

Before Serena could complete the thought, her sisters were aiming weapons as well as lights. With hands that trembled, she lifted her own, her prepared speech frozen on her lips.

I think I may be your mother. You were taken from me long ago, before I ever even got to hold you. I've devoted every moment of my life since to searching for you, finding you. You're beautiful, and I love you, and you can trust me. And these guns won't harm you. They're only for your own protection, just until I can make you understand. I've come to help you, because I would never hurt you. And everything's going to be all right now. And thank God, thank God, thank God I've found you.

But none of those words made their way past her lips. Her brain froze on one simple fact. If this was her baby girl, then what Callista had told her was true. Her daughter was a vampire.

She managed to say something — something ineffective, by all evidence — because in the next instant someone shot, and then the two vampires exploded from the cave. Sisters fell like dominoes as what seemed like a dark twister crashed through them. And then the vampires were gone.

Serena found herself lying faceup in a clump of brush. "No," she whispered. And then, scrambling upright, she shouted, "No, wait! You don't understand!" She began running in the direction they had taken. "Come back! You have to listen to me!"

But there was no response.

She kept going, using her flashlight to scan the ground for tracks. The Sisterhood had trained her, and trained her well. She could track better than the most avid hunters. All the sisters could.

Eventually she came to a spot where signs of the vampires' passing met up with hoof-prints in the soft, damp ground. She followed the prints, moving as quickly as she could, but she knew she would never catch them. Her daughter — her one chance at finally finding her baby — was vanishing practically before her eyes.

Her whole body trembling, she stopped at

last and stood staring into the distance.

"I'll find you, baby. I swear to God, I'll keep searching until I find you."

Wiping away her tears, she turned and walked back along the path to the clearing outside the cave. And there she saw her sisters, some injured, others tending to them. Shaking her head slowly, she drew a breath and got to work.

In my dream I was back there. I was back at The Farm. . . .

Ethan was gone, and I had been dejected since I'd awakened one morning to hear the gossip that claimed he had escaped. He wouldn't have done that, would he? I thought. Not after that tender kiss we'd shared. I'd thought there was something between us — something unspoken but real. He wouldn't have gone and left me behind. Or maybe he *would*. Maybe he knew that if he stayed, I'd get us both killed.

I was the rebel, the untamable one. The one constantly being punished. The one whose mind-bending drugs were being increased beyond anything that had even been attempted before, in order to bring me into submission.

I'd heard the keepers talking about that. And I was afraid, because since this last time, I hadn't felt right. My thinking was clouded. My temper was dulled. Part of me wanted to just give in and do what the keepers told me to do. Part of me wondered if maybe being there wasn't so bad after all.

And then I heard one keeper mention an antidote by name — something that could be used on me in case of accidental overdose. "Melanine," she said. And I knew I had to find it somehow. Because I could feel my mind slipping from my grasp.

And so I'd been very obedient that day and pretended that I no longer cared enough to disagree with the teachers. I worked hard and fell into bed. And they relaxed a little. At least enough that I didn't wind up in the punishment barracks again. Then, in the dead of night, I sneaked out of my barracks and made my way to the medical facility. I knew where it was located, but I had never ventured into that part of the compound before. I'd never had reason. I did on that night, though, and I hoped I would be able to find the right building.

Unlike most other places on the compound, the medical center was only lightly guarded, and I wondered at that. As I headed closer, I passed another building. A small tin shack, perhaps six feet square. No windows, and only one door, with two guards stationed in front of it.

Two guards. For a shack so tiny it couldn't possibly hold more than one person. Who was so important — or so dangerous? There was a barbed-wire fence around the men and the shack, and signs that warned against stepping past it.

I paused, hidden from the guards' view by the shadows, something compelling me to halt there for just a moment.

And then I heard it. A voice — in my head, but far too real to ignore.

Young one. Lilith. You're a special one. I sense it in you. I am very weak and will not be able to help you much longer. So come to me. Come to me, Lilith.

I swallowed hard, my eyes widening, my heart racing. I knew the voice came from inside that tiny, well-guarded building. I *knew* it.

I need your help, child, as much as you need mine. Please, find a way to get inside. I promise you won't need any help at all getting back out.

Something wouldn't let me disobey. He sounded weak. He sounded as if he were suffering, in great pain. And I didn't like seeing anyone tortured. I knew all too well how that felt.

Licking my lips, I tried to think of a way

to get the guards' attention away from their duty, and I came up with a method quite easily. I backed away until I was near the huge electrified fence that surrounded the entire compound. We all knew it was deadly and rigged to sound an alarm when touched.

I picked up a rock from the ground and threw it as hard as I could at the nearest metal fence pole. The rock hit, and a shower of white-gold sparks sizzled from the point of impact and the alarm began to shriek. The guards raced away from their post.

I ran very fast toward the tiny building, diving over the barbed-wire fence, landing hands first, and tucking and rolling to break my fall.

Then, wasting not a single second, I scrambled to my feet and ran to the door. Even as I stood there fumbling with the lock, it clicked open all on its own. I wondered if the person inside were magic. A wizard?

I stepped inside, and then I caught my breath.

It was stifling inside, like an oven. And . . . *he* was lying on a hard table, beneath a white sheet, and his face was gaunt, bleached white skin stretched so tightly over sharply delineated bones that I thought it could easily be peeled away.

His cheeks were hollow, the cheekbones and jaw as prominent as a naked skull's. White matted hair covered his scalp in tufts, with pale skin in between. And his eyes . . . ice-blue eyes that seemed to be clouding over with — well, to me, it looked like death.

"Who . . . who are you?" I whispered.

"Can't you guess? Who else could open a lock without touching it? I'm a vampire, child."

"A real one?" I'd been taught of them in my studies. I knew they existed.

And I knew, even then, of my own unique connection to them as one of the Chosen.

But I'd never seen one before.

"Yes, a real one." He spoke very slowly, each word seeming to emerge only with extreme effort. "But not for much longer, I fear. I'm dying, child."

"You are?"

He nodded.

"You and I have a special bond, child, and I do not have time to explain it to you. But I *will* tell you that I'll be far happier dead than living in this hell any longer."

"Why are you here? What are they doing to you?" I asked.

He blinked, and I thought with alarm that I could see through his eyelids. His hands

166

moved as if to gesture, but they fell again with a clanging and banging noise. Manacles and chains, I saw now, at his wrists and feet.

"When they want to make a vampire, they get the blood from me. Every vampire in this place is my offspring. My bloodline. They're afraid I'll regain my strength and destroy them, so they don't give me enough in return. I grow weaker every day. But my bloodline is strong, Lilith. If you'll take the gift I offer, you'll become a vampire, too, this very night, and you'll be strong enough to jump the fence and run away. But it has to be *now.* Right now. I'm not going to live another night. Perhaps . . . not even . . . another hour."

I thought about all the others here. I thought about the revolt I had hoped to instigate, the coup I'd hoped to lead that would put this place into our control. But I thought perhaps those things would be better accomplished from the outside. I could grow strong. I could learn more. I could solicit help.

I blinked and, meeting the old man's eyes, nodded my acceptance. "What do you want me to do?"

He lifted a hand, the chain jangling as he moved it, and gestured me closer. I moved, and when I was near enough, he closed his hand on the back of my head and jerked me forward. He was remarkably strong, far stronger than I would have imagined. If this were weak — if this were dying — then what had he been like in what he called life?

He whispered in my ear, and I shuddered, then gasped as he yanked my head right down to his and forcefully pressed my neck against his dry, shrunken mouth. I felt it open. But then his head fell, and I knew he was too weak to do what needed doing on his own. Looking around, I spotted a blade, well beyond his reach, and, taking it, braced myself and drew it cleanly across my wrist.

I woke all at once, my eyes flying open wide. My head felt as if it were being pounded from within by an oversize mallet. My limbs didn't respond to my mind's commands right away, and when they did, they were uncoordinated and weak. Focusing my eyes required no small effort, but I managed it, though it seemed to take an inordinate amount of time.

As I blinked away the sleep fog, I tried to get my bearings. I was lying on my back. There were pillows beneath my body. Soft ones. I was . . . I was naked. Yes, I felt the chill air touching my skin. And something else, just as cool, but more substantial.

Hands.

Ethan's hands.

As I lay there, his palms moved over my right arm, skin brushing across skin, his touch more than a caress that made me tingle down deep. He was . . . looking for something. *Feeling* for something.

As I frowned and tried to lift my head, only to have it refuse to obey, Ethan moved his hands to my other arm, running them over it in the same thorough, tender way. From my fingers to my wrist, over my forearm to my elbow and along the tender skin inside the bend. He skimmed and squeezed and felt my biceps and triceps and up to my shoulder, and even underneath, and I bit my lower lip against the swell of unbearable pleasure. I bit it hard, but I couldn't feel my own teeth sinking into my flesh. I could only feel Ethan's hands on my skin.

And then he moved to my foot, and again he began that delicious, sensual hunt, as if for some tiny treasure. His hands skimming, his fingers pressing and moving in small circles. The ball of my foot, my ankle, each and every toe. And then to the calf, not missing an inch of flesh as he went. His touch moved higher, to my thigh, to the tender skin inside it, and then still higher.

I slapped his hand, a reflex that halted his progress. He turned his head, meeting my eyes, holding my gaze. "You're awake," he said, and he sounded relieved.

"Obviously. The question is, why was I otherwise?"

"Those women — do you remember? At the cave?"

I nodded, impatient to hear the rest. Meanwhile, I scanned my surroundings, beginning with those nearest to me. My bed, I discovered, was a chaise longue, a big one, deep and plush and brown. It was situated in one corner of a smallish room, a nice room.

"The weapons they used were tranquilizer guns."

I lifted my brows, curious. "I wouldn't think any ordinary tranquilizer would be effective on a vampire."

"I wouldn't, either. But then again, I've only been on the outside for a couple of years, and I've had no direct contact with other vampires. Apparently someone has come up with a tranq that *does* work on us." He touched my upper arm, just below the shoulder. "One of the darts grazed you here. You must have received a small enough dose that the effect was delayed."

"That makes sense." Except that I hadn't felt the dart graze me. And yet, there on my arm was the evidence of it. A narrow cut, like a furrow in my flesh. Perhaps the heat of the moment had distracted me.

He had lost interest in explanations. His eyes were once again focused on my body, and his hands had resumed their intense exploration. He was about to continue his examination-by-touch of my inner thigh.

"And yet," I said aloud, "it doesn't begin to explain why I am currently naked, or why you are currently touching every part of my body in an apparent attempt to drive me insane."

My words stopped him again. He drew his hands away from me and sat up straighter on the edge of the chaise. "Sorry. I . . ." He paused, then looked me in the eye. "My brother was there."

"Your brother? He was where?"

Ethan leaned over me once more, but this time only long enough to reach past me for a blanket that had been tossed over the back of the chair, beyond my peripheral vision. He draped it over me before speaking. "He showed up in the woods just after you passed out and fell off Scylla. He was on horseback, too."

I frowned hard, my vision sharper now as

the drug began to wear off, and searched his face. "Are you sure *you* didn't get nicked with a dart yourself?"

"He was there. He rode up to within thirty feet of us, said you'd likely been hit by a tranquilizer dart, told me to bring you here because it would be safe, and then he took off in the opposite direction before I could even ask him . . . anything."

I felt the pain in him.

He sighed and went on. "He was . . . like us," he said softly. "He was a vampire."

I blinked, knowing instantly what that suggested even before he repeated my own thoughts back to me.

"That means he was probably changed by the keepers and sent into the service of the DPI. He probably works for them."

I nodded. But despite the fact that I was in complete agreement with him, I found myself wanting to give him hope that things were not what they seemed. "Not necessarily," I said. "*I'm* a vampire. So are you. And neither of *us* works for them."

"That's true."

"And," I went on, "you still haven't come to the part where you explain why you're groping me."

He lifted one brow, sending me a wounded look. "Groping? I thought I was employing the tenderest of caresses."

"All right. That, then."

"Gee, thanks."

I shrugged. "I didn't say I minded."

He met my eyes, and the heat in his own was palpable. "You didn't?"

"Mmm, no. But on the other hand, I didn't get the feeling it was intended as foreplay."

"It would have been much better if that's what I was doing."

"No doubt," I said, pouring sarcasm into it. In fact, I *didn't* doubt it. We would be good together, he and I. We would be . . . explosive. We'd been explosive when we'd done no more than kiss, and now I could hardly wait to have sex with him, even though I knew next to nothing about it. The desire was instinctive — and irresistible.

"I was looking for a tracking device." I frowned, but he went on. "I've been thinking about what you said before. About how if they have some way to track you, it has to be something on the inside. And it makes sense. After I escaped — after James and I escaped, I mean —"

"If he *did* escape."

"After *I* escaped, then, they might have decided to find a way to keep tabs on any future runaways. Maybe they implanted some kind of microchip or something." He frowned, searching my eyes as thoroughly as he had been searching my body. "You said you remembered me. What else do you remember?"

Frowning, I thought back. "I lived in a room with another woman. Her name was . . ." I squeezed my eyes tight. "God, I can see her face. She was a strawberry blonde, with freckles just across the bridge of her nose, and blue, blue eyes. What was her name?"

Ethan's hand covered my clenched fist. "Don't try to force it. Just let it come, holes and all, and tell me about what comes to you."

But it infuriated me that I couldn't remember her name, when I could so clearly remember her face. Even her voice. "She had the brightest smile — when we were younger. I remember noticing that she smiled less and less as we grew up. By the time I decided to escape, she was like . . . like a —"

"I know. I know."

"We bunked together. There were ten rooms in each of the little painted cinder-block buildings. Two of us to each room. Ours was called Cabin Ten. It was yellow. The twenty of us had a little kitchenette, a

174

tiny living area, a television and some easy chairs. There were two bathrooms, one at each end."

"Sounds just like my cabin. Twenty-one, other end of the compound. There were barracks, too, with two rows of cots and just enough space to walk between them. We'd spend thirty days in the cabins, then thirty in the barracks."

"I don't remember that."

"Anything else hitting your memory just yet?"

I lowered my head and thought of the dream, of the old man, but I couldn't bring myself to talk about that. Not yet. So I pushed it aside and searched elsewhere in my mind.

"I remember martial arts classes. I remember that's where I was going when I used to pass you every day. And I used to look forward to that as if it were — I don't know, a highlight of my existence. The way you would always look at me, right into my eyes, the way you would hold my gaze and how it made my stomach knot up and filled me with . . . joy, just joy. And hunger. And —" I stopped talking there and bit my lip, because the memory was so real and so vivid that I was beginning to feel those things again now.

Drawing a breath, I steadied myself.

"It was the same for me, Lilith. Don't ever doubt it."

"It can't have been," I said softly. And I felt a burning in my eyes that I was sure was a very rare thing for me. "It can't. Because I never could have left you behind in that place. Not in a million years."

He averted his eyes, but I felt the rush of guilt that filled him then. Clearing his throat, he started to speak, then seemed to change his mind.

Sighing, I went on. "What I do *not* remember is someone implanting me with any microchip or tracking device."

I sat up slowly, looking around the house, my eyes pausing on the windows, my senses suddenly picking up. "They weren't implanting anything before you left, right?" I asked.

"No. Not that I know of, and I assume if they had been, they'd have found me long before now."

"So if your brother found us by means of a chip that wasn't in use until after he left, then . . ."

"Then he really *has* been working for them all this time." He rose to his feet in a rush of motion. "But that doesn't make sense. If he's working for them, why would he help us? He *helped* us, Lilith."

"Did he?" I asked softly. "Or did he just set us up for a DPI trap?"

He went tense, his eyes widening just a little. There was a moment of silent intensity, in which I knew he was scanning the night for any sign of someone else — friend or enemy, vampire or mortal — nearby. I knew it, because I was doing the same thing. And feeling nothing.

Yet.

"I don't believe he would do that," Ethan said softly. And then he fetched a handful of clothes, handed them to me. I took them. Jeans close to my size, a T-shirt, even socks and tennis shoes. I looked at him, noticed he was wearing different clothes himself. "I found them here. James must have left them for us. Another effort to help us. But I think it would be a good idea for us to leave here, just in case."

"I think that's wise." I rose, unashamed and unembarrassed, and dressed. "We'll find a better place to rest, and if we get there early enough, I'll finish inspecting myself for any lump or bump that might be a subcutaneous bit of electronic gadgetry."

"I really don't mind doing it for you," he said. And he said it without changing his inflection, so that in the midst of the ten-

177

sion, the fear that we were sitting in the jaws of a trap that might spring closed at any moment, the remark truly made me smile.

"We'll see," I promised.

He handed me a glass filled to the brim with something red. "Here. James told me there would be sustenance here. He was honest about that much, anyway."

"Aren't you afraid it might be drugged?"

"No, since I drank some almost an hour ago."

"That's reassuring, at least," I told him, and downed it as Ethan quickly moved through the house, probably in search of any other items the sainted James had left for us. Within moments he rejoined me, a small bundle under his arms.

We left the house, moving quickly to a large shed in the back, where I felt Scylla and Charybdis's presence before I heard or smelled them. They were alert already. Aware we were coming, I wondered, or sensing something else — like impending danger?

As we walked, it was as if I could feel eyes on me from the woods around us and from the house itself, as if we were surrounded by our enemies and would be attacked at any moment.

Yet I knew that was not my preternaturally

sharp senses talking. It was my own fear.

We opened the barn door, and Ethan quickly reached into the stall for Charybdis, speaking soothingly and walking the massive stallion outside. As soon as he was out of the way, I gripped Scylla's halter and led her out, as well, swinging myself onto her back the moment she reached the open, where there was room.

Let's go slow and silent. Ethan spoke to me with the power of his mind.

How, when everything in me is telling me to launch her into a full gallop?

He rode directly beside me, on the right, and his eyes met mine, his smile as reassuring as it could possibly have been. *Patience.*

Even the horses wanted to run, though. I could feel it. They were sensing exactly what I was. Picking up on my fears? I wondered. Or was something more substantial about to take place?

And then I felt it. And I knew he felt it, too. Something was coming, and it was coming from above. Ethan shot me an alarmed look just as the warning bells rang in my mind. And then he clenched his knees on his stallion's sides and shouted, "Run!"

We took off, the horses, magnificent beasts that they were, nearly flying through the night, their hoofbeats pounding so loudly that at first, I didn't recognize the sound of the helicopter blades slicing the very fabric of the night sky. But then the spotlights poured down from above and there was no more mistaking them. Even in the darkness, I could see the logo on the sides of the three black insectlike helicopters. A white-hot lightning bolt piercing a bloodred crescent moon. And suddenly something flashed through my mind, and I realized I knew that symbol well. I'd seen it often enough on The Farm. It was stamped on everything, from the labels of the clothes they gave us to wear to the boxes, cans and wrappers that held our food and drink, to the furnishings, the bedding, even the lightbulbs. Everything bore that same symbol. One I now equated with captivity and pursuit and danger.

How could the idiots still living on The Farm not see the things that Ethan and I had seen? How could they be content to live a life imprisoned?

Gunshots shocked me from my thoughts. They were firing at us from the choppers! Ethan gripped Scylla's halter and veered Charybdis toward the sheltering trees. As if I wasn't going to follow at a full gallop! I smacked his hand away and took control of my mare as we raced in a zigzag pattern across the small patch of open ground toward the trees and the mountains beyond them.

We galloped as if competing in a race — and maybe we were, a race for our lives — and we crouched low over the horses' necks as they ran. I held on to Scylla's mane for dear life and hoped I wasn't tugging too hard as her powerful stride jostled me from one side to the other. All the while I clung as hard as I could with my legs.

Finally we pierced the forest wall and dove into its embrace. Deeper and deeper into the forest we went, while the three choppers circled overhead. But not *right* overhead. After only a few moments, they were buzzing this way and that, and I realized they couldn't see us anymore. But soon enough they would. They would cordon off the forest and send in searchers. Somewhere their fearless leaders might very well be organizing that already.

"We've got to make for the mountains," Ethan called to me. "It's our best chance."

Maybe, I thought, our *only* chance.

10

Ethan began leading the way through the woods and toward the rugged mountains beyond. The sight of them frightened Lilith. He knew that. She had no idea how they would survive in the wilderness — much less how she would, if something should happen to him.

He felt her eyes on him as she tried to read his thoughts, a skill he knew she hadn't yet perfected. If she had, she would realize that he wasn't thinking about their situation at all, nor about those in pursuit of them, the ones they had temporarily left behind. His mind was indeed working overtime. But it was focused on something else, something that hurt to think about.

"You're so quiet," Lilith said to him at length. "But I can feel the darkness coming off you in waves, Ethan. What is it? What's wrong?"

He looked at her and could barely force

the words, but knew he had to. "We're going to have to leave the horses," he said at last.

"Leave them? We can't just —"

"We have to," he said. "It's the only logical thing to do. In this terrain, we can move faster without them. We need to get beyond the boundaries of this forest before it's completely surrounded, if that hasn't already happened. When we do, we need to keep our options open, take a car if one becomes available. We couldn't do that with them depending on us. This is the best possible place to turn them loose. We have no other choice."

Lilith was still for a moment as she seemed to scan the woods, her senses sharp. She was learning fast how to use them, he thought with no small amount of admiration. And yet he knew she felt responsible for this — for all of it. Intended or not.

"It's my fault, isn't it?" she asked at length. "It's my fault you no longer have a safe place to live, my fault you've got to give up your beloved horses." She lowered her head, her body moving in a gentle rocking motion in time with Scylla's careful plodding gait. "I'm sorry I brought all this down on you. Maybe you should just take the horses and go your own way. It's me they're somehow tracking. If I go off alone, I'm the one they'll follow."

He looked her up and down, and he knew she was terrified of being on her own. Not that Lilith was a needy, dependent, clinging female. She wasn't. Never had been. But she barely understood her own nature, and there were unimaginable forces hunting her down. In those circumstances, anyone would feel better in the company of someone else.

"I have a better idea," he said softly. "If there's a tracking device on you, let's find it and get rid of it. Otherwise, it's not going to matter where we go. They'll follow us to the ends of the earth."

She shook her head as if she couldn't care less about that. "What about the horses?" She leaned down over the mare, stroking the velveteen neck. "What will they do on their own?"

"They'll be fine, Lilith," he told her, and he hoped it was true. He honestly thought it was. "They'll wander, they'll graze, they'll drink. Maybe they'll even find their way back home. They could, you know. We're not more than twenty miles away."

She pulled Scylla to a halt. Charybdis, sensing it, stopped, as well, several paces ahead on the trail. "That's the answer, then," she said.

Ethan turned to look at her. "What is?" But she was already jumping down and, to his utter astonishment, peeling off her T-shirt. "What the hell are you *doing?*"

"We need to find it, Ethan. The tracking device. *Now.*"

"We don't have time."

"We don't have time not to. Listen, we find it, you cut it out —"

He grimaced at the very thought of it, at the same time remembering that he'd found a knife at the house and taken it. Though he'd never had an inkling he might have to use it on Lilith. An icy chill shot up his spine.

"And then we attach it to one of the horses. They wander to wherever, and the bastards chasing us think they're still on track. Until they catch up, that is. And by then we'll be long gone."

Ethan sighed, because she was right. He couldn't have come up with a better evasion technique if he'd tried for a month. "That's a very good plan, Lilith," he told her with a firm nod. "If we can find it. If a tracking device even exists."

"If it doesn't, then how do they keep finding us?"

"I . . . don't know," he admitted.

She nodded hard. "Come on, Ethan. Let's get on with this." Already she was running her own hands over her body, the nape of her neck, the front of her chest.

He dismounted and walked to where she was. When he stood right in front of her, she met his eyes, and her hands went still. For a long moment they just stood like that, only a few inches between them. She, naked from the waist up in the middle of the forest. He, more aroused than he'd ever been in his life. And he couldn't stop his eyes from exploring her, moving up and down her magnificent body.

"Ethan? As flattering as the fire in your eyes is right now, we're in a hurry. Remember?"

"Yeah." He cleared his throat, gave his head a shake. "Yeah. Uh, I already checked the front of you fairly, um, thoroughly. Here, turn around."

"All right," she said, matching her action to the words. The horses stood nearby, not impatient, not pawing, just nibbling on the plants that grew alongside the game trail they'd been following, and blowing gently now and then.

Night in the forest was fragrant. He could smell every plant that grew, along with the scent of warm horseflesh and the stream nearby. And he could smell her — the feminine, unique scent of woman.

Again he stared. His eyes traced the gentle line of her shoulders, the length of her back. Girding himself, he moved closer and pressed his fingertips to her spine, following the line of it down to the base.

And then he halted, because that was when he felt something. A hard little knot beneath her supple skin. A bump that didn't belong.

"Ethan?" She craned her neck to look over her shoulder at him.

"There's . . . something here," he said. "I . . . think."

"Got a blade on you?" She said this without a single tremor in her voice, without hesitation. Without even a tremble of fear as far as he could sense.

"I found one back at the house." He went to Charybdis and undid the makeshift pack he'd put together, digging around until he found the jackknife he'd tossed inside. And the entire time, he was feeling more and more physically ill at the thought of what he had to do to this woman. A vampire's senses were heightened. All of them.

She would feel ten times the pain a mortal would feel in the same situation. More than that, perhaps. It could be debilitating. So debilitating that he could lose her.

"If you don't do it, you'll lose me anyway — and die along with me, more likely than not," she said softly.

He looked at her in surprise. "You're eavesdropping. Reading my thoughts."

"Just practicing my skills," she told him.

"Hmm." He swallowed hard and opened the blade. Then, bending low, he picked up the blanket she'd been wearing as a cloak and draped it over a gently rounded boulder. "Lie here, facedown. It's curved, so it'll arch your back toward me. Should make this a little easier. Faster, at least."

She nodded, her expression one of stoic resolution, even as she complied. She unfastened the jeans, lowering them just a little, then bent over the boulder, and he wished to God it were for another reason.

He moved to one side of her and knelt to get the best angle. "In a vampire," he told her, "pain is magnified. So this is going hurt a lot more than you can possibly expect."

"Thanks for telling me."

He thought he detected sarcasm in her tone. "I just thought you should be forewarned."

"Just do it, Ethan."

This time her voice shook. He knew he needed to get this over with. "All right."

Positioning the blade over the bump in her lower back, he used his other hand to pinch the hard little knot and force it up. Then, clenching his jaw, he swept the blade through that stretched bit of skin, slicing it off cleanly and knowing the sound of her anguished scream would haunt him for the rest of his days.

Her head rose, neck tipped back, eyes wide, mouth even wider as her cry filled the forest, echoing endlessly through the night and the mists. It could have been the cry of a tortured animal. But it wasn't. It was the cry of a beautiful woman. A woman who had never harmed anyone, as far as he knew, and certainly didn't deserve this kind of pain. He felt that he was as guilty as her tormentors back at The Farm.

The echoes of her scream faded, and then, as her head fell forward upon her hands, the sounds died completely.

Ethan sliced a bit of cloth from the blanket and pressed it to the wound. Then he took her hand, pulled it behind her and held it there. "Keep pressure on it, Lilith," he told her.

She didn't reply, but she did keep her hand there, even when he folded one side of the blanket over her body, so she wouldn't be quite so exposed.

Rising, Ethan looked at the bloody bit of flesh he held between his thumb and forefinger. He turned it over and carefully peeled the tiny electronic gadget from the underside of her skin. Then he took the device toward the horses, moving quickly now that the deed was done. This ruse would only work if they could get out of this patch of woodland before they were boxed in.

The horses were drinking from a stream, so Ethan knelt and rinsed his hands and his knife in the water. Then he rose and used the blade to slice a tiny hole in the double-layered leather of Scylla's halter. He slid the tracking unit into the hole, then pushed it deeper with the tip of the blade until he was sure it would stay put.

Then, after patting the horse he loved, he moved on to the stallion's side, removing the bridle and patting him, as well. He looked into the horses' eyes, trying hard to make them understand. It seemed as if they did. He hoped to God it was true.

"I want you to go home. All right? Go home. Go on."

They grew very alert, no longer drinking, but lifting their heads, watching him with their paintbrush-fringed eyes. Their ears flicked as if they were listening hard.

"Go home. Go on!" Ethan clicked his

tongue at them, and as they turned, he slapped their hindquarters just hard enough to really get them moving. The pair took off into the woods at a happy trot in the general direction of his place. He wondered if they would make it, or if they would even try to return to their own familiar stable.

Finally he turned his attention back to Lilith. She was still lying there, exactly as she'd been before. Almost exactly. Her hand was no longer pressed to the small of her back. Instead it hung limply over the boulder. The bloody scrap of cloth had fallen to the ground.

His nerve endings tingled with alarm, and he moved rapidly to her side, lifting the blanket that covered her back. Apparently she'd passed out from the pain, and she was still bleeding. Badly.

He ran back to his sparse cache of supplies. Bandages. Medical tape. Items he'd been glad to find. Vampires bled. It was a fact, one he'd learned early, and he should have thought about that sooner, instead of worrying about losing his precious horses.

Kneeling beside her again, he pressed gauze to the tiny wound, pressed hard, as he added layers and layers of it. Then he began wrapping her in tape, all the way around her waist, and he wrapped her *tight*.

191

When he finished, he returned to the stream, dipping a cloth from the pack into the water. He carried the soaked, icy-cold rag back to her and carefully washed the excess blood away, watching the entire time for any sign that the bleeding might be starting up again and seeping from beneath the bandages.

So far, so good.

Dammit, though. She needed the day-sleep. It would heal the wound completely, but until then, she could easily bleed out. He would have to watch her. And more than that. He was going to have to get her some blood. Powerful blood. Or she just might not make it to the dawn.

He put the T-shirt back on her, lifting and turning her body so he could ease her arms through the sleeves, wincing every time he had to move her. He was so afraid of making the bleeding start again. But he managed to dress her, and the gauze covering her wound remained white and unstained. He wrapped the now-bloodstained blanket around her, too. And then he lifted her into his arms and carried her. They had to get out of this forest.

If only he had some idea where they were going.

"Where . . . where are we?" I opened my eyes briefly, but only because Ethan had been telling me to open them for several minutes. He kept shaking me, saying my name over and over, patting my cheeks. Why couldn't the man just let me sleep?

"Lilith? Thank God you're awake."

"Not by choice." Slowly, I opened my eyes again, and for a bit longer this time. I narrowed them, willing them to clear as I looked at our surroundings and blinked my vision into focus. I appeared to be lying on a hard wooden bench, with my head and shoulders cradled in Ethan's lap.

Frowning, I shifted my gaze to his face, looming above me. "Are these . . . pews?"

"Yes, and that's an organ. There's an altar up front, and if you'll direct your attention to the wall beyond it, you'll note the giant crucifix with Jesus looking agonized and near death."

"Cheerful image," I muttered. He smiled very slightly and I wondered why. I was being sarcastic and unpleasant. Why would that make him smile? "We're in a church, then?" I asked, although the answer was already quite obvious to me, and he had to know it. I was killing time while waiting for my strength to return. It didn't seem to be in any hurry.

Ethan nodded. "It was the first place I found once we got clear of the forest."

I blinked, then started to sit up as I recalled the gravity of our situation. We'd been surrounded, or about to be, by armed assassins determined to see us both dead.

And then I blinked. "Wait a minute. Wait. A. Minute."

"What?"

I focused on Ethan's face, his eyes, and then his lips. And I felt a warmth uncurling in the pit of my stomach at the intimacy of lying there that way. So close.

No, no, I was losing focus. I'd had a point to make. "Those people in the helicopters were shooting at us."

"Yes," Ethan said.

"With real bullets."

Ethan nodded. "Big ones. Big enough that if one had so much as nicked us, we would have bled out in short order."

"So they wanted us dead."

He nodded. "*Want* us dead. Present tense."

I tipped my head slightly to one side. "But before that — those women, they weren't shooting at us with bullets. They were using

194

tranquilizer darts. Why were the women shooting tranquilizers at us instead of bullets, Ethan?"

"I don't know. I'm not sure it matters."

"Of course it matters. One bunch of attackers wants us dead, but the other intended to take us alive."

Ethan frowned, studying my face. "That *is* puzzling."

"Ethan, could there be more than one set of enemies after us? Can you think of anyone besides the DPI and our former keepers and the vampire assassins they've probably sent to hunt us down — anyone besides them, who might be after us?"

"No." He didn't even have to think before answering. "There's no one else."

"What if the Wildborns found out about us?" I asked. "Would *they* try to hunt us down?"

"Those women outside the cave were no vampires. They weren't the Chosen, either. They were just . . . humans. Ordinary humans."

I lowered my head, shaking it slowly. "I don't get it." And then I started to get up. I sat up and lowered my legs to the church floor, braced my hands on either side of my hips and went to stand up . . . only to discover that my legs would not support me.

I sank back onto the pew where I'd been lying. It was the last one toward the rear of the church. Dizzy, I lowered my head into my hands. "God, what's wrong with me?"

"You lost a lot of blood when I cut the transmitter out of you. Between the blood loss and the debilitating power of pain over our kind, you're extremely weak. I had to carry you all the way here."

That caused a hitch in my breathing. The knowledge that he'd carried me. Protected me. Taken care of me. No one had ever done that. I didn't remember every detail about my past, but I knew that much. And I didn't know what to say to him. The knowledge nearly overwhelmed me for a moment as I sought to understand it and to form some kind of reply. But I found none, so I changed subjects, vowing to think more on it later. "Where, exactly, is *here?*" I asked him.

"I don't really know. The outskirts of a small town in the middle of nowhere, I think. We emerged on the east side of the forest, and I didn't sense any of *them* around or hear any choppers. I think your ruse with the horses might have worked."

"Mmm. Perhaps. But for how long?" I asked. "How long will it take them to catch up to the horses, figure out what we did and get right back on our trail again?"

"We got rid of the transmitter," Ethan said. "How can they track us without it?"

I lowered my head. I was sitting upright, beside Ethan on the pew, but I would have far preferred lying down. "I have a feeling they'll find a way."

"Don't worry, we've got an ace in the hole. One they don't know about."

"We do?"

He nodded. "My brother, James. He found us once. He'll find us again. And with his help, we're going to get out of this mess."

"And rescue the others. And shut The Farm down for good. Right, Ethan?" I watched his eyes as I awaited his answer.

"If we possibly can," he said, "then I promise you, we will."

"I would have preferred a simple 'yes, or die trying,'" I told him.

He smiled a little. "You're weak. And still in pain."

"Does it show that much?"

"I can feel it." He sighed, looked away from me, then back again, spearing my eyes with his. "I can fix that, too."

"Can you?" I was surprised, but also in too much discomfort to want to doubt him. My back felt as if there were a red-hot poker thrust into the base of my spine. And I was

197

so weak that it was an effort just to hold my head up.

"Yeah, I think so. You need to . . . feed."

"So you have a victim tied up and unconscious somewhere?"

He smiled again.

"Why do you smile every time I say something sarcastic?" I asked him.

His smile faded, and another look came into his face. It softened. "Because that's who you are, Lilith. And it does my heart good to see the real you coming through."

"Oh." I couldn't look away. "So . . . are there bags of blood stashed here somewhere?"

"No." He couldn't look away, either, it seemed. His eyes never left mine, and the intensity in them grew hotter, brighter. "There's . . . just me."

I felt my eyes widen. "You want me to . . . ?"

He nodded. Then he put his hand at the back of my head, his palm cupping, fingers moving ever so slightly in my hair as he pulled me toward him, pulled my head toward his neck.

I kept my eyes open as I drew nearer. I smelled his skin, his scent, and the hunger quickened inside me. My body tensed, and my mouth literally watered for him.

"Are you sure?" I whispered, my lips grazing his skin as I spoke.

I felt him tremble. "More than sure." And his voice was deeper, softer, than I'd ever heard it, slightly rough-edged.

I let my lips taste his skin first. Salty, good. I sucked gently, and he moaned, and I knew he was as aroused by this as I was, that he wanted it every bit as badly. I opened wider, settled my mouth over his luscious neck and bit down. My incisors sank through his tender skin easily, then popped through the jugular, then — then I tasted him. I sucked at him. I drank him into me.

With the first swallow came an explosive shock that made me go rigid, and I bit down harder. He clutched me to him, letting his head fall to one side to give me better access, and I took advantage of it, devouring him as every sip made my hunger grow. I felt the power of his blood spreading through me, making me stronger, taking away my pain, my weakness.

Eventually he clasped my head between his hands and whispered, "Enough, baby. You don't want to drain me."

At that moment, though, I *did*. I could think of nothing I wanted to do more. But I withdrew my fangs, lifted my head and saw his eyes glowing red with passion. I knew mine were, as well, and, being nowhere near sated, I kissed him.

He kissed me back, pushing me down until he was lying on top of me, one hand between us, tugging at the shirt I wore, shoving the jeans down my hips. He was too slow, though, so I shoved him off me and tore off my clothes. Then I yanked him to me again.

He swore as he ground his hips against mine, taking my mouth with a ferocity that set me on fire. Again he took one hand away, but this time it was his own clothing he struggled to be rid of. Soon enough it was gone and he'd dropped to his knees in front of the pew, in front of *me.*

I lifted my legs to wrap them around his waist, then tightened them to pull him to me — hard. He sank into me deeply — so deeply I felt entirely possessed by him. My mouth open wide, sounds of intense pleasure issuing from the depths of me, I moved with him as he drove inside me. Deeper. Harder. Back and then in again, stabbing into the core of me, touching places that had never been touched and now — longed to be. *Had* to be.

My hands couldn't stop moving over his back, his shoulders, his neck, and he fed from my mouth as I had from his throat —

desperately, hungrily. He clutched my buttocks and jerked me harder, tipping my hips up, giving him even greater access, so that his thrusts went deeper still, and I cried out in a mixture of pleasure and pain at being so deeply probed, so widely stretched, so completely taken by him.

In that moment, I wanted nothing more. . . .

"Oh God, yes!" I cried. "Yes, Ethan, yes!" My body coiled tighter and tighter, until I felt as if my muscles were about to tear free of my bones — and then, at his mastery, I broke free in a release that made me scream. It was an animalistic cry of pure, powerful ecstasy. And then I was left shuddering as he poured himself into me with one final, powerful thrust. He held me as he pulsed into my body, and I was certain there had never been a feeling this good. This perfect. This mind-altering.

Never.

Nor was there ever likely to be again.

He slid out of me, only to pull me from the pew onto the floor. He groped, finding our blanket, which, I realized sleepily, he had rinsed free of my blood and somehow dried. He pulled it around us and wrapped me up close to his side. My head rested on his magnificent chest, and his arms enfolded me utterly.

I pressed my lips to his skin and whispered, "I never — I *had* never —"

"I know." He held me tighter. "Did I hurt you?"

"Yes." I lifted my head and stared up into his now-troubled eyes. "Please hurt me again?"

His smile was slow and full of mischief, but before it was complete, I was climbing on top of him, straddling him, rubbing myself over him. "Please?" I asked again.

He frowned. "We shouldn't have even once. Your back —"

"It's not bleeding." He looked for himself as I rushed on. "Besides, it will be dawn soon, won't it?"

"Soon," he said. "Still, I don't think —"

I didn't let him think for even a second. I slid myself over him and began bouncing up and down, and he threw his head back and closed his eyes.

"Done thinking yet?" I asked as I took him, harder and faster every second.

"Not . . . capable of . . . oh hell, yeah . . . right there . . . thought."

I giggled. It surprised me, because I didn't recall having ever giggled up until then, and moreover, I didn't think I was the giggling type. And yet this — this melding of body

202

to body, this taking and giving of such exquisite pleasure, this building and building toward release, this moving as one, *feeling* as one — was heady and beyond anything I had ever imagined.

I was fast approaching climax yet again, and even as I strained to take him harder, he pressed his palms to my back and pulled me forward so that my breasts were bouncing right in front of his face. Then he caught one of them in his teeth and held it there, nibbling, sucking, biting me. I whimpered in pure delicious sensation and pressed closer to that teasing mouth, only to be rewarded by more pressure, the flicking of an eager tongue, more little bites that grew harder as I got closer, and then . . .

I shouted his name as I exploded and my body contracted around his, milking him until he spilled into me yet again. Then I fell upon his chest in utter bliss.

We lay like that for long moments, his hands stroking my back, right down to the small of it, only stopping before he reached my bandaged wound, then sliding upward again.

"I don't want to go find your brother. I don't want to go rescue the captives. I don't even want to try to destroy The Farm," I whispered.

"No?" His touch was maddeningly gentle, and it just went on and on.

"No. I just want to stay here and do this. Over and over and over until I die of pleasure."

He clasped a handful of hair at the back of my head and gave a teasing tug so I leaned back so he could stare at me, and then he pulled my face to his to kiss me just as hungrily as before. When we broke the kiss, he said, "Your wish is my command, beautiful Lilith."

"Really? You'll do this to me until I die?"

"Or until *I* do. Can't think of a better way to go."

Laughing, I rose just a little and turned around on top of him, straddling him again, but facing his feet, and slid down over him once again.

He moaned and pushed me forward so that my chest brushed his thighs, and his hands on my backside moved and squeezed and lifted, so I knew he was looking at me.

"Enjoying the view?" I teased.

"You're every man's fantasy, you know that?"

"Mmm, that's nice. Say it again."

He smacked my ass lightly, teasingly, making me want more. "Don't be greedy."

"Oh, but I am. I am, Ethan." My hands

closed around his calves, nails sinking into flesh just a bit.

He drove up into me harder, his hands sliding to my hips to hold me down, to make me take it. And I loved it. "Okay, then," he said. "Be as greedy as you want."

"I intend to."

"Thank God."

I rode him like that, sometimes leaning forward to tease him, and myself, as well, by dragging my breasts over his thighs. Sometimes sitting upright, arching my back and pounding myself down onto him to take as much of him as I could get. And for a third time we exploded into ecstasy together.

At last I turned around and collapsed atop him. "I shouldn't be this tired, should I? Not yet. We're vampires, for God's sake."

He smiled, pleased as hell, I thought, that I still wanted more of him. "It's the dawn, Lilith. And not even we can keep the sun from rising, I'm sorry to say."

I drowsed as he carried me down a set of stairs into a musty storeroom that felt as if no one had been there in years. He settled us in a corner, on a pile of old tablecloths, and I felt my eyes falling closed. I quickly reached down to find him still erect. I moved until he was sliding inside me, then settled comfortably over him once again. "If we have to sleep," I whispered, "let's sleep like this."

"Mmm, and wake like this," he promised.

"I can't wait." I lifted my head to receive his kiss, and then I felt myself slide into the blackest form of slumber, with his tongue in my mouth and him buried deeply inside me.

I didn't particularly care if I never woke up again.

11

She was amazing and he was in trouble, Ethan thought, as Lilith sank into sleep on top of him. He didn't *want* to lose his life in a futile attempt to rescue those who preferred captivity. He didn't *want* to ever set foot on The Farm again. Had never intended to, at least not until he'd found his brother and learned all he could about the place and the people behind it. He had a plan, dammit, and he'd intended to follow it step by step.

Until now.

Now his desire for this woman had him actually considering chucking the plan and charging in there without a clue or a chance. Just because she wanted him to. God, he must be losing his mind.

She fell asleep before he did, and he assumed that was because her body so needed it. He'd been surprised that she'd even had enough energy for the frantic sex they'd just shared. Surprised — but even more delighted. Gratified. Grateful. It had been incredible. Amazing. Beyond anything he'd ever dreamed, and he'd dreamed a lot about making love to a woman. To *this* woman.

Dreaming about it, though, was all he'd done. Until now.

Since leaving The Farm, he'd led an almost solitary existence. He came into contact with others — humans — only when he had to. Buying feed or fence posts or other necessities meant making contact with the outside world. But aside from those essential interactions, he kept to himself. Even when searching for his brother, he was careful to avoid direct contact with others.

He'd had no idea, all this time, what he'd been missing. And he wondered, as she rested in his arms, if sex was always this way — or if this was unique, specific to the power that pulsed between the two of them. He couldn't imagine it was always this . . . explosive. Not even between two vampires. Surely it couldn't be. Not for everyone. There was something special and unusual happening here.

He felt the dawn creeping closer, its power siphoning the strength from his limbs, the clarity from his mind, and he pushed aside the newfound thoughts and feelings that combined to produce an avalanche of questions in his mind. He pushed aside everything except for the vital task at hand. Because he was running out of time.

Focusing on the image of his brother in his mind, he called forth the essence of James. The new one, the one he'd tasted so briefly when he'd seen him in the forest. That brief encounter had been enough to help Ethan understand why he'd been unable to contact James before now. James wasn't the same. Ethan had been focused on the old James, the mortal James, one of the Chosen. He'd been focused on the brother he remembered. Not on the vampire James had become.

Now that he'd felt the essence of the new James, he called it to mind, felt it again, filled his senses with it, and, focused on that, he called out mentally, as he'd done a thousand times before.

James. I need you. Can you hear me?

The reply was instant, and so clear and powerful that despite the looming sleep, Ethan jumped, his eyes widening in surprise.

I've been waiting to hear from you, Ethan. Worried. I went to the place where I told you to hole up, but no one was there, and I felt a sense of danger everywhere. Are you all right? Are you both all right?

209

We're all right. But . . . James, why did you send us there? Did anyone else know about the place?

It's a place I've used in the past, his brother explained. *A place where I'd left a supply of blood and other essentials, and a place that's always been safe.* He gave his answer without hesitation, without taking time to think about his words first. *What happened there?*

Ethan hesitated, and James pressed on.

I know something did. I could feel the energy of it lingering. It felt like fear, like attack, like betrayal.

Yes, Ethan replied. *That's exactly what it felt like. It was an ambush, James. The DPI knew we were there. They came for us with choppers and weapons and troops. It was as if they knew we'd be there even before we arrived. What I didn't understand — perhaps don't want to understand — is how they knew.*

He felt his brother's shock and wondered if it was genuine or manufactured, even as he berated himself for doubting his only kin.

Ethan, tell me you don't think I tipped them off. You can't believe that. I'm your brother. . . .

You're a vampire. They create vampires to work for them. To carry out their orders. How can I know that's not what happened to you?

There was a long pause, and when James spoke again, his words rang clearly inside

210

Ethan's head. *I could have suspected the same of you, brother. It did cross my mind, in fact, to wonder if they had sent you out, staged your escape, only to draw me out of hiding. I wondered if you were the one they sent to kill me, Ethan, because you were the one I wouldn't suspect. But I told myself it wasn't possible. And if it was, I would rather trust you and die for it than mistrust you and be wrong. You're my brother, Ethan. You're all I have in this world.*

Ethan's guilt tripled, burning in his gut. He licked his lips and forcibly squelched his suspicions. *I'm sorry, James. You're right. We're brothers. We need to stick together. It just — well, it seemed like we were set up, Lilith and I. I never should have suspected you.*

Bastards must have figured out that place was one of my hideouts, James's voice whispered in Ethan's mind. *That's the only possible answer. They were there for me, not you, Ethan.*

It's possible, Ethan concurred, then admitted, *But they might also have tracked us there. We found a tiny electronic device embedded beneath Lilith's skin. I think it was a tracking device. I think they must have begun using them after I escaped, to prevent it happening again.*

What makes you think that? his brother asked.

I've checked thoroughly, and there's nothing in me. You can feel it. Lilith's was beneath the skin of her lower back. You can check yourself to be sure. Just run your hands over the skin there. If there were anything, you'd feel the lump.

His brother was silent for a moment. Then, *You're right. I didn't find anything.*

Exactly. Besides, if we'd been implanted with them, they'd have found us by now. You've been at large almost three years, and I've been free for two.

Makes sense. So . . . you removed the device from her?

Ethan shuddered at the memory. *It wasn't easy — or pleasant. She bled a lot, passed out.*

Is she all right now?

Yes. She's all right. He looked at her as she slept, and warmth suffused him, even as he felt his body growing heavier. *Daylight is near. I need to rest, and you do, too.*

Before that, Ethan, tell me . . . where are you?

Ethan hesitated, then reminded himself that this was his brother, and that he'd been searching for him all this time. If he couldn't trust James, he couldn't trust anyone. Then again, not trusting anyone had kept him alive this long. But this was James. This was his *brother*.

We're holed up in an abandoned church in the middle of nowhere. The only sign I saw said Leister.

I know where that is, James replied, relief evident in his thoughts. *Wait for me come nightfall, Ethan. I'll join you there.*

Ethan didn't agree or disagree. He mulled it over, but the sleep was pulling at him too heavily for him to give it any serious consideration just then. He decided to wait for nightfall and full wakefulness to discuss it with Lilith, and decide then. He thought momentarily about telling his brother of Lilith's plan to return to The Farm and rescue the other captives, but that, too, would be best saved for another time.

Rest well, James, he said to his brother. *I've missed you.*

And I've missed you, James replied. *Sleep well, Ethan.*

Ethan relaxed then, wrapping his arms more snugly around Lilith, and let the day-sleep take him.

I woke still lying on top of Ethan's gorgeous, naked body. My head rested near the middle of his chest. My left leg was lying along his side, foot against his calf, with the right one tangling with his left.

As I came awake, my body was flooded with the most luxuriant, languorous feelings I had ever experienced. My eyes felt heavy as they opened, and my body moved as if in slow motion as I stretched. I rubbed my hands and feet softly against whatever part of him was closest. My hand made lazy circles in his hair, and my hip arched against his thigh.

It was surprising to find myself acting — much less *feeling* — this way. Utterly physical. Utterly sensual. Completely female — and powerful and beautiful and . . . alive.

And then I forced myself to turn my attention outward, away from my own thoughts for a moment to try to pick up on his. Was he feeling as . . . transformed as I was this evening?

He lay on his back, his body relaxed, one hand resting in my hair. I closed my eyes against his chest and felt his fingers moving as if in the most erotic caress, though it wasn't. Or shouldn't have been. And yet it set me on fire.

His other hand moved to the small of my back, and his fingertips dragged very lightly up and down my spine, seeming to leave a trail of sparkling energy everywhere they touched. I couldn't stop myself from making a soft sound of pleasure.

Beneath my belly, I felt him growing hard, and I was eager to feel that hardness inside me yet again.

But then he lifted his head and pressed a kiss to the top of mine. "We don't have much time, Lilith. I wish we did."

I sat up, frowning, and met his eyes. "Why not?"

"Because my brother will be here soon."

And all at once, all the sensual pleasure I'd been feeling drained from my body more quickly than blood through a severed jugular. "Your *brother?*"

"Yes. I spoke to him before I slept, and he agreed to meet us here right after sundown, so —"

"You *told him?*" I asked in disbelief. Scrambling off him, I found my clothes, wishing I had something fresh to put on. "You told your brother where we are? God, Ethan, why would you do something so stupid?"

He blinked at me, wounded, I thought, by my words. And I *had* been harsh, yes, but for the love of God, how could he be so naive?

"I trust him, Lilith. He's my brother. He

won't betray me." He got to his feet, as well, and gathered up his clothes, along with the small bundle he had taken from the house where we'd nearly been ambushed. He thrust it at me. "I trust him," he said again.

"And what about me, Ethan? My life is on the line, too, and I *don't* trust him." I spun away from him, and untucked the ends of the bundle to discover it was a blanket with more clothing rolled inside.

I frowned as I looked through it. No fresh jeans, but there was a clean tank top, and a green button-down cotton shirt. There was even an unopened package of underwear.

I looked up at Ethan.

"He knew you were with me," Ethan said. "He must have put those things in the house for you before he even located us. How can you doubt him?"

But then another thought occurred to me. I turned my tennis shoe over and looked at the number stamped on its sole.

"And how did he know my size?" I asked, then looked at the jeans and the shirts and added, "All my sizes. Hell, Ethan, even the underpants are the right size."

"He's a vampire." Ethan shrugged. "He's been one longer than either of us. He's probably discovered powers we haven't even thought of yet."

"Yes, I'm sure every vampire can guess a woman's panty size without having seen her in over two years, and then only in passing. It's a basic survival skill, after all." And yet I couldn't resist tearing the packet open. I examined the clothes thoroughly, including those I'd already worn, and wishing I'd thought of it sooner, just in case his elusive brother had placed another electronic tracking device in them. I checked all the clothes, and especially the shoes, which had more places to hide something like that.

"He's a refugee, just like us," Ethan said as I examined each scrap of clothing and then got dressed. "He can help us, Lilith. He's already trying, by leaving us the clothes and supplies."

"Yes, remind me to thank him — if he doesn't get us both killed."

He rolled his eyes as I pulled on my jeans, followed by the clean tank top. It was black, with a red rose painted on the front.

"Why don't you trust my judgment on this, Lilith?" Ethan asked. "Who would know my brother better than I do?"

"The people who programmed him, perhaps?"

He was getting angry with me. I could tell by the tightness of his jaw and the way he was pacing the small room. I didn't want to

217

make him angry, but I couldn't ignore my suspicion about his brother, and I felt compelled to make him listen.

"Ethan, how is it that those DPI hunters knew where we were going last night? How is it that they got there fast enough to nearly catch us? When no one but the two of us and your precious brother knew where we were planning to go? Have you even wondered about that?"

"Of course I wondered about it! But now that I've spoken with him, I know I was wrong to suspect him."

"Then how did they know? How did they find us? And don't tell me it was the tracking device, because we both know it wasn't. They got there too fast, and with too much firepower. They knew where we were going *before* we arrived. They were almost there in time to intercept us, for God's sake."

He stopped pacing and turned to stare directly at me, his eyes trying to convince me of the truth of his words. "I know. And I know it looks bad. But James thinks it was him they were after. That place was one he's used before. They must have found out, somehow, and set a trap for him there. For *him,* Lilith. Not for us."

"So, us nearly being caught in the teeth of

that trap was merely a coincidence?" I asked.

He lowered his head, probably because he knew how lame the explanation sounded to me. "Yes."

"There's no such thing as coincidence, Ethan." I said it softly, trying to temper my words a bit. I'd pulled on the green shirt and left it hanging unbuttoned. I rose and ran my hand up the side of his face, then softened the tone of my voice, reminding myself that he was not the enemy.

"I know it's hard for you to believe your own brother could be working for the DPI, Ethan. But we can't afford to act as if it's impossible. Not when it could cost us our lives."

His head came around, eyes spearing mine. "But we *can* afford to risk our lives in a doomed attempt to rescue the others?"

"I can't afford not to," I told him in all honesty. "That place has to be shut down, Ethan. Those people must be stopped. The prisoners need to be set free. I could never live with myself knowing I hadn't at least tried."

"They don't *want* to be set free," he countered. And he lifted his hands to cup my face, his gaze urgently probing mine. "Those prisoners would turn you in just as soon as look at you, Lilith. You're risking your life for people who didn't ask for it, won't appreciate it and wouldn't know what to do with freedom if it were handed to them this very night."

"Only because they've been deceived. More than deceived, they've been brain-washed. You and I were strong-willed enough to withstand it, Ethan, but not everyone was. It's not their fault they've succumbed to deceptions and lies."

"Maybe not, but it's not *our* fault, either."

I lowered my hands and took a step away from him. "I saw him, you know."

"You saw who?"

Sighing, I sank back down to the floor. "I saw the Wildborn vampire they keep at The Farm."

His expression shocked, Ethan sank down beside me as if his legs were too weak to support him.

"I was looking for the medical unit," I said, "and he sensed me passing and called me to him. He told me that he would rather die than remain there."

"A Wildborn? Are you sure?"

I nodded. "I don't know how I know, but I do. There was something . . . about him. Ethan, he was in chains, locked up in this tiny tin shack that was like an oven. Fed

220

only enough to keep him alive, drained of blood every time they needed it to transform one of us. To make us what we are now."

"Did you — did you try to free him?"

"I wanted to, but he was dying. Nothing I could have done could have saved him. And . . . and he said I would have no chance to get away unless I became a vampire first. He convinced me to come close, and it frightened me, but before I could back away, he yanked me closer and tried to sink his teeth into my neck."

"God, how did you get away?"

I lifted my eyes to Ethan's. "I didn't. He wasn't attacking me, Ethan, he was saving me. Giving me the gift. But he was too weak. That's why I found a blade. That's why I cut my own wrist. He drained me until my mind was nearly as empty as my body, and I collapsed on top of him, barely alive. But then he held my face to his neck, and then I was . . . drinking from him. Drinking and drinking and drinking. And he didn't push me away, and I didn't know. I didn't *know*."

Ethan stroked my hair gently. "You didn't know what?"

"He was so weak — far stronger than any mortal, but so weak for what he was. His skin was gray, his face and eyes, just sunken.

221

It was as if he were already dead. He seemed like a living corpse, and I know he was in agony.

"As I drank from him, I felt his pain. I felt his anguish and heartache and grief and hopelessness. I felt it all, and I thought I would lose my mind with the intensity of it, because that was what he felt. That he would lose — perhaps had already lost — his mind. I felt it all. And I drank it all into me. I drank . . . until there was nothing left."

Ashamed, and barely able to force myself to do so, I looked into Ethan's eyes. "I killed him, Ethan."

"You didn't know."

"That doesn't matter. I still did it. And then I escaped. Just like you did. I left everyone else behind, just like you did. But I killed to do it. *Unlike* you. So I have a lot more to make up for. To atone for. I have to do this. And I'm sorry, Ethan, but I cannot and will not wait here for your brother. I'm not risking my life for nothing." I jumped to my feet, unable to contain my energy anymore.

"It's not nothing to me." He got to his feet, too. "I understand your reasons so much better now, Lilith, but you have to see that there's no benefit in rushing this. James can help us. And besides, getting my brother back, seeing him again, it's important to me. He's all I have, Lilith."

I closed my eyes against the pain that statement stirred to life in me. But I didn't call him on it. I didn't say to him, "What about me?" even though the words were burning on my tongue. There was no point.

I lowered my head and let it rest on his shoulder just for a moment. His arms came around me, holding me lightly, tenderly, against him. Being together had been good. And all too brief, I thought.

"I'll go on alone," I said softly. "You wait here for him. If he betrays you and you end up back in captivity, I'll do my best to get you out along with the others. But I don't know if they'll keep you alive this time, Ethan. You're a vampire now. You fooled them before. But now they know you were only pretending. And if they couldn't break you before, they have to know they have no chance of breaking you now."

I turned away from him, but his voice came after me even as I began to walk up the stairs toward the church's large red entry doors. "The same thing applies to you, you know."

"I know." And I kept walking.

"Lilith, wait!" I stopped, listening. "You can't go alone. You don't even know where

The Farm is."

I still didn't turn to face him. Leaving already felt nearly impossible. Looking at him even once more would make it even harder. "My memory has been returning to me bit by bit. This morning, more of the pieces are there. The night I escaped, the route I took. I think that if I return to the place where I first awakened, I can find my way back to The Farm."

He came up behind me, caught my shoulders and turned me around to face him. There was desperation in his eyes as they searched mine. "You'll be killed if you go back there, Lilith. Please, don't go."

"I have to try." I felt tears burning in my eyes. Not for fear of what I was about to do, but for the pain of leaving this man. How had he come to mean so much to me in so short a time? No, not such a short time, really. There had been something between us long ago. I knew that now. The memory of it burned in my heart. "I'm sorry."

He shook his head slowly, even as I turned away again.

"What happened between us, Ethan . . . it was magical. It . . . meant something to me."

"To me, too. Don't doubt that. I had never —"

"Nor had I. I'll never forget it, Ethan. Or you."

And with that I walked up the stairs to the door. I gripped the cool brass handle and pushed the door open. The night breeze kissed my face in welcome, warm and scented with autumn leaves. Traces of the postsummer warmth still lingered. I stood there for a moment, staring up at the stars that spread like a glittering blanket over the earth. I loved the night.

A fortunate thing, given what I was.

I took one more step, and then he was there, wrapping me in his arms, turning me around, bending to kiss me. And in spite of my resolve, I kissed him back. There was heat between us, an attraction I couldn't deny and a kinship that I wished he could see was far more potent than the one he shared with his brother.

And yet, I had to leave him. I knew that.

As he lifted his head, his eyes glittered like the stars overhead. "I'm going with you."

My eyes, heavy with the beginnings of passion, widened as I searched his. "But . . . what about your brother?"

"I never promised to wait for him. We'll go. Right now. I can't let you do this alone, Lilith. If you were taken or killed, I'd never forgive myself. I'm going with you."

He put an arm around my shoulders then, and started down the church steps to the sidewalk, as if the matter were settled. But then I planted my feet two steps from the bottom, forcing him to stop, to turn and search my face yet again.

"What is it?" he asked.

I licked my lips, nervous that what I was about to ask of him would be too much. But I had to ask — no, demand — one last thing.

"If you come with me, I need your promise that you won't contact your brother again, Ethan."

"What?"

"I know he's important to you, but I — I have to insist on this. Once our mission is done, you can find him again. It won't be so hard this time. He'll be waiting, expecting your call. But while you love and trust him, Ethan, you have to try to understand why I don't. Can't. There's too much at risk here."

He stood staring at me, hurt and bewildered. "Lilith, he's my *brother.* It's been three years."

"Then a few more days can't hurt so much, can they?" I watched his face as he wrestled with the decision I was asking him to make. "I'm not asking you to choose between us. Only to delay your . . . reunion a little bit longer. If you want to come with me, you have to promise not to contact him again or respond when he attempts to contact you, because you know he will. Not until we return from this mission."

I waited as seconds ticked past.

"Ethan, please. You have to at least acknowledge the *possibility* that the DPI were successful in turning him. Brainwashing him. That he's working for them now to recapture me. Us."

Still he said nothing.

Sighing, I lowered my head. "If it's a promise you can't make, I understand. Stay here, and let me go on my own. I won't think less of you, Ethan, I swear I won't. And I'll find you again when it's over."

Alone, I descended the final steps. My feet met the pavement and I walked into the night. And with each step I took, my heart broke just a little bit more. The tears that had been burning in the backs of my eyes welled and then spilled over, burning their trails down the pale, sensitive skin of my face. "Goodbye for now, Ethan," I whispered.

"No!" he shouted, and an instant later he was at my side, his arm again around my shoulders. "No, I can't let you go. I'm going with you. On your terms."

I looked up at him in stunned surprise. "I have your promise?"

"You have it." He smiled tenderly as he lifted a hand to my face, his thumb swiping the tears from my cheeks. "You were crying?"

I didn't answer.

"At the thought of leaving me?" he asked.

I looked away quickly. "I cried — a little — at the idea of facing the rest of this journey on my own. That's all."

"Oh."

The single word held myriad meanings, the main one being that he knew full well I was lying. His arm tightened around me, pulling me closer to his side, and we walked steadily away from the church.

"How far is it, I wonder?" I asked him, still marveling that he had made such a promise, that he was still by my side.

"I have no idea. What we need is a map, and perhaps a car."

"And where are we supposed to find those things?" I asked him.

"In the nearest town." He closed his eyes, and I felt him opening his senses, hunting for the scent of a dense population of humans. When he opened his eyes again, he nodded. "Farther east," he said. "I think there's a town that way. We can find a car there. A map, too, if we're lucky."

"Do you — even know how to drive a car?" I asked.

"It was part of my training. Wasn't it part of yours?"

"No."

He smiled a little. "I imagine, as rebellious as you were, they were afraid you would run them down, then smash through the perimeter fence, if they put you behind the wheel. They probably intended to break you first, then teach you to drive."

"I think they'd given up on breaking me at all. I think they had marked me for death."

He was silent for a moment. Then, "You realize you're still marked for death, don't you? Or worse. If it were only your death they intended, they'd have killed you by now. But if they catch you again, Lilith . . ."

"I know." I lowered my head. "I know."

We came to a crossroads then. Ethan turned me in the direction we needed to take, and we continued walking.

Eventually I saw his head perk up, and after a moment's confusion I knew his brother must be calling out to him. He looked at me quickly and kept on walking. He gave no sign of attempting to reply. And

I knew it was possibly one of the most difficult things he'd ever had to do. And yet he did it . . . for me. All for me.

My heart jumped a bit inside my chest, a feeling like joy suffusing it and flowing into my veins until it filled me. Not because he'd rebuffed his brother — I wanted James to be one of the good guys. I wanted to see the two of them reunited and as close as ever. I wasn't jealous of or threatened by their closeness. No, what made me happy was that Ethan was showing me a level of caring I hadn't believed possible — from anyone.

Was there anything he wouldn't do for me? I wondered.

Maybe he *did* feel as strongly as I did. Maybe. Just maybe.

12

Ethan! James called. *Where the hell are you? I'm at the church where you told me you would be, and it's empty. I thought you were going to wait.*

As carefully as he could, Ethan answered mentally, guarding every thought from Lilith and keeping his face impassive, so she wouldn't be able to tell by looking at him.

I couldn't. Something came up, James. There's going to be a . . . slight delay. There's something I have to do first.

Ethan glanced sideways at Lilith, and she met his eyes and smiled. God, she would never forgive him if she knew. But he felt justified in this small deception. She was wrong about James. Dead wrong.

Something you have to do? James asked. *What? What are you up to, little brother?*

I can't discuss it now, James. I'm going to ask you to trust me. I just need a little time. A few days, at most, and —

You still don't trust me, James accused. *God, I can't tell you how much that hurts me, Ethan. I'm your brother.*

It's not that I don't trust you. I do, but —

If you trusted me, you'd tell me what's going on. What are you up to, Ethan? Is it risky?

Swallowing hard, Ethan glanced at Lilith. She was walking along beside him with an expression of bliss on her face. And he wasn't so dense that he didn't know why. She was relieved that he'd agreed to her terms, that he'd insisted on coming with her. She trusted him.

And he trusted his brother. And he couldn't let her rob him of his only family. It was too much to ask. He was risking his life for her. Shouldn't that be enough?

We're going back to The Farm, James. We're going to try to rescue the other captives.

There was no reply.

James? Are you there?

Nothing.

James! Are you all right?

Still no reply. A sickening feeling began writhing in Ethan's stomach. He had a sudden fear that he knew why his brother had broken off contact once he'd gleaned the information he'd been seeking.

The information Ethan had promised not to give.

Again, he looked at Lilith.

She stopped walking, her smile blossoming wider as she met his gaze, her own adoring and utterly trusting.

"Thank you, Ethan," she whispered. "Believe me, I know that mere words aren't enough, but somehow, on the other side of this, I promise you, I'll find some way to repay you. This means . . . well, it means everything to me. Just . . . everything."

Oh God, he thought, unable to hold her steady gaze. He lowered his head, focusing on the road ahead of him and the lights of the town coming into view just ahead. And all the while he prayed silently that she was wrong. That his brother was not, even now, betraying him.

"There's the village," Lilith said, spotting the cluster of lights and pointing.

"Part one of our mission is all but accomplished. Thank you, Ethan."

Ethan thought he might throw up. But he managed to paste a confident smile on his face and mutter, "You're welcome."

Ethan scanned several parking lots, peering into one vehicle after another. At last he found keys stuffed under the visor of a dark green older-model Ford Bronco. Four-wheel drive and solid, with a powerful engine and plenty of room. It was exactly what they needed, equal to almost any challenge they might encounter. Any transportation-related challenge, at least. As perfect as it was for their driving needs, the vehicle couldn't wipe out a compound full of armed keepers, much less the vampire assassins who would be sent after him and Lilith in the unlikely event that they escaped alive.

Who was he kidding? The vampire assassins had likely already been dispatched. Just because they hadn't yet seen them, didn't mean they weren't out there, lurking in the night. And he and Lilith were running toward them, rather than away. It was insane.

This mission was suicide. His only hope, he decided, was to talk her out of it before they got themselves both killed. There had to be a way.

They got into the Bronco, and Ethan put the keys into the switch and glanced toward the bar where the vehicle's owner was presumably spending his time. It was a small establishment housed in a slab-sided wooden building with a neon sign in the window advertising a popular brand of beer.

A wooden placard nailed above the door proclaimed it the Dirty Dog Bar & Grille. For the life of him, he couldn't find anything appealing about that name.

Lilith shot him a look. "What are you waiting for?"

"It's just what we need, but when we start it up, it'll be loud. The owner's going to hear it."

"There's music pouring from that place. He won't hear a thing."

"And if he does?"

"We're *vampires,* Ethan. What's he going to do?"

"Call the police, report it stolen. We can't afford that. We're being hunted, don't forget."

"Oh, for Pete's sake." She wrenched open the door and got out before he could have known what she was thinking, and even as he got out to go after her, she was marching up the steps of the Dirty Dog, pushing open its dark stained door and stepping inside.

Ethan followed, but stopped in the doorway, wondering what on earth she intended, even as she strode boldly through the dimly lit barroom and straight to the jukebox, where she bent slightly to yank its power cord from the outlet in the wall behind it.

Then she straightened and turned to face

the crowded room.

Dressed in her snug-fitting jeans and tank top, with the green shirt dangling open, her hair long and curling, she made quite a picture, especially with the jukebox cord dangling from one hand. Conversations stopped just as suddenly as the music had, and every eye turned toward her. Men who'd been sitting on stools in front of the polished hardwood bar stared at her. Couples sitting at small round tables set their glasses down, and those standing here and there around the plank floor turned toward her. No one said a word.

"Sorry to interrupt your evening," Lilith said, her voice confident and sexy as hell — to Ethan, at least. "I need to speak with the owner of the green Ford Bronco in the parking lot."

People frowned, murmured to one another. Male eyes devoured her from head to toe. A big man slid from his bar stool and said, "That would be me. Did you ding it or something?"

"Ding it?"

"Hit it? Dent it? What?"

She flashed him a brilliant smile. "Nothing like that. I want to borrow it."

His face split in a grin, and he glanced behind him at some other men. "She wants to borrow it. Hell, well, if that's all, I'll just hand over the keys."

A round of boisterous laughter burst from the patrons. Lilith only blinked and kept smiling. "No need. You left them under the visor. I wanted to just take it, but my friend was reluctant."

The laughter died. The man's smile faded. He took three steps closer, bringing him to within a few feet of her. Ethan started forward from his spot in the doorway, but Lilith quickly held up a hand toward him.

"Are you freakin' crazy, lady? I'm not loaning you my truck."

"Yes, you are." She took a single step closer to the big man. Then she pressed her palm to his cheek, and Ethan could feel the intensity in her eyes as they bored into the man's. Her voice dropped to a mere whisper. "You trust me. We're old friends. You were only playing with me before. It's a running joke between us, my showing up to ask for favors. You know I'll return your truck unscathed and with my undying gratitude, and you want that more than you want to draw another breath — which is also an option. You won't worry about the Bronco. You won't give a second thought to this arrangement. It will all make perfect sense to you until I return your vehicle — one week

from today and just as good as new. I promise."

As she spoke, Ethan watched the man's
face change. It seemed to lose all expression. His eyes emptied, and his jaw went
lax. When she straightened away from him
and met his gaze again, he only nodded.

"So it's okay if I borrow it, then?" she
asked, louder now, for the benefit of his fellow drinkers.

"Yes. It's okay."

Ethan heard some of the others gasp,
heard them speaking softly to one another.
Finally one man spoke louder. "Have you
lost your mind, Sam?"

Sam blinked and turned his head toward
the other man. "She's an old friend. I was
only playing with her before. It's a running
joke between us."

"*I'm* an old friend," the man said. "How
come I never heard of her?"

"She's an old friend," Sam repeated.
Then, as if unable to do otherwise, he
returned his attention to Lilith. "Take it.
It's full of gas."

"Thank you, Sam. I'll see you in a week."

He smiled a little crookedly and stood
exactly where he was as she turned, bent
and plugged the jukebox in again. The
music resumed as she walked to the door.

Ethan stepped aside to let her pass.

"You're out of your mind, you know that?" he asked, following her.

She smiled at him as they hurried across the parking lot. "I remembered that I was trained in mind-control techniques, the power of vampiric suggestion, back at The Farm. So were you, I bet. But it was only theory. I couldn't put it to the test, because I wasn't a vampire yet." She opened the passenger door. "But you were right, Ethan, when you told me about it before. It really works. I can really do it!"

"Apparently so." He was standing behind her as she climbed into the Bronco. She reached for the door, but before pulling it closed, she frowned at him. "Will you get in? We have work to do."

Indeed they did. And he was beginning to realize that finding a way to convince her to change her mind was going to be as big a challenge as the mission itself. He'd been thinking of her as a child, a newly transformed vampire, alone in the world, weak and uncertain. But he could see now that the old Lilith was alive and well inside her and returning to the fore at a frightening pace.

Sighing, he went around to the driver's side, got behind the wheel and started the engine. The powerful machine roared to life, its deep, noisy growl providing little comfort. He backed carefully out of the parking space, planning his words carefully as he turned on the headlights and began to drive.

"This bridge where you woke up — one of them saw you there. They could still be watching for you."

"Yeah, I've thought about that. You were at The Farm. Don't you remember where it is? How to get there?"

He shook his head slowly. "No. The only thought I had that night was getting away. I ran, just like you did, and I never looked back."

She studied him, and he knew she was trying to see inside his mind, read his thoughts to determine if he was lying or not. And he was. He knew, more or less, how to get back to that place. But he blocked his thoughts from her, wondering whether she knew that, or if she just assumed she wasn't very good at mind-reading yet.

"You couldn't even get us into the general vicinity?" she asked. "I'm sure if we got close, we could sense the others. Couldn't we?"

"I don't think we could. There's some kind of barrier around the place. A force field or . . . something like that. As soon as

240

I was beyond the fence, I noticed it." That much, at least, was true.

"How could you know? You'd only just become a vampire."

"I'd been taught that vampires sense the presence of the Chosen. You were taught that, too, weren't you?"

She nodded, saying nothing.

"I tried to feel that, to sense them, to see if I could tell whether my escape had been detected. And I felt nothing. Just . . . emptiness. I wondered if they'd lied about that, but I've felt it since."

"I see," she said softly, probably not believing him. "Then I guess we'll just have to take our chances at the bridge and hope I can find my way back from there."

"There is another way."

She looked at him, and this time she knew what he was thinking, though he didn't think it was because she was reading his mind. "We're *not* contacting your brother. I don't trust him, Ethan. But I do trust you. I trust you to keep your promise to me. I hope I'm not making a mistake."

I waited for Ethan to reply, to reassure me that I could trust him completely. But he didn't, and that worried me.

Still, after hours of driving, he managed

to get us to the bridge where I had awoken. He drove through the town that bordered his home, and I knew that being so close was difficult for him. He wanted to check on his horses, to see whether they'd made it back safely and see to their comfort if they had. But he never spoke of those desires. It would do no good. We both knew we couldn't return there. So we drove on through the little town, and when I saw the field through which I had run, I pointed. "There's another road on the far side of that field," I said. "That's the road that leads to the bridge."

He nodded. "Then we'll take the first left we find and hope for the best."

"Can't we just drive across the field?" I asked. "Wouldn't it be faster?"

"That would draw attention, Lilith. We need to remain undetected for as long as possible."

"It's the dead of night. Who would notice?"

"Why take the risk that *anyone* would?"

I sighed my frustration, but I knew he had a point. So he kept driving, and soon we found a road that went in the direction we wanted; he took it, and we drove some more.

"It seems too far," I said. "We should have come to the road by now."

"You were running full bore, certain you were being pursued, Lilith. You're a vampire, don't forget. You could have covered miles in a very short time."

"I suppose — Wait! There's a crossroads. Could that be it?"

"I don't know." He drove until we came to the stop sign where the two roads met. As we sat there, I looked left, then right.

"Which way?" he asked.

"Right . . . I think."

He turned and drove. When I spotted the bridge looming ahead, I nearly bounced in my seat with exhilaration. "There!" I shouted. "There it is!"

"I see it," he said. I could feel him trying not to let any emotion come through in his tone. But damn, it felt as if he'd been hoping I wouldn't be able to find my way quite this easily.

Then again, we weren't at The Farm. Not yet, anyway.

"We found it, Ethan!" I said, unable to contain my excitement, despite knowing that he didn't share it. "We found the bridge. I *know* we can find The Farm from here. I just know it."

I felt a wave of emotion from him, but it was brief. As if he'd slammed the doors on it the instant it began to flow. It didn't feel like what I was feeling. It wasn't excitement or triumph. Far from it.

"You're not happy about this, are you, Ethan?"

"I have a deep feeling that we're driving this borrowed Bronco straight to our deaths, Lilith. So no, I'm not happy about that."

"And yet you're doing it."

He didn't answer.

"Go straight from here, and then take the next possible left-hand turn. I remember that much, at least."

He nodded and kept driving. He checked the mirrors often, and I did, too, but no one appeared to be following us. So far.

"You were wrong about them watching this place," I said. "No one's spotted us."

"They can hardly follow every vehicle that passes. They may not have known it was us."

"You have a very negative attitude, you know that?"

He sighed, and I sensed his frustration. "What's going to happen to them, Lilith?"

"To whom?" I asked, unable to follow his train of thought.

"These captives you're risking your life to save," he said. "What do you think they're going to do once they're free?"

"Live, I imagine."

"They all have implants, just as you had.

If they didn't when you left, you can bet they do by now. They'll be tracked, followed. Hunted like animals."

"I'll tell them about the devices. They can get them removed."

"Half of them will be caught before they can do that."

"Then half will go free." I shook my head. "Or more, if they remove them quickly enough. And I intend to decimate that place. I intend to cripple the keepers, to buy the prisoners more time to get away."

"How?"

The word burst from him as if driven.

I blinked and stared at him. "I don't know yet. I'll . . . I'll think of something."

He lowered his head slightly but kept on driving.

"It's a long way from here," I told him. "I know we're going in the right direction, but . . . I ran for a long time. Hours, I think."

"We only have a little more than an hour until dawn," he said. "We should start looking for a safe place to rest."

"But —"

"We'll need time once we find The Farm, Lilith. Time to plan, time to carry out the attack, time to get the others to safety. Even if we were two minutes away now, it would be better to wait."

I sighed, rolled my eyes and tipped my head back until it hit the seat behind me. "All right. All right. We'll find a place to rest."

"It's for the best," he said, and I felt the relief in his tone. He wasn't afraid; I didn't get any sense of fear from him. But he was in no hurry to face this battle, and I was beginning to fear he would rather try to stop me than help me as he'd promised to do.

"You don't have to do this, you know," I told him. "If you would rather part ways here, I would understand."

He shot me a look that roiled with emotions I couldn't begin to name. "I don't want to see you killed," he said slowly, and I sensed him choosing his words with great care. "I don't particularly want to die, either, but, Lilith, it's the thought of what could happen to you that's making me dread what's to come."

"Why?" I asked him, nearly shivering with suspense as I awaited his reply.

"I-I'm not sure." He stared deeply into my eyes for a long moment, then tore his gaze away. "I just know that I don't want you hurt or killed, or tortured or captured and returned to that hell, or —"

"Stop," I said. "I'm afraid enough as it is."

"You are?" He sounded surprised. "You

246

don't seem afraid. You seem like a warrior, eager for battle."

I shrugged. "I don't like to be afraid. I'm trying to refuse to let my fear control me. But don't confuse that with the idea that I'm fearless. I'm not. I know what could happen as well as you do."

"Then why do this?"

"Because it's what I want to do, what I'm compelled to do. If I didn't do it just because I'm afraid, that would be letting fear control me. And nothing controls me, Ethan. Nothing and no one. Never again."

He glanced sideways at me. "It's like you have something to prove. Or is it vengeance driving you?"

"Maybe it's both. Or maybe it's Justice, using me as her tool. I just know it has to be done, Ethan. I know that every time I close my eyes and see the lifeless face of the Wildborn I killed to gain my freedom. You know it, too. Someone has to do this. If not me, then who?"

He nodded. "I know."

"Look, there's a barn up ahead."

He looked and nodded. As he drove closer, he said, "It looks abandoned. There, across the road from it, that must have been a house once."

Now the "house" was little more than a

crumbling foundation, with the worn black shingles of a peaked roof lying broken and cockeyed on the ground.

The barn was in far better shape, but it, too, showed signs of deterioration. He drove past it slowly, his sharp senses scanning the area just as mine were.

"No one's around," I said. "At least no one I can feel."

He nodded, turned the Bronco around and started back. "If we can get the door open, we can drive right inside, so the truck won't be seen."

"You're good at this," I told him.

"I've been hiding for a long time."

"And now I'm taking you back to the people you've been hiding from." I thought just then that it might have been better for him if I'd never found him that first night of my new life.

His gaze snapped toward mine instantly, and he said, "Don't think that, Lilith. You were *meant* to find me."

I started, surprised that my thoughts had been so easily heard by him. "Do you really think that's true?"

"I do."

"So that you can help me rescue the others?" I asked.

"So that I can keep you alive."

13

"Lilith is your daughter," Ginger said softly. "I'm putting you in charge while we're here."

Serena had been with the Sisterhood of Athena for twenty-one years, but being in charge had never been one of her goals. She was content to be a soldier in the cause. Giving orders wasn't her forte.

"I don't need you to do that, Ginger," she said.

The three of them were parked in front of Ethan's home, with its long curving driveway, rolling fields, immaculate stable and pristine house. Red, with white trim to match the picket fences, the place was warm and welcoming. It was also abandoned.

"I need to do it," Ginger said. "This plan is in direct violation of our rules. If it goes badly, I don't want to shoulder the blame. Neither do any of the others. It would drive a wedge into the heart of the organization."

Serena felt the weight of the world settling heavily onto her shoulders. "You're right. At least they might forgive me — once the whole truth comes out — chalk it up to a mother's love."

"Besides," Terry added, "who better to know what's best for Lilith than her own mother?"

Serena tried to slow her racing heart. She'd been the one to suggest they put a team out here, in case Ethan and Lilith returned. It was a long shot, but she hadn't been able to think of anything better. It had taken a couple of days to organize after Ginger had not only agreed but insisted on coming along.

Then again, she was still trying to keep the truth about Serena's relationship with one of the Undead under wraps, so it made sense.

"All right, then, let's go," Serena said, giving her first order.

As one, the three women exited the blue Ford Taurus, which they'd parked at the end of the driveway that snugged up beside the house, making it less obvious, though not invisible. They strode toward the house, and then a soft beeping sound brought them to a stop.

"It's the GPS!" Serena yanked the small

gray box from its belt clip and stared at the flashing light on the screen, blessing the day they'd managed to hack the DPI's tracking program. "They're close and coming closer." She turned, scanning the horizon, and then a nickering call brought her head around.

Serena smiled as she saw two horses galloping across the meadow toward the stables, their glorious manes flying as their hooves thundered over the earth, and with every stride, the beeping on her tracking unit got louder and faster. Then she realized that the horses were riderless, and her smile froze and then died.

"Something's happened to them," she whispered.

Terry clutched her shoulder. "Not necessarily."

"No," Ginger said. "They're smart. They must have found the transmitter, attached it to one of the horses and sent them home. Freaking ingenious."

Serena felt as if her heart had fallen to her feet, but she tried to hold back tears. God knew she'd shed far too many of them over the years, and not one had done any good.

Terry gave her a squeeze. "Look, you get the door open, so we can spend the night in the house. Ginger and I will check out the

251

horses. Okay?"

Blinking, she nodded and fished in her backpack for the tiny zipper pouch that contained her lock-picking tools. Breaking and entering was one of the skills the Sisters mastered during their training, and she was no exception.

She opened the door without too much trouble, then stepped inside and lifted her head. She went stone-still as she spotted the painting above the fireplace, a portrait that bore the same name as her daughter.

Lilith.

And it looked like her, in subtle ways. The hair, the skin tone, the height.

Serena swallowed the lump in her throat and blinked her eyes dry. She dragged her gaze away from the painting with no small effort, tossed the tracking unit onto a coffee table and forced herself to check out the rest of the house, beginning with the kitchen. They would need to eat, after all. As she had suspected, the cupboards were bare, and the fridge held only a stack of plastic bags with the familiar Red Cross logo on them.

She'd moved on to the dining room, in search of clues that might lead her to her daughter, when she heard the others come in and returned to the living room.

"How are the horses?" she asked.

"They're fine. Tired, I think, but they came inside without any trouble," Terry said. "Walked right into their stalls, once we'd cleaned them and put down fresh straw."

"You rubbed them down? Fed them?"

The two women nodded in unison.

"That's good. God only knows how far they've run." She returned to the window and sank into a chair.

"Have you found anything here, Serena?" Ginger asked. "Any sign of where they might have gone?"

"No." She glanced at the gray electronic box that lay uselessly on the coffee table. "And we can't track them with this anymore. But then again, neither can the DPI."

Ginger moved closer and pressed a hand to Serena's forearm. "I'm sorry. To have come so close, after searching for her for so long —"

"It's not over, Ginger. I'm determined to find her, and I will."

"I know you will," the older woman replied.

Terry stood looking around the room. "I doubt they're coming back here tonight. It's too close to dawn. They would have taken shelter by now."

"I doubt they'll come back here at all," Serena replied. "They have to know the place is being watched."

"*If* it's being watched," Terry said, looking nervously toward the window behind Serena's head, "then should we still be here?"

"We're not vampires," Ginger said. "They might be watching, but they won't bother us, probably won't even approach us. They won't risk knowledge of their activities leaking to the public, and as far as we know, they have no idea the Sisterhood even exists."

Terry nodded, but she still looked nervous. She had been with the organization nearly as long as Ginger had, and in the years since Serena had joined their ranks, she didn't remember ever seeing her shaken before.

"If we're staying, we'll need supplies," Ginger said.

"Yeah, there's not a crumb here to eat," Serena told her.

"Should I go into town and get food?" Terry asked.

"Not alone," Serena said. "You should both go." She glanced at Ginger then, because she was so unused to giving orders. But Ginger nodded her approval, encouraging her to continue. "I want to stay here, just in case they come back."

"Anything else?" Ginger asked — almost as if it were a test.

Serena licked her lips and thought. "Be discreet, and stick to our cover story. Keep a sharp eye out, too. It wouldn't hurt us to know whether those government goons are keeping tabs on us. Notice everything."

"Will you be okay here alone?" Terry asked. "Maybe we should all go. It won't take long, and if they come back —"

"Go." Serena smiled, even though she was far from feeling it. "I'll be fine. I have a hankering for an omelet. Bacon on the side. Oh, and coffee, for God's sake."

"We'll be back in no time," Ginger said, taking Terry's arm and heading for the door.

Serena waited for the sound of the car, and only as it faded did she lower her head into her hands and let the tears she'd been holding back come pouring out.

She'd been so close! But she hadn't had the reunion she'd dreamed of, the fantasy that had kept her going for so many years. Only a glimpse, a teasing glimpse of her flesh and blood, and no more.

Lilith — the name those bastards had given her — was a grown woman now. A vampire, yes, but her daughter, still. And she was beautiful. More beautiful than even Serena had imagined. She wished she'd been able to look at her more thoroughly, to drink in every feature, to talk to her, to touch her. . . .

"I'm closer than I've ever been before," she whispered, wiping the hot tears from her cheeks. "I'm going to find her this time."

A knock at the front door startled her, and Serena shot to her feet, darting a quick look in that direction before dashing into the kitchen to splash cold water on her face. The tears must not show. The Sisters of Athena did not weep. Not in front of others, at least.

As she grabbed a hand towel to dab her face dry, she called, "I'm coming." Then she hung the towel neatly where she'd found it and walked to the front door. "Who's there?"

"Police, ma'am."

She peered through the window beside the door. The man wore a dark blue suit. No uniform. She didn't see a car in the driveway, either. "Police, my ass," she muttered. But she moved to open the door all the same, replaying her cover story in her mind.

She opened the door and fixed a calm expression on her face as she looked up at the tall man who stood on the other side.

"Ma'am," the man said with a respectful

nod. "Are you the owner here?"

"Oh, I wish," she replied with a smile. "No, I'm just house — and horse — sitting while the owner's out of town."

"I see." He looked around. "I don't see a vehicle."

"No, I don't, either. Did you walk here, *officer?*"

He looked back at her quickly. Had her sarcasm been a little bit too evident? "I parked down by the road."

"What an odd thing to do."

"Where's your car, ma'am?"

"Oh, I'm not here alone. I have two colleagues with me. They took the car into town to get us some junk food and DVDs."

"I see. And can I get your name?"

"Sure. If I can get yours. I imagine it's on your identification, isn't it?"

He frowned at her. "There's really no need to be defensive, ma'am. Unless you have something to hide."

"I'm a woman alone in the middle of nowhere, with a strange man standing at my door. I'm not being defensive, I'm being careful."

He smiled a little. "How well do you know the owner?"

"Not well at all. I've met him once or twice, and we share a love of horses. He phoned to ask if I could care for his, and I said yes." She waved a hand. "How could I not? It's a gorgeous place, and like I said, I love horses."

"And where are these horses now?"

"Munching oats in the stable," she said, hoping that nasty little tracking device had been crushed to dust by now.

"Do you know the owner's name?"

"It's on the mailbox, Officer. Dan Smith."

"Mmm. And how long will *Mr. Smith* be gone?"

"It's open-ended. I told him I could stay as long as he needed."

"Do you know where he's gone? Did he leave any contact information with you?"

"No. And no."

"Don't you think that's a bit odd? What if something happened to one of the horses?"

"I imagine I'd call a vet. You still haven't shown me your ID."

He stared at her silently for a moment, as if trying to decide whether she was what she said she was. She probably ought to stop taunting him and play the obedient citizen, intimidated, as most people were, by authority figures.

"Oh, hell," she said, reaching into her pocket and pulling out a business card. "Here."

He read the card out loud. "Peggy Johnson. House-sitting and In-Home Animal Care."

"That's right."

"There's no address."

"I go where I'm needed."

"Work is that steady?"

"You'd be surprised." She smiled. "Why don't you call my office if you don't believe me?"

His eyes narrowed a little, and he pulled a cell phone from a pocket, quickly dialing the number.

The phone that was clipped to her jeans pocket rang, and she quickly picked it up and said, "Peggy Johnson, House-Sitting and In-Home Animal Care. Can I help you?"

The "cop" almost smiled as he closed his flip phone and returned it to his pocket. "Very funny," he said.

"I couldn't help myself. You're so serious. Is Mr. Smith in some kind of trouble?"

"No. I just need to ask him some questions about a few things."

"I see. Well, I'll tell him you were here if he calls in. Or if not, then when he returns."

"You do that, Ms. Johnson." He nodded, his eyes taking their time scanning the room beyond her before he finally turned and walked down the driveway, back to where she saw he'd actually parked his car. Why? Did he have a partner waiting in the vehicle? Weapons? What?

She watched him all the way there, then watched him get into the vehicle, visible now that she knew where to look. Though it was too dark outside to see many details, she could tell it was a big, darkly colored SUV. She remained where she was until it pulled out of sight.

She wondered briefly whether he'd believed her, and knew that whether he had or not, he would be checking out her story. She was grateful that she and Ginger had planted enough information to satisfy at least a surface investigation. There was a Web site advertising her services, complete with testimonials from satisfied customers, all of whom were, of course, Sisters of Athena.

No matter what he thought at the moment, once he checked on her, he would believe her story. What other theory would explain the presence of a harmless-looking mortal woman in the home of a vampire?

Nothing he could imagine, she ventured.

After he drove away, she turned, noticing again the framed print that hung above the mantel. It was meant to depict the legendary first wife of Adam, the one who refused to submit, and was expelled from the garden and replaced by the obedient Eve.

Well, obedient for a while, anyway.

Ethan must have cared a great deal for her daughter when they'd been at The Farm. Maybe he'd even loved her.

She hoped he still did. That he would continue to. That he would protect her, the way Serena wished she could do herself.

Moving to the window, she gazed out at the slowly fading night. "I'll find you, sweetheart. I will. And I'll make everything all right for you again. I promise."

The sound of a car, moving far too quickly along the driveway, startled her, and Serena turned and rushed to the front door, fully expecting to see the faux cop and a dozen friends swooping in on her.

Instead she saw the familiar Taurus, Ginger behind the wheel, Terry gripping the dashboard as if for dear life.

Opening the door, Serena rushed outside, meeting them halfway as they hurried toward the house. Ginger was holding up her cell phone, her eyes eager. "We had a message from —"

"Not here!" Serena flung up a hand in traffic cop fashion, stopping her in midsentence even as she looked left and then right

261

in search of eavesdroppers. When Ginger blinked in confusion, she said, "I had a visitor while you were gone. Can't be sure he's not still lurking."

Terry and Ginger exchanged glances, then nodded. Terry had two bags in her arms, and Serena felt her stomach growl in spite of everything on her mind.

The three women went straight to the kitchen, where Terry set the bags down and began putting things away.

"Is it safe to speak in here?" Ginger asked.

"Yes, but softly." She cranked on the water taps and turned on the range's vent fan just in case.

"Who was he?" Terry asked, opening the fridge and wrinkling her nose in distaste.

"DPI." Serena grabbed one of the grocery bags, and, edging Terry out of the way, quickly put the blood into the bag and tucked it into the vegetable crisper, out of sight. "He said he was a cop, but he never showed any ID. I gave him the cover story, and I think he bought it."

"For how long?" Ginger asked. "Not that it matters. We won't be here long anyway. Here." She held out her cell phone.

Serena took it and looked at the screen, which showed the text of an e-mail. Glancing up, she asked, "From Callista?" The other two nodded.

Serena looked back at the phone and began reading the message aloud. " 'Sending this risky — but risks necessary now. E and L plan return to Farm to rescue rest. Everyone knows and they're waiting. It's a trap. Find this place and intercept them first. Stop them at all cost or they will both be killed. Farm is former military base, if that helps. Must return phone before missed. Will leave on. Number 555-0689. DO NOT CALL THIS NUMBER. Use to triangulate signal.' "

Serena tried scrolling down for more, but that was the end of the message, except for an odd little symbol, two zeroes with a V underneath them.

0 0
V

It vaguely resembled the face of an owl. Owls being sacred to Athena, and one of Her symbols, this simple design told Serena that the e-mail was genuine.

"How could they know?" she asked, and even she wasn't certain who she was asking. The phone? The woman who'd sent the message and could not hear her? The two who stood staring at her now? Or the gods themselves? Maybe all of the above.

"They must have told someone about their plan," Ginger said. "Someone who betrayed them."

Nodding, Serena fished out her own cell phone and placed a call to the Sisterhood's Appalachian headquarters — the place she called home. "It's Serena. I need you to find the location of a cell phone signal. Can you do that?" She listened, then nodded and gave them the information. "Call me back when you have it." Then she hung up. "As soon as we know where The Farm is, we'll head out."

"I'm not quite sure how we're going to do that," Ginger said. "Lock the doors, ladies."

Serena frowned, turning. Ginger was standing at a window, holding the heavy curtain aside and looking out. The other two quickly looked, as well.

There were people out there. Two at the end of the driveway. One near the stable. Three more in the trees to the right. Just standing there, pale as ghosts.

Terry jerked back from the window, ran to the door and threw the locks. "Are they . . . ?"

"Vampires," Ginger said. "And if they want us, I don't think locks will keep them out."

Serena stood silently, staring at the creatures, wondering why they were lurking, what the hell they wanted. None of them were moving any closer. They were just standing there. "Callista told us that the Chosen at The Farm are transformed when they reach adulthood and sent on missions for the DPI. I'd say we're their latest mission."

Terry was shaking visibly. "So what do we do, then?"

Ginger backed away from the window and strode toward the fridge. "I don't know about you, but I'm going to get something to eat."

"I'm going to take a quick look around before the sun rises."

"Hell, Ethan, there are two hours before dawn. At least." Lilith leaned on a post inside the barn as he headed for the door. The place smelled of musty hay long past its usefulness.

"I know. But still . . . just to be on the safe side," Ethan said.

Lilith nodded, then returned to her task, spreading her blanket-cum-cloak over the straw on the floor to create a soft place to rest.

Ethan stepped outside and swung the barn

door closed behind him, but he walked only a short distance before he lowered himself onto the grassy ground, closed his eyes and focused on blocking his thoughts from everyone except the one to whom he spoke. There was no longer much reason to keep James in the dark. He couldn't find them now, even if he wanted to. They were walking into the lion's den of their own free will.

James? James, can you hear me?

I've been waiting all night! Where are you? Are you still all right?

Ethan nodded, letting the feeling of the motion move from his mind to his brother's. *We're fine. But she's remembering her way back, and I'm beginning to think there's no talking her out of this insane notion.*

Then stop trying.

Ethan went still, shocked into silence by his brother's suggestion.

Maybe she's right, Ethan. Have you thought of that? I've entertained the notion of returning to that place and freeing everyone there ever since I left.

But you didn't. The thought rushed from him before he could censor it.

And you resent it, don't you? That I didn't come back for you. But think about it. You didn't go back for Lilith, either. You left her

266

there, because you knew you would have no chance.

No, that wasn't why. I was waiting.

For what?

For you! I knew that if I could find you, you'd help me. You'd know things, you'd have ideas, you'd . . . help me.

He felt his brother's hesitation before he finally replied. *And that's exactly what I'm going to do, Ethan. I'm going to help you. There are three of us now. That's three times the chance of success.*

Three times zero is still zero. I can't believe you're going along with this insanity.

I thought you said you planned to go back yourself?

For Lilith! Ethan shouted mentally. *But she's free now, and there's no reason to risk my life for the others. They don't even want our help.*

Some of them might, James returned. *Just tell me when you get there. I'll be waiting.*

We'll hit the road again at sundown, and we don't have far to go. I'll delay her, try to steer her off course, pray to God she can't find her way and that we aren't spotted while she tries. But if we get there, we'll be there before sunrise tomorrow. Well before, I imagine.

I'll be there, James promised. *And, Ethan . . .*

267

I'm sorry. I'm sorry I didn't come back for you.

"Ethan?"

He started, spun around and tried to wipe the guilty look off his face as he spotted Lilith standing there staring at him. And then he didn't need to try anymore, because she was completely naked. She'd pulled her long hair around in front of her shoulders, so that the endless coils spilled over her breasts and waist and hips, all the way to her thighs. But they hid nothing, only made the tantalizing glimpses even more erotic.

He felt himself growing hard, and he wanted her right then, more than he'd ever wanted anything.

"If you don't hurry it up, we won't have time for sex before we sleep."

He felt his lips pull into a smile. "I thought you said we had two hours," he said, rising and moving toward her slowly.

She walked toward him, holding out her hands. "It was so good before, Ethan," she whispered. "I want as much of that as I can get. Don't you?"

"Oh, *hell* yes."

She flashed him a smile that was more than pleased, but then, as he reached for her hands, she dropped them to her sides, turned and walked away from him, back into the barn.

Ethan practically ran after her.

14

I relished Ethan. Every touch, every sensation, every incredible, mind-bending orgasm. And maybe part of the reason was that I knew we might not get another chance. The very next nightfall would bring us to our goal — well, *my* goal, not his. And I knew we could die in the effort if things went badly.

And yet there wasn't a cell in my body that truly believed that could happen. We would be successful, I knew we would. We would free them all. We would shut that horrible place down for good. I felt buoyant. And I knew part of that was because of him. Had I been facing this challenge alone, I thought I would have been much less optimistic about my chances. But I honestly felt as if there was nothing I couldn't accomplish with this man by my side.

I lay there then, in his arms, and he held me as if I were the most cherished thing in the universe.

"We're going to make this work," I told him. "We'll be successful, and we'll escape unscathed. I know we will."

"I hope you're right," he said. "And if we do . . . then what?"

I felt my brows furrow in a tight little frown. "What do you mean?"

"I mean — what's going to happen afterward?"

I lifted my head from his shoulder to better see his face, but there was no reading his expression. "We'll live freely. Without being hunted. We'll have others of our own kind to interact with."

He shook his head slowly. "Not of our own kind, Lilith. Not really. We're vampires. The captives at The Farm are the Chosen — not the Undead. They're *not* like us."

I lowered my eyes and nodded reluctantly.

"But that wasn't what I meant by my question," he said softly. "I meant, what will *you* do if we survive this?"

I blinked, my head coming up again, my eyes meeting his. "I don't know. I . . . could stay with you, I suppose. If . . . if that's what you're asking."

He smiled. "I guess it is. I feel like we have something together, Lilith. Something more than just this physical bliss we've been enjoying. And I'd like to take some time to find out just what it is."

"Oh, I already know what it is," I told him. And I ran a hand over his cheek. "It's trust."

His eyes shifted to the left, away from mine.

"I don't think I've ever trusted anyone before," I told him. "It's a new feeling for me. All those years at The Farm — I've been remembering more and more, and I know I didn't trust anyone there. Or anything they told me."

"Does that include your fellow inmates?" he asked.

"Oh, yes. I cared about them, but I wasn't stupid. I don't think I've *ever* been stupid. So no, I didn't trust them." I lowered my head to his shoulder again, pressed small kisses to his neck. "But I trust *you*." It felt so good to be able to say that to another being, and to mean it.

His arms tightened around me, but he didn't say a word.

Ginger put her superior on speaker, so the others could hear the entire conversation. They all knew this was going to be a delicate negotiation. While the heads of the organization knew about the existence of The Farm, they didn't know that Ginger's branch of the Sisterhood had placed a woman inside. They didn't know that Serena was the mother of an escaped vampiress. They didn't know that Ginger, Serena, Terry and Callista had been waging a four-woman campaign to uncover the DPI's secrets and rescue Lilith for her mother.

When Phaedra answered, Ginger said, "We have discovered the location of The Farm."

"How?" Phaedra asked.

"Anonymous tip."

"Anonymous?" Phaedra hesitated. "Do you realize that would suggest that someone not of the Sisterhood has learned of our existence?"

"Well, we already know there are a handful of vampires who know. It may have been one of them."

"But you don't know for sure?"

"No, Lady Phaedra, I don't know."

There was silence on the other end. Ginger glanced from Serena to Terry and back again, cleared her throat and said, "There's more."

"Do tell."

"Well, we know of two vampires who escaped captivity. And we believe they're on their way back there to try to free the others. We suspect the DPI knows it, too, and

273

are waiting in ambush."

"This anonymous source of yours seems to have a lot of information."

"Yes," Ginger said. And Serena knew the other woman had also heard the skepticism in Lady Phaedra's tone, the suspicion. "We'd like to intercept the vamps. To warn them."

Phaedra sighed into the phone. "And you believe this meets with our criteria for intervention?"

"I do. Humans — the DPI, in this case — are tampering with the supernatural order. It's our sworn mission to prevent that kind of tampering, to protect that order and allow it to evolve as it's meant to. Besides," she added, "they won't stand a chance if they walk into that trap."

Serena could almost see the older woman nodding slowly, eyes narrowing as she considered every option. She was thinking, and Serena, Ginger and Terry stayed silent, giving her time to strategize.

"I agree," Phaedra said at length. "Although I'm going to insist on a full accounting afterward, you realize." Her voice had a water-over-gravel quality, probably from years of sneaking cigarettes, despite the Sisterhood's ban on smoking. The Sisters of Athena had to be healthy and strong, and

274

Phaedra was both, in spades. But she still loved her Marlboros. "What is your plan?"

"I'd like to send several groups out today. Have them waiting along every route to The Farm, with orders to intercept the vampires if and when they try to pass."

Serena nearly held her breath as she awaited the reply. Terry was listening, too, but also constantly peering outside at the vampires standing sentry all around them.

They hadn't tried to come inside yet. They hadn't attacked. They were just . . . watching. Waiting. Probably for Ethan and Lilith.

"Ginger, you'll have to keep your women far enough from The Farm to be safe. You'll have to make it look innocent. As if they've stopped along the road to — I don't know — change a tire. That sort of thing."

"Yes, naturally."

"And they'll need to be armed with tranquilizers — every single one of them. I will not risk my women being killed by vampires who may not realize they're only trying to help."

Ginger swallowed, her eyes shooting to Serena's. "All right."

"I want the intervention to be fast. Instantaneous. If the DPI forces catch you, God only knows the damage that could be done. We cannot risk the government getting a clue as to our existence. They would destroy us."

"They would try," Ginger agreed.

"So this is how it will unfold. The vampires begin to pass, our women stop them, tranquilize them and get them to hell out of there. Immediately. No conversation. No reasoning. You strike, and you get out."

Serena closed her eyes, not liking the plan at all. And yet it was probably the only thing that would work.

"Once you get them to safety, they are to be physically restrained until they wake and we can explain the situation, and determine that they are not a threat. And even then, I want most of the Sisters well beyond their reach. Understood?"

"Yes, Lady Phaedra."

"All right, then. It will take place tonight?"

"I'm almost certain of it," Ginger said.

"I'll expect a report as soon as it's done."

"Yes, ma'am. Thank you."

"Be extremely cautious, Ginger. Your main objective is to protect the anonymity of the Sisterhood of Athena. That above all else."

"Yes, ma'am," Ginger said again. "I'll call you tonight, when it's done."

"Do that. And text me the location of The Farm as soon as you hang up."

The click of Phaedra disconnecting

seemed to be the period at the end of a sentence. "In case we die tonight," Ginger whispered. She sighed and lowered her head. "It's the best we could have hoped for."

"You didn't mention that we were sitting here surrounded by DPI-trained vamps," Terry said. "You should have had her send help."

"We won't need help," Serena said softly. She nodded toward the grandfather clock, with its slowly swinging pendulum, in the corner of the room. "It'll be dawn in another hour. They can't very well stand there watching us while the sun comes up. They'd be toast."

"You really think they're alone?" Terry asked. Then she shook her head slowly, in answer to her own question. "Their mortal puppetmasters must be nearby. They'll take over watching us like vultures once the vamps take cover for the day."

"Maybe. Maybe not," Ginger said. "It's vampires they were sent to find, after all. Ethan and Lilith. And they have to rest by day, too. Once they fall asleep we'll be able to slide right out of here unnoticed."

Serena nodded. "We'll have to make sure of that. I don't want to find Lilith, only to learn that I led the DPI right to her." She thinned her lips and began picking up the empty plates. They'd made bacon, lettuce and tomato sandwiches for their predawn dinner. "We need to get out a map and start planning this out in detail."

"We have everything we need back at Athena House," Terry said.

"Yeah, and that's where we're heading, the minute the sun comes up," Serena said. "Let's try to rest, okay? I'll set my phone alarm to wake us in an hour."

"Yeah. Like I'm going to be able to sleep," Terry muttered.

As dawn came, I fell asleep — perhaps for the last time — in Ethan's arms and that was where I awoke at dusk. I tugged myself free and sat up slightly, so I could look down at him. He was a beautiful man. Reluctant to help me in my mission, yes, but surely he would soon see that it was necessary.

He opened his eyes slowly, and his lips pulled into a soft smile as he saw me looking at him. Drinking him in.

"You look happy this evening," he said.

I let my smile grow. "I am. Tonight's the night we're going to find that place and free the captives."

He blinked, his smile fading a little. "Oh.

278

I thought — Never mind."

Realizing my mistake immediately, I hurried on. "Besides, what woman wouldn't wake up happy after the time we spent together and sleeping in your arms all day long?"

He nodded, but I didn't think he bought it. Not entirely, anyway. He knew I had a one-track mind, and right now that track was leading me to The Farm.

Still, he pulled me to him for a deep kiss that grew deeper and hotter in a hurry. I enjoyed it thoroughly, until I began to suspect his intent. And then I pulled away and blinked at him.

"Are you trying to distract me?"

He sighed and let his hands fall away from my shoulders. I missed his touch immediately, but I knew it was necessary. "I was hoping to. But I didn't think it would work."

"You know me very well, then, Ethan."

He nodded. "I like to think so. Listen, once we locate the place, we should take enough time to do some careful surveillance. Map it out, note all the ways in and out. We should know how many guards there are, when they change shifts, what weapons they carry, things like that."

I sat on my heels. "You *are* trying to delay us."

He sat up, too, smoothing my hair as if soothing my temper. "I'm only trying to keep us alive. And we'd be more likely to stay that way with more help."

I rolled my eyes. "Not this again."

"Lilith, my brother —"

"I don't trust him. I don't *know* him."

"He's one of us. What more is there to know?"

"How about whether or not he's working for *them,* Ethan? How about whether he's only in touch with you now because he's hunting you? Or me?"

"He's my brother."

I lowered my head, lifted it again and got to my feet, then gathered up our few possessions, walked to the Bronco and tossed them inside. I moved to the barn doors to open them wide.

The night spread out before me, smelling of alfalfa and wildflowers. It was warm, and barely a breeze stirred the air.

I heard Ethan sigh, but he got up and pulled on his clothes. Then he joined me outside, looking around, but not listening to the night birds and crickets as I was, I thought. No, he was searching for signs of trouble.

His caution irritated me. I went back inside and got into the vehicle, and then, growing impatient when he took his time joining me, I turned the key, starting the noisy engine.

He took the hint and got in beside me, shoving me over to the passenger seat. "I've never seen anyone in such a hurry to face her own demise," he muttered. He said it as if he was joking, but I knew that deep down, he wasn't. Not really.

"I'm in a hurry to get my siblings out of that place."

He looked at me sharply. "You have family there?"

"So do you," I told him. "We're all family. It's in the blood, and it's a bond every bit as strong as the one you have with your brother, Ethan, whether you like to admit it or not."

"It's not the same."

I pressed my lips together and said nothing as he backed the vehicle out of the barn and, once clear, drove over the bumpy ground to the road beyond. I half expected him to turn in the opposite direction from the one I wanted him to take, but he didn't. He continued on the same course we'd chosen the night before.

We drove in silence for quite some time, and then my head rose, my senses perked. "I think — yes, this is familiar. I came this way, I'm sure of it. I cut through those woods, to stay out of sight, but I followed the road all the same. This very road, Ethan!"

He nodded. "I think we must be close, then," he said.

"Yes, I think we —" I broke off there and looked at him. He was slowing down. But I'd felt his thoughts as he'd spoken. He didn't *think* we were close. He *knew* it. "How do you know we're close?" I asked him.

He didn't look at me, not even a quick glance, and I could feel the shields going up in his mind, blocking mine from entry. I couldn't read his thoughts, which made me both suspicious and . . . hurt.

"It's only a guess," he said.

"No, it's not."

He looked at me sharply. "I'm just going by how far I estimate you could have traveled in a single night and how far we've already come, and —"

"Then why are you guarding your thoughts from me?"

"I'm not." And that was so obvious a lie, even a mortal would have detected it.

"You're lying to me, Ethan." I blinked, stunned at this revelation. "You *know,* don't you? You know where The Farm is. You've known all along!"

"Lilith, I —"

"I *trusted* you," I whispered. And the pain in my chest was so intense that I almost couldn't bear it. I wondered at the enormity of it but brushed the questions aside as I rushed on. "I've never trusted anyone before. Not ever. But I trusted *you.*"

He pulled the truck onto the shoulder, sending up a cloud of dust, and braked to a stop. Then he closed his eyes briefly. "You can still trust me, Lilith."

"How?" I asked.

"Look, you're right, okay? I *have* known the location of The Farm this entire time. But I thought if I just had some time with you, I could —"

"Where?" I demanded.

He was silent, so I said it again. "Where is it, Ethan? You said I could trust you, so prove it. Tell me the truth, for once."

"Ten miles, straight ahead." The words seemed to be wrenched from his chest, as if he were speaking against his will. "Then there's a dirt track that veers off to the right, twisting into the woods. The compound is just beyond the end of the tree line."

I nodded just once, then wrenched the door open, got out and began walking.

He caught up to me in seconds. "Lilith, I

wasn't trying to deceive you. I just wanted more time to try to change your mind."

"You lied to me."

"I want you to stay alive, dammit."

"By keeping me from doing what I have to do? What I'm willing to die to do?"

"I can't bear to see you die. How can you hate me for that?"

"You left me behind in that place. And all the others, as well. You didn't come back for us. You wrote me off to embrace your own freedom. Where was all this concern for my well-being then?"

"That was before. I was young and naive, and I felt powerless. But I never stopped thinking about you, Lilith. You know that's true. You saw the proof of it in that print I keep hanging above my mantel. I intended to return, to try to free you — you know that, as well. I only wanted to find my brother first, so I could —"

I whirled on him. "Your brother, your brother, your *brother*. I'm so sick of hearing about your damned brother!"

"He can help us, Lilith." He gripped my shoulders, as if trying to force-feed me the words.

"Go find him, then. Be with him. He's all you've thought about from the beginning. Just go. I'll do this alone." Pulling free of him, I turned and began walking again.

And that was when I felt the stabbing pain in my shoulder. I flinched, my hand flying to the spot as my eyes searched the night for its source. I felt a dart embedded in my arm and yanked it free, then hurled it away with all my might, even as I whirled and saw people crouching in the brush along the roadside. And then, just as I spotted them, they began to blur before my eyes.

"Lilith!" Ethan ran toward me, but even as I turned to look back at him another dart hit me, squarely in the hip this time. I felt myself weakening, falling.

"Run, Ethan," I whispered. "Save yourself."

He came toward me anyway, but I didn't see what happened next. My vision went dark as I hit the pavement.

Ethan was stunned by the attack. He'd been so focused on Lilith that he'd failed to detect anyone waiting in ambush. Darts flew from the brush along the roadsides, one grazing him even though he ducked.

Then, suddenly, he heard squealing tires, saw bright lights and blinked, confused, as the Bronco sped up beside him.

He fought to keep his footing, his eyes ahead, on Lilith. But the door opened and someone yanked him into the truck.

"No," he managed, though his tongue felt thick. "Have to save . . . Lilith." He fought to stay conscious, peered through blurry eyes as the Bronco lurched into motion.

Lilith was lying on the pavement ahead, a hooded figure bending over her. He sensed it was female and mortal, but no more. She was blocking. An ordinary mortal, blocking her thoughts from a vampire. It had to be one of the keepers or some other agent of the DPI.

And then the Bronco looped around in a semicircle and began speeding in the opposite direction.

"No!" he shouted, finally turning his attention to the person driving his borrowed vehicle.

James. His brother shifted into a higher gear and stomped on the accelerator.

"James, no! We have to save her!"

As he spoke, he twisted around in his seat, looking back. He saw another vehicle skidding to a halt in the road, and Lilith being lifted and shoved into the backseat. Panicking, he reached for the wheel, tried to pull it from his brother's powerful hands, to turn the truck around himself.

But he was weak, and his brother easily pried his hands off the steering wheel.

"We'll get her back. But not here," James said. "We're outnumbered, out-armed. You try it here, they'll get you, too, little brother. They'll have both of us. And then who'll be left to save your Lilith?"

"But —"

"Ethan, trust me. This is the only way to save her. We get away, we find out where they're taking her and then we attack. They'll never expect it."

Ethan's stomach lurched as they sped farther away from Lilith. He gagged and lowered his head to the seat. "We know where they're taking her," he told his brother. "Back to The Farm."

James patted his shoulder. "I don't know who that was, Ethan, but I don't think they were DPI."

Ethan's head came up slowly. "What makes you say that?"

"They were women. Every last one of them."

15

I woke in a comfortable bed in a comfortable room that had bars on the windows and door. As I spotted them, I sat up fast, eyes wide, fists clenched, ready for a fight.

Beyond the barred doorway, a woman stood watching me. She was slender, tall like me, with auburn hair that curled wildly to shoulder length and green eyes that glittered as they took me in.

"Hello, Lilith." Her lips smiled at me, but her eyes were wary and extremely wet. "I've been waiting for a very long time to say that."

I frowned as I studied her, puzzled, because though I appeared to be her captive, the emanations I felt from her were peaceful, loving and kind. She was clearly on the verge of tears, something that made no sense whatsoever.

I glanced around the room, which didn't resemble any memory I had of The Farm.

It was pale green, with dusky pink roses hand painted in the corners. The woodwork was cream colored, and there were lace curtains on the windows. The flowers on the bedspread that covered me matched those on the walls. And the furnishings were delicate and old-looking.

Where was I?

"Lilith," the woman said softly.

I shot my gaze back to her, all my defenses going up. "Why have you taken me prisoner?" I asked her. "What is this place? What have you done with Ethan?" I frowned at her. "You're not with the DPI, are you? This isn't The Farm."

"No, we're not the DPI, and this isn't The Farm. I'm sorry we had to act so . . . violently, Lilith, but you'd have been killed if we hadn't."

I lifted my brows, recalling the ambush and the fact that there had been many, not one, who had attacked me. "So you and your friends ambushed, drugged and abducted me to save my life?" I asked skeptically. "And these bars? If you're trying to help me, why am I imprisoned?"

"Only to keep you from killing an innocent before you've had a chance to hear that we're on your side. We need to protect you — but also to protect our own."

"How noble of you."

She nodded. "Any mother would do the same for her only daughter."

I was silent. Her words slithered around in my mind like snakes seeking a home. They had to be lies. They *must* be lies. I stared at her as I probed her mind, seeking the lie. But I didn't find one. She was completely open to me, and I felt no hint of deception or malice.

She looked like me, I thought in growing amazement. But no. It couldn't be true.

"I was told my mother died giving birth to me."

"And I was told my daughter was still-born, even though I heard you cry. I knew it was a lie. One of my nurses did, too. She tried to help me and was murdered for her efforts. But it was because of her that I found these women — this order. And because of them that I finally found you."

I blinked as I stared at her. "This . . . order . . . ?"

"It hasn't yet been decided how much I'm allowed to tell you about us, Lilith. But they are good women, devoted to a just cause. They would never do harm to one of you."

"One of me?" I rolled my eyes even as I averted them. "What on earth do you mean by that?"

"You're a vampire. So is your friend Ethan. You were kidnapped at birth because you were one of the Chosen, as so many other children and babies have been, only to be raised in captivity by the DPI and their keepers. We still don't know the entire purpose behind that. We only recently even learned where The Farm is located."

"How?"

She lowered her head. "I can't tell you that. Not yet. But we do know, from an unquestionable source, that the DPI knew you and Ethan were on your way there, intending to rescue the others. They were waiting for you, Lilith. You'd have been killed before you ever got inside."

I pushed back the covers, putting my feet on the floor, realizing only now that I had been re-dressed while I slept. I was wearing a long, pretty nightgown of soft white linen. For a moment my hands trailed over the fabric and my heart softened. I found myself wanting to believe this woman. And yet, how could I? I had trusted only once in my life, and Ethan had betrayed that trust by lying to me and — and maybe more.

"How could anyone know what Ethan and I intended to do?"

"I don't know the answer to that," the woman said softly. "Did you or Ethan tell anyone?"

I knew I had told no one of our plan. And I could think of only one person Ethan might have told, though he'd promised me he wouldn't. And yet he had. He must have. And that made twice that he had broken my trust in him. He must have told his damned brother.

"What happened to Ethan?" I asked, not answering her question, and regretting instantly that the words emerged in a coarse whisper, betraying my emotions.

"He was taken."

My head swung toward her as my breath caught in my throat. "The DPI?"

"I don't know. It was just one man. He got Ethan into your SUV and then drove away."

I closed my eyes. If Ethan had told James where we were going, and James had told the DPI, then it was clear James was working for them. And by now they had undoubtedly taken Ethan back to The Farm. God, was he even still alive?

I got to my feet. "I have to find him. I have to get to him before it's too late, if it's not already." Moving to the barred door, barefoot, I clutched the bars in my hands. "If you are truly my . . . mother —" I could scarcely say the word "— then you'll let me go to him."

Her tears spilled over then, rolling slowly down her cheeks, and I found it hard to doubt that she had been telling me the truth. "Lilith, please," she whispered. "You can't go back to The Farm. They'll kill you."

"They have Ethan."

"You can't be sure of that."

"I'm as sure as I need to be," I told her. "Please — I have to try."

"Then let us help you."

I blinked at her, shocked by the offer. "A handful of mortal women, against the DPI and their army of vampire killers? You wouldn't stand a chance."

"A better chance than you'll have going alone." She sighed when I didn't answer, then said, "You've been unconscious for hours, Lilith. It's too near dawn for you to do anything tonight. You might as well rest here today. You'll be safe."

"It doesn't look as if I have a choice about that," I said.

She frowned, and then, with a heavy sigh, reached up to what must have been a switch in the hallway. A moment later, the barred door slid into the wall. The bars on the windows rose, as well, disappearing into the wall above them.

"I won't hold you against your will, Lilith.

293

I only wanted to keep you here long enough to tell you who I am and why we acted as we did."

As she spoke, she stepped inside, hesitating after a few steps, then moving closer, until she stood right before me. With a hand that trembled, she reached up to me, and her fingertips touched my face, then slid back to my hair. Fresh new tears welled in her eyes as I stared into them, and something gripped my heart and squeezed.

"You're so very beautiful," she whispered. "I knew you would be. I didn't get to see you. To hold you. To be a mother to you. But I knew —"

"We look alike," I told her softly. "I always wondered if I resembled my parents. But the keepers got angry when I asked about you, and then they claimed not to know anything anyway."

"I'm sorry I couldn't protect you. I was young and alone, and I didn't know."

I nodded. "And my father?"

"I barely knew him," she told me. "He was a one-night stand, a date that went further than I'd intended. I never even knew his last name."

"And . . . what is *your* name?" I asked her.

"Serena," she told me. "Serena Monroe." She lifted her chin, swallowed hard. "Lilith, what did they do to you at that place? Were you . . . were you mistreated?"

I averted my eyes and thought that if she truly were my mother, she was far better off not knowing the worst of it. The punishments, the torture, the drugging and mind-control techniques. "We had classes, lessons. They taught us about the nature of vampires, and about combat. Armed and hand-to-hand. They tried their best to squelch any hint of independence or rebelliousness in us. When we became vampires, they told us, we would work for them, serving our government for the good of all."

"And do you believe that?"

I met the woman's — my mother's — eyes again. "I never believed it. That's why I had to leave. They couldn't defeat my will, so I knew they were going to have to . . . to kill me. I was running out of time."

"I can't possibly imagine what you've been through. All these years . . . When I think of you as a newborn in their hands, as a little girl —" A sob escaped and seemed to choke her. She pressed a knuckle to her lips, sniffed hard, took a breath. "I'm glad they couldn't break you."

"So am I." I moved toward the door, almost experimentally, walking at a mortal's pace, and not entirely because I wanted to.

I was still weak and shaky from the drug.

Serena stepped aside, and when I looked her way, she lowered her head and blinked away the new tears filling her eyes.

I reached the door, and another woman stepped into my path, blocking it.

"It's all right, Ginger," Serena said softly. "I've told Lilith who I am and what's awaiting her at The Farm. I've done what I wanted to do. Besides, we don't hold captives here."

Ginger looked from Serena to me, her eyes wide with what looked like disbelief and hurt — not her own, but hurt on behalf of her friend. Her mind — unblocked, perhaps untrained, or maybe just that honest — spoke volumes. She thought I must have no heart, that I must be the coldest being in the universe, to walk away from the mother who'd devoted her entire life to finding me. The mother whose heart was being broken all over again.

But as I neared the door, Ginger stepped aside, refusing to look at me.

I stopped, licked my lips and turned. "You really are my mother, aren't you?"

Lifting her head, Serena met my eyes, no longer even trying to hold back her tears. She nodded. "I am."

Swallowing hard, I moved back toward

296

her, an odd tight — and unfamiliar — feeling in my chest. "Perhaps you're right and it *is* too near dawn for me to accomplish anything tonight. And I do still feel weak from that drug, as well."

"I'm so sorry, Lilith. It was the only way we could think of to stop you from walking into the DPI's trap," Serena — my mother — said.

"Yes, I'm beginning to see that."

My mother pressed a hand to her forehead, moving toward the window. "We had every intention of saving Ethan, as well. That man who intervened —"

"I know you tried." I walked closer to her, lifted a hand and let it come to rest on her shoulder. "This probably isn't the reunion you've been dreaming of all these years, is it?"

She looked over her shoulder at me, her smile a bit shaky, her eyes filled with more emotion than I'd ever seen before. "But it *is* a reunion. You're alive, and I've finally found you. Nothing else matters."

I felt something stirring in my belly, but I didn't know what it was. "I don't really know how to . . . how to be a daughter. How to have a mother. I don't know what it is you want from me, but I sense your disappointment. If you tell me, perhaps —"

297

A sob escaped her, and then she wrapped her arms around me, held me close to her, and I could feel her body trembling. One of her hands moved in small circles on my back, with the other slipping gently into my hair, pulling my head down on her shoulder.

I was surprised and yet also soothed by the warmth that moved from her body into my naturally cool one. I was touched by the rush of feelings I felt coming from her, for she erected no barriers in her mind. This woman, I realized, loved me.

She *loved* me. She would die for me.

That was real, and it was true, and it was beyond my ability to comprehend. Here was a person I could trust beyond all others. Beyond anyone. And I didn't even *know* her. But I couldn't deny the purity of her feelings for me. I could feel them. She didn't hide from me the way Ethan did.

I wrapped my arms around her and squeezed gently, letting my head relax more thoroughly on her shoulder. My eyes burned, and my chest still felt tight. It was powerful, this emotion that flowed between us, more powerful than anything I could have imagined. And quite suddenly I didn't want her to let go. The realization came out of the blue, washing over me with a softness and warmth and a feeling of utter relief that left me almost limp in its wake. It was as if I'd been waiting my entire life for this woman's loving embrace.

And I knew in that moment that I would never regret trusting her, that she would never deceive me the way Ethan had. This woman — my *mother,* I thought again — would suffer slow torture and death rather than betray me. She loved me in a way that no other being ever had, ever could or ever would.

I clutched her tighter, and my shoulders trembled. I felt my own tears rolling down my cheeks. Gently, she held me away from her to look at my face. I wasn't ashamed of my tears. I didn't need to be ashamed of anything with her.

With the most tender touch I had ever felt, she brushed my wet cheeks with her fingertips. "It's all right. This must be overwhelming for you."

Sniffling, I nodded. "I don't know you, but it's as if a part of me does."

"The part that came from me, perhaps?"

"All of me came from you."

She smiled at me. "Including the stubbornness that wouldn't allow those bastards to tame you."

I blinked and smiled back at her. "Yes, it must have. For you to have refused to give up trying to find me for so many years — you must be as stubborn as I am."

Serena nodded, wiped at her own eyes then, and smiled.

"I'll stay here for today," I told her. "I'll rest and recover. But at sundown, I have to go after Ethan."

"You love him?" she asked.

I blinked, then frowned. "How can I answer that? Until just now . . . Mother . . ." I smiled as I called her that for the first time. "Until just now, I didn't think I could love anyone. But . . . I . . . love you."

"And I love you, Lilith." She slid an arm around my waist, walking me along the hallway toward a massive staircase. The other woman, Ginger, stayed behind, but I heard her sniffle and clear her throat. "We have more than an hour until sunrise," Serena said, leading me past the staircase to the farthest reaches of the corridor. "And so much talking to do. Let's sit in the solarium while we can still look out at the stars."

"Yes. I'd like to know about my family."

She nodded, opening a door and leading me up a flight of stairs. "Yes, and you can tell me about your escape, and what you've done and seen since then. And you can tell me about your Ethan."

My Ethan. I hadn't thought of him that way, and it made my heart jump a bit when she said it. But I didn't know if he truly was mine in any way. He'd lied to me.

For the first time, though, I thought I might have a clue as to why. His brother was his family. The bond I felt with my mother was a revelation to me, and perhaps he felt a similar one to James. That bore some consideration, didn't it?

We emerged into a circular room, with walls only about four feet in height. Everything else, from there up to the domed ceiling, was made of glass. The frame that held it looked like a spider's web. And beyond the glass, the stars glittered like icicles in moonlight.

She led me to a pair of comfortable chairs, and I sat, staring upward. "This order of yours — can you tell me its name?"

She was silent for a moment. "It's secret. We couldn't continue in our work if word of our existence leaked out, Lilith."

I nodded. "I won't repeat anything you tell me in confidence," I promised her.

"We are called the Sisterhood of Athena," she told me. "We're more centuries old than even we know for sure. We go back as far as the written word, that much we know."

"And . . . your work?"

She looked at me, trust in her eyes. "We observe and protect the supernatural order. We watch over vampires, Lilith. We seldom interfere in the affairs of the Undead, but when others do, then we step in. This Farm that the DPI is running, the abduction and imprisonment and, apparently, the indoctrination of the Chosen — that's not natural. It's not allowing you, and all of them, to grow and live and choose with your own free will. They're trying to own and control, perhaps even to enslave, an entire race. And that cannot be allowed."

I watched her and frowned. "But what can you hope to do about it? You're just a group of ordinary mortal women."

"Mortal, yes. Ordinary?" Her smile widened a little. "No, we're far from ordinary. We're strong. We're fast. We're skilled. We spend our lives training, so that if and when we are needed, we can be effective, even deadly if necessary. The Sisters of Athena are warrior women, Lilith."

I tipped my head to one side. "Then why have you allowed The Farm to continue as long as it has?"

"We couldn't find it. We finally got a lead on a handful of individuals we felt might be connected, and we sent a member out to make inroads with them. She made one of the men fall in love with her, and eventually he brought her in as a keeper. But when she was taken in for the first time, she was blindfolded, and once they're inside, the keepers aren't allowed to leave until their time has been served. Three years. She's been there more than two now, and in all that time she's only managed to contact us twice, both times just in the past few days, to tell us of your escape, and then the fact that the DPI knew you and Ethan were coming and would be waiting in ambush."

I went tense in my chair. "I know who she is!" I said, as the image of a kind-faced blond woman flashed into my mind. The one keeper who'd always shown kindness, humanity and concern, but only when the others weren't watching. "Her name is Callista, isn't it?"

She blinked in surprise. "Yes. How do you know?"

I shook my head slowly, remembering. "She was . . . different. Kind when she could be, without being observed. Of course, she had to pretend she was one of them, but I always knew there was something more to her."

My mother looked troubled then. And I understood why. "She took a great risk, sending out that warning for my sake, didn't she?" I asked.

"Yes, she did. If they find out, she'll be killed. But she knew that, and she took the risk of her own free will."

"So she told you where The Farm is?" I asked, already worried about finding my way back.

"We have the coordinates. We triangulated the cell phone's signal."

"And what will you do, now that you know where it is?" I asked.

"We'll take a few more days. We'll surveil the place, map it, know it by heart without them ever knowing we've been near. We'll come up with a plan, and then we'll move in and destroy The Farm in the most efficient, safest way we can come up with."

She sounded almost like Ethan when she spoke about time and surveillance and plans, I thought.

"Our goal," she went on, "is to free the prisoners, save our sister Callista and prevent innocent blood from being shed."

I sighed and lowered my head. "I'd go with you if I could, but I can't wait for all that. If Ethan was taken there, they could be planning to kill him at any time. If they haven't already."

"Can't you try to contact him? Mentally?" she asked.

I closed my eyes. "I've been trying ever since I woke up. But there's no response. Ethan thought there was some kind of barrier around that place — one that prevented mental contact between the prisoners and anyone outside." My throat went tight. "Or perhaps he really is already dead."

"Lilith, I think the man who took him was a vampire."

I frowned and opened my eyes. "How would you know?"

She tipped her head and frowned back at me in an almost amusing way. "I've been studying them for a long time now. I know a vampire when I see one, and I'm almost certain it was a vampire who took Ethan."

I blinked rapidly as I processed that information. "It could have been his brother, James. He vanished from The Farm almost three years ago. Some believed he escaped. Others believed he had been transformed and sent out to work for the DPI."

"Do you know what kind of work they make their Farm-raised vampires do?"

"I only know what they told us. That we would be serving our country for the good of all. And that anyone who escaped would be hunted down and killed." I swallowed a lump in my throat. "By someone like James, maybe."

"He wouldn't kill his own brother!" Serena said it as if she were willing it to be true.

"You don't understand what they do to us there, Mother. They — they brainwash. They program. They drug. Most can't withstand it. They become loyal, obedient unto death."

"I can't imagine any vampire being so thoroughly controlled."

I glanced at her, wondering how many vampires she had known.

She read my look. "I've met some, but none who were raised as you were."

"You've met the Wildborns?" I was stunned. "And lived to tell about it?"

She smiled. "Wildborns? That's what you call them?"

I nodded. "And we're Bloodliners," I told her. "That's what they call us at The Farm. They say we're all the same bloodline, once we're made over."

She frowned, a troubled look crossing her face. "But . . . how are you made over?"

"Through transfusions. They drain our blood and infuse us with vampiric blood."

"But . . . where are they getting the vampiric blood?" she asked.

I blinked, remembering the horror. "They

306

had a captive vampire there. I saw him, before I left. He was in so much pain. He . . . he made me take his blood. I think I killed him, and I think that's what he intended."

She closed her eyes and leaned over in her chair to hug me gently. "You couldn't have known."

I lowered my head to her shoulder. "It was cruel, the way he was kept. And I felt for him. But he must have been different from the rest. The Wildborns are vicious. They're savages. Killers. Like wild animals."

She met my eyes, her own gleaming with utter disbelief. But even as she parted her lips to speak, the door to our haven burst open and another woman surged inside. My mother shot to her feet.

"Serena, we have to evacuate immediately!" the newcomer shouted, all but breathless.

"Why? What's happened?"

"The vampires have found out where we are."

16

"Ophelia was servicing one of the cars we took on the mission, and she found this."

I lifted my brows as the newcomer handed Serena a tiny metallic object. It was round and silver, spattered in mud.

"It was up in the wheel well. Ginger says it's a tracking device, so it's only a matter of time until they get here. She's ordered a 3-D."

My mother's face went pale, and she shot me a look. "We have to go." Grabbing my hand, she tugged me to my feet. The other woman had already disappeared from sight.

"I don't understand," I said. "What is that thing? And what's a 3-D?"

"That," my mother said, holding the thing up as she pulled me beside her into the hall, "is a tracking device. 3-D stands for Depart, Destroy, Defend. It means we evacuate the house immediately. And since there's no time to remove every sensitive document, we burn the place down behind us as we leave. Then we gather in a safe location to figure out just how badly our secrets have been compromised."

"But —" I began.

"There's no time. Whoever planted that unit could be here any second. They could be here now, for all we know."

"Where will you go?" I was running now, to keep pace with her.

"Don't worry, Lilith. We have safe houses all over the continent — all over the world. We'll go to the closest one, and I promise to keep you safe until we get there, as I so miserably failed to do on the day you were born."

I blinked in amazement and touched her arm. "I do *not* blame you for that."

"I blame myself." She squeezed my hand. "Come on. We need to hurry."

Together we raced downstairs, where I saw women rushing around. But it wasn't chaotic. Each one seemed to know exactly where she was going and what she had to do. Mother and I rushed to the bedroom I sensed was hers, and I watched in awe as she yanked a bag from beneath her bed, fully packed already.

She handed a second bag to me. "I packed this for you while you were sleeping. You needed clothes."

"And you? How did you know you would need to pack for yourself, too?"

"We always have a bag packed with our essentials inside. We're constantly prepared for trouble, Lilith. Come with me. Now."

My hand in hers again, we ran back into the hall and down the stairs to ground level and a room that could easily have been called a great hall. It was huge, ornate, echoing with every footstep. I glimpsed fireplaces, a crystal chandelier, Oriental rugs of massive size and little else. We were quickly joined by a dozen other women, each with a bag. There were suitcases, duffels, backpacks and everything in between.

My mother opened the door and, stepping out, stared into the night. And that was when I felt it — the presence.

I grabbed her shoulder and jerked her back inside, even as a shot rang through the darkness. The bullet hit the ornate light that had been glowing beside the door, right next to my mother's head. Glass shattered as she and I tumbled inside, and someone else slammed the heavy door closed.

"Are you all right?" I asked my mother, pushing her hair aside to examine her head, seeing no damage, smelling no blood.

"Yes. But who . . . ?"

"I felt them — two of them. Vampires," I told her, staring at the closed door as tears burned in my eyes. "One I don't know. And one I do. It was Ethan. And from what I sensed before he shut me out, the other one has to be James." I lowered my head. "I can't believe Ethan would do this. I trusted him."

For the second time in as many hours, tears flooded from my eyes and my chest went tight. Ethan. How could he turn on me this way? Or had his *help* been only a part of some game he and his brother had been playing the whole time?

Ethan, I thought, but only to myself, closing my eyes and clutching my chest. Ethan, why? Why, when I could have loved you?

Ethan went rigid when he saw his brother leveling a weapon — a real one, not a tranquilizer gun — at the woman who was silhouetted in the open doorway. And then he spun and back-kicked, even as the shot went off. The gun flew in an arc and hit the pavement several yards away, while James gripped his own hand, hissing in pain.

"What the hell do you think you're doing?" Ethan demanded. "Dammit, James, that could've been Lilith."

"I could see that it wasn't."

"How? I've slept with her, and I couldn't tell."

James went still, turning to stare at his brother's face. His own had gone solemn and dark. "You've slept with her?"

Ethan averted his face. The partial dose of the drug had finally taken effect, and he'd awakened only an hour ago to find himself still in the Bronco, his brother still at the wheel. His eyes had immediately been drawn to a small device stuck to the windshield, held there by a suction cup. It had a flashing light and an intermittent beep that would, he imagined, become maddening in very short order.

"I told you I'd find Lilith for you," James said with a nod at the thing. "I slipped a tracking unit onto one of the cars they had hidden off the roadside, just before they attacked you."

It had occurred to Ethan then to wonder just where his brother's priorities lay. If their situations had been reversed, he would have been thinking about saving his brother first and foremost, with tracking the perpetrators far below that in importance. But he'd brushed that thought away, telling himself that it had ended up working to his advantage, now that their attackers were holding Lilith prisoner.

Now, though, all Lilith's doubts about James were ringing in his mind. And he wondered . . .

"You've actually slept with her?" James asked again, his voice registering intense displeasure and bringing Ethan back to the present with a jolt.

"I didn't mean to say that."

"But you *did* say it. You're involved with her. Good grief, Ethan, is it just sex? Or is there more to it than that?"

"That's none of your business." But Ethan wondered how he would have answered the question if he'd chosen to. He didn't even know himself what was between him and Lilith. But he knew it was driving him crazy to believe she was in danger right now and beyond his reach. He realized, though, that his brother was waiting, almost demanding that he say something more. He shook himself and tried. "I just — God, you could have killed her."

"It wasn't her."

"Then you could have killed whoever it was!"

"And why would you care if I killed your girlfriend's abductors?"

Ethan shook his head and turned again to face the mansion. It was built of rough-hewn blocks of glittering white granite. The front door was brick red, with stained-glass sidelights that matched the peacock's-tail window in the door itself. The knocker was brass. An owl.

They must have a thing for owls here. There were two others perched atop the pillars at either side of the front gate. Giant white stone owls, like sentries guarding the entrance. The gate itself was wrought iron, and a fence of the same design encircled the entire place, as far as he could see.

From within, he picked up the clear sense of women. Many of them. Mortals, all. The only vampire essence he felt was Lilith's own alluring aura, and it did things to him, even then. And there were none of the Chosen there, either.

"I don't think these people — these women — are DPI, James," Ethan told his brother. "They don't give off that stench, if you know what I mean."

"They have a more pleasant energy about them, true," James agreed. "But could it be just that they *are* women? Certainly they're some other branch of the DPI, just a less maleficent one, perhaps. Maybe even unaware of the . . . less palatable things the DPI has been doing."

"If that's the case — if they don't know — then maybe we can reason with them.

Maybe if they knew —"

"You want to *reason* with them?" James's words were heavy with sarcasm. "You want to *reason* with the people who drugged and kidnapped your woman?"

"She's not my woman."

"I hope that's true. But either way —"

"I'm going to the door. We have to get her out of there."

"They'll drug you and imprison you, too. Hell, it's probably what they're waiting for. It's probably the only reason she's still alive."

"Thank God she is," Ethan muttered. Heaving a sigh, he focused his mind on Lilith, brought the image of her face into his mind. His gut clenched as he envisioned her arched, slightly heavy brows, her cheekbones and the smoothness of her skin. The intensity that was always swirling in her emerald eyes.

Lilith, he called mentally. *Are you all right? Have they harmed you?*

She didn't reply. Frowning, he tried harder. *Lilith? I'm with James. We've come to rescue you. How many of them are there? Are you under guard?*

And still there was nothing. He tipped his head to one side.

Then James said, "I've stopped feeling

315

them." He met Ethan's eyes. "Only moments ago I sensed them, all of them, near the front of the house. But now — there's nothing."

"They must be getting away!" Ethan surged from their hiding place beyond the shrubbery that lined the lane, leaping the bushes, crossing the road at a sprint no human could match. As the tall iron fence loomed before him, he bent his knees and sprang upward, sailing easily over it. And then he was racing up the drive, toward the front door. He didn't stop there. He didn't knock. He didn't even slow down. He just hit the door with one shoulder, and it flew open. Bits of wood flew like shrapnel, and the door hit the wall so hard its knob cracked the plaster.

He ran a few steps inside, then stopped, turning his head left and right, scenting the air, but feeling only emptiness. "Lilith!"

"She's not here, little brother." James had been only a few steps behind Ethan on the way in. "There must be some other way out."

"How about you tell me something I don't know, James?"

James frowned, wrinkling his nose. "Okay. This place is about to go up in flames."

"What?"

"Run!" As he said it, James gripped Ethan's arm and propelled him back through the front door even as a series of explosions ripped the night. From the front step, they leapt as one, landing on the grass just inside the giant fence. Behind them, windows shattered, glass flew wildly and flames sprang to life as if from nowhere.

Getting to his feet, Ethan turned to look back at the place, stunned beyond belief. "What the hell — Why would they . . . ?"

Brushing himself off, James gripped his arm. "There were things there they didn't want us to find. Secrets."

"But we already knew they were DPI," Ethan said. "What other secrets could they possibly have?" He frowned and turned his head slowly. "Unless . . . they're not."

"Of course they are," James said. "Who else would kidnap Lilith?" He turned, looked briefly at the fence, then bent low and jumped, clearing it easily. He landed on the other side and looked through the bars at Ethan. "You coming?"

"Whoever they were," Ethan said, "they knew where to wait for us. They knew where we were going."

"Ethan, will you get out of there before the entire house blows up? You're too close to the flames for my peace of mind."

Ethan nodded and jumped the fence. But his mind was on other things. He landed beside his brother, straightened and searched James's eyes, his mind. "How could they have known where we were going last night, James? How could they have known that Lilith and I were heading back to The Farm? I removed the tracking device they'd implanted beneath her skin. And I told no one but you."

"Don't even think it, Ethan. Don't even. Maybe they had you under surveillance the whole time. Maybe they spotted you out of sheer luck. Maybe they had another tracking device implanted in Lilith — one you *didn't* find. There are a thousand maybes."

"Or maybe you told them. Maybe you've been working for the DPI all along."

"I thought you just decided those Amazons were *not* the DPI? How does that fit with this new theory of yours?"

Ethan didn't answer, just continued watching James, praying he was wrong in what he was starting to think.

"You're a real disappointment, you know that?" James said. "I freaking risk my neck to help you and your insane lunatic girlfriend, and at the first sign of trouble, you accuse me of betraying you. What the hell, Ethan? I'm your *brother.*"

318

"I know."

"Yeah. Right." James lowered his head and started walking.

"Where . . . are you going?"

"We need to put some distance between us and that inferno before the fire department gets here. And it'll be daylight by the time they leave. We need shelter."

Ethan walked a little faster, caught up to James and fell into step beside him. "I'm sorry, James."

"I don't suppose I blame you. I mean, we've been apart for over two years, and neither of us is the man he was before. We're vampires now."

Ethan nodded.

"At sundown we'll come back here and figure out how they got out, where they went. Then we'll find your Lilith."

"We have to," Ethan said softly. "We have to, James."

"I will not rest, my brother, until I do what I came to do. On that you have my word."

As Ethan stared into his brother's eyes, he felt a little chill and didn't know why. But then James smiled warmly, and whatever had been there was gone. He clasped Ethan on the shoulder, and drew him farther along the road to where they'd left the Bronco.

Serena and the other women had trooped through the house as if it were a long-practiced routine, and I was beginning to think perhaps it was. They led me to a sun-room in the back and out through its glass doors into a mazelike garden. We made our way along its twisting paths until we reached the center, where a massive white statue stood: a Greek goddess, with an owl on her shoulder.

Athena, I guessed.

Leaning over, Ginger, the redhead who appeared to be the group's leader, pushed at the statue's base, and I gasped as an entire section of the thing simply slid open, revealing a dark stone stairway descending into the earth.

"Quickly, ladies. Hurry now," Ginger ordered.

Swiftly, silently, the first women stepped down those hidden stairs and vanished into the earth. I saw lights appear, flickering like flames, and realized there must be candles positioned along the way.

Serena and I entered after the first few women had gone down, and she turned to call encouragement to the others as they came. Ginger came last, and I heard the stone sliding back into place a second later.

As we moved deeper into the underground passage, my mother found a candle in a wall sconce and took it down. She pulled a lighter from somewhere and put its flame to the wick, then offered the light to me.

I drew back. "That's all right. I prefer to keep a little distance between myself and open flames."

She smiled, and her face in the candle's glow was beautiful. "I'm very glad you found me," I told her. "Thank you for never giving up the search."

"Thank you for staying alive and keeping your sanity in that place. Otherwise there wouldn't have been much to find." She lowered her eyes. "I'm sorry about Ethan."

"I never should have trusted him. From the first it's been, 'my brother' this and 'my brother' that. I can't compete with that, nor do I want to."

"Blood ties are powerful, Lilith."

"He took his brother's side against me." My voice broke a little when I said that, because it hurt so much to acknowledge the truth that had become so glaringly obvious.

"You don't know that. He could have been deceived by his brother, just as you thought from the start. He might still be unaware of what James is up to."

I said nothing, but I felt a swell of something in my chest, as if my heart were admitting a small rush of hope. I hated that feeling. I would only be let down all over again if I let myself hope.

And yet that tiny flame flickered in my heart, refusing to die away, no matter how I tried to ignore it and pretend it wasn't there.

"Where are we going?" I asked.

"To our secret library. It's well hidden. There are some things that the world must never know — and though we keep careful records of your kind, we would never risk our knowledge falling into the wrong hands."

Ahead, I saw a doorway opening, lights coming on from within. "There's power way down here?"

"Yes, and everything else we could need, including an entire network of escape tunnels. Any pursuer would find it difficult to decide which one to follow. But we won't use those just yet. We'll be safe here for today."

"But . . . what if they find the entrance?"

"If the hidden passage opens, an alarm light will flash in the library. We'll know they're coming long before they reach us. But it's highly doubtful anyone — even a vampire — could locate that passage or figure out how to open the door." She glanced at me with a reassuring smile. "*You* didn't guess it was there, did you?"

I breathed a sigh of relief. "No. Not until I saw it sliding open."

My mother smiled and patted my hand. "I told you I'd keep you safe. Come, I want you to see this."

And with that, she led me the last few steps along the corridor and through the open door. Before me, a room opened out: round, with a domed ceiling and not a window in sight. Its walls appeared to be made of books. Nothing but books and more books, and more and more books. There were computers on desks in various spots, too, and on the farthest curve of the circular walls, another doorway.

"Where does that one lead?" I asked.

"To the vaults. We have a lot of artifacts that need to be just as well-guarded as the records." She nodded to her right. "That bookshelf opens to reveal the entrance to four escape tunnels. The one to the left, four more. They open by a switch hidden in the light fixture there." She pointed.

I nodded. "I don't like the idea of spending the day here," I told her. "I'm helpless when I sleep. And if someone does find the passage, I'd be right here, waiting for them to find me."

"How could anyone find the passage?" she asked.

I shrugged and averted my eyes. "Ethan and I have been . . . close. Or I thought we were. There was a connection between us. I think it was real, even if it meant nothing to him in the end."

"I see," she said softly, and I got the feeling she really did.

"He might be able to sense me, even if no one else could," I told her.

She nodded. "We'll all be awake. We'll protect you. If the passage opens, we'll carry you out of here, if necessary."

I looked slowly at the women who shared the library with us. One had located a closet and was pulling blankets and pillows from its depths, and handing them out to the rest, so they could nap on and off throughout the day — in shifts, no doubt. Another was entering what looked like a pantry. I smelled food coming from it, and I felt jealous that these mortals would eat while I had to go hungry.

Unless I decided to eat one of them, I thought, with a private, inner grin. I wouldn't, of course, but I amused myself with my own little joke, even while deciding not to share it. They likely wouldn't find it very funny.

"You can trust them," my mother told me. "These woman have worked as hard as I have to find you, most without even knowing you were my daughter, though they all know it now. Some have been here for as long as I have. A few, even longer. They love me, and because of that, they'll be loyal to you. You have nothing to fear from any of them, I swear it."

"I'm sorry. I'm just not used to trusting anyone. Ethan really was the first, and you've seen how that turned out."

"You don't yet know how that turned out."

I looked at her, frowning and wishing with everything in me that I could believe her.

She stroked my hair, her touch tender and loving beyond measure. "You have a set of circumstances that seem to suggest he has betrayed you. But you don't *know,* Lilith. Try not to judge him until you do."

I nodded, and felt the pull of the unseen sun upon my body. My limbs were growing heavy, my movements clumsy and labored. My eyelids kept dropping closed.

A young woman touched my shoulder, and when I looked her way, she handed me a blanket and pillow. "Pick a spot near the escape tunnels, so we can get you out first if anything should happen."

I shot a swift look at my mother, then returned my probing but sleepy gaze to this girl, with her pixie brown hair and twinkling blue eyes. "Why would you want to get me out first?"

"While you sleep, you're helpless, right? Naturally we'd take you out first. You'd be the most at risk." She smiled a little. "Besides, you've been a pet project of ours ever since long before I came here. We *couldn't* let anything happen to you now."

I nodded, and the girl turned and hurried away. Looking once more at my mother, I said, "I guess I *can* trust them." I didn't though. Not fully, and not deep down. How could I? I didn't know them.

But I trusted Serena. My mother. I trusted *her* and hoped I wasn't wrong . . . again. Taking my pillow and blanket, I chose a spot, spread the blanket on the floor and lay down on it, resting my head on my hand, my elbow on the soft pillow. "They look up to you here," I said.

She nodded. "I'm Ginger's second. Though if you'd told me I would ever rise to this position twenty years ago, I would have said you were crazy." She shrugged. "I came here, joined this order, for one purpose and one purpose only. I thought it was my best chance to find you."

"But that changed, didn't it?"

She nodded and looked around the library, pride beaming from her eyes. "Their cause is so good, so noble and just. The more I learned about them, the more I believed in what they were doing. Fighting to protect an entire race that has as much right to exist as any of us do."

I nodded slowly. "Have you known many of them, then? Vampires?"

"Known? No, I wouldn't say I've really ever known any of them. I've encountered a handful, and I've helped a great many, though always without their knowledge."

"Even . . ." I was having trouble staying awake, and soon I would be helpless to try. "Even the Wildborns?"

"Until you, I never knew there were any other kind," she said.

I frowned. "I don't understand . . . why anyone would help them." My eyes fell closed, and my mind faded to black. The last thing I heard was her voice.

"Rest now, daughter. We'll talk again at sundown."

17

At sunset Ethan awoke all at once, a feeling of urgency snapping his senses to full awareness. He sat up fast, then blinked away the remnants of the sleep-haze and looked around the falling-down shack where he and his brother had taken shelter.

James lay a few feet away from him, stirring slowly to life, stretching his arms as he sat up. Ethan got to his feet, paced from the sheltered area where they'd slept to the nearest gap in the broken boards and stared outside. "You ready?"

"I've barely opened my eyes, Ethan." But James got up and came to join him. Already Ethan was climbing through the opening to the outside, then standing and scanning the night.

"Anyone around?" his brother asked.

"I don't feel anyone. Including Lilith."

James clapped a hand to his back. "We'll find her. Let's get back to that burned-out mansion, see if we can find some clue as to who those women are, what they're up to, where they've taken her. And why."

Ethan nodded, but he felt a grim foreboding that didn't leave much room for hope. "I can't understand why she hasn't contacted me."

"Maybe her captors are preventing it. And even if she does, Ethan, you'll need to exercise extreme skepticism about anything she says. They might be coercing her into misleading you."

"Nobody *coerces* Lilith into doing anything, brother," Ethan said as they made their way through the woods to the road. The mansion wasn't far. They'd deliberately remained close.

"Anyone can be turned — or forced — under the right circumstances. Even your feisty Lilith."

"You wouldn't be so sure of that if you knew her." Ethan spotted the sodden wreckage of the mansion. There were no mortals near, but the sense of those who had been here earlier permeated the place. Not just the women — but the firefighters and others who'd rushed to the scene. Tire tracks marred the once-perfect lawn, and ashes coated the grass. The stench of burned wood still filled the air. Yellow tape surrounded the area, woven through the bars of the wrought-iron fence that guarded the place. The house had collapsed into a pile of blackened wreckage. It didn't look as if much had survived.

"The women must have left through the rear or we'd have seen them," James said, then headed across the narrow road. The two of them jumped the fence and headed around the mansion's remains. Beyond it, there were shrubs and flowering trees, rose bushes, lilacs, plants of every imaginable sort, all interwoven with footpaths. Those plants nearest the house were destroyed, their leaves blackened or burned entirely away. Others were only wilted, but Ethan doubted they would survive what must have been a blast of extreme heat.

Ethan hurried into the garden, feeling with his mind for any sense of Lilith. There was one, but it was faint, and already fading. "She's been here," he said. "This way." Choosing the path where his sense of her felt strongest, Ethan followed it, pausing at every fork to feel for her and then moving on.

The trail came to an abrupt halt at a giant sculpture of a goddess. The thing was as tall as two of him and must have weighed tons. He touched it, circled all the way around it, but couldn't pick up any trace of Lilith's vibration anywhere. It was as if she'd walked up to the statue and vanished.

"It's odd," he said softly. "It's as if she disappeared right here."

"That *is* odd." James put his hands on the sculpture, feeling every bump and ripple in the stone as if in search of an answer.

Ethan did the same, but he did it with his eyes and his senses, not his hands. He tried to see what Lilith had seen here, tried to feel whatever she'd felt before she'd vanished. His eyes were drawn to the sandaled foot of the giant goddess, and he saw a seam in the stone there. Tracing it around the base with his eyes, he realized it was not some ordinary crack in the stone but a man-made cut. Part of the statue would move away from the rest — and there had to be some sort of lever to trigger it.

He turned to James, parted his lips to speak, but hesitated at the intense and furious expression on his brother's face, and the sudden sense of frustration wafting from his brother's mind. As soon as James felt his attention, the doors of his mind slammed closed. The angry expression faded and was replaced by an innocuous one.

"What do you think, Ethan?" he asked.

Ethan blinked and decided he wasn't as

sure of his brother as he'd been trying to believe he was. He'd ignored the warning signs up to now, allowed his brother to explain them away. All because he wanted so badly to believe in James. But maybe — just in case — he should exercise caution this one time.

"I think it doesn't much matter where she went from here," Ethan said softly. "I know perfectly well where she's heading. To The Farm."

"But she's being held captive by those women."

"Yes, that's true," Ethan said with a nod. "But if they're DPI, that's where they'll take her. And she'll probably let them, because that's where she wants to go."

"And what if they're not DPI?" James asked.

And Ethan got the distinct impression just then — though only briefly, so slight he couldn't even be sure it was real — that James already knew very well that those women were not associated with the DPI.

But he didn't press the point. "If they're not," he reasoned, "then she'll escape and go to The Farm anyway."

"And you really think she's capable of escaping from that many armed females?"

Ethan nodded. "There's no question in

my mind, James. She's an amazing woman."

James sighed deeply. "If that's the case, Ethan, then I'm afraid there's nothing more we can do for her."

"We can intercept her," Ethan said. Then he sank onto a nearby bench and lowered his head into his hands. "Maybe. I don't know. I can't think straight, I'm so damn hungry."

"We should get sustenance, then," James said. "There's a small clinic nearby. Maybe we can find blood there."

Ethan lifted his head, nodded, then closed his eyes. "I'm feeling really weak. I don't know what's wrong."

James studied him for a moment. "Do you want me to go for the blood, then? Bring it back to you here?"

Ethan nodded. "Yes. That would be great. Will you?"

James's eyes were narrow and probing. "Of course I will, if that's what you want. I'd do anything for you. You're my brother. My only family. And I'm yours."

He held Ethan's eyes for a moment, until Ethan, racked with guilt, had to look away. "I'll wait right here," he said, nearly choking on the blatant lie. If he was wrong, he hoped to God that James would forgive him for mistrusting him so completely. And he hoped he *was* wrong. He hoped it with everything in him.

James looked at him hard for a moment longer, but then turned and took off at an easy pace. Ethan watched him go, waiting until he was certain his brother was out of earshot, even feeling for him before proceeding. Then he knelt and began examining the statue again, trying to find the trigger that would open the door hidden in the base. There had to be one.

Within a few moments he located it, a bump of concrete in the shape of a flower bud. When he depressed it, the base of the statue slid back, revealing a set of stairs leading downward. He felt the touch of subterranean air, damp and cool, and with it, his sense of Lilith returned. She had gone down this hidden stairway. She had descended into the depths of the Earth Herself.

Ethan glanced back once, then started down those stairs, searching along the way for a means to close the door behind him. He found it, a switch in the wall that no one had bothered to try to conceal, and when he flipped it, the statue's base slid closed, grinding and scraping all the way.

He watched its progress until it had completely closed out the night, and then he moved on. And as he did, another thought occurred to him.

What if his growing suspicions about his brother were correct? He'd been worrying about whether his brother would ever forgive him if those doubts were wrong, but what if they were right? Would Lilith ever forgive him for not believing her from the start? Was it, in fact, his own fault that she was in the dire situation she faced right now?

Closing his eyes briefly, he leaned against the wall, a wave of weakness sweeping through him. He hadn't been lying about being hungry and needing sustenance. That much had been utterly true. But it was the thought of losing Lilith's budding trust in him that had turned his bones to water just then. And it was the even more debilitating thought — that he might be responsible for her impending demise — that he found nearly paralyzing.

"First things first, Ethan," he told himself aloud. "If she doesn't survive this, it won't much matter if she forgives you or not. And if it's your fault she's in this mess, then it's up to you to get her out of it. So buck up and get moving — before it's too late." He drew a breath and prayed in desperate silence that it wasn't too late already.

■ ■ ■ ■

As soon as night had fallen, I had awakened with a smile tugging at my lips and opened my eyes expecting, for one brief, blissful moment, to find Ethan lying beside me, staring into my eyes with that look I'd glimpsed in his before — that look of deep and intense caring. That look that had been a lie.

As I sat up and the reality of that returned to me, I felt the most crushing sense of loss I had ever experienced. He had betrayed me — and who knew to what extent? Had he only trusted his brother with information he'd promised me he wouldn't share? Or was it even worse than that? Was he truly conspiring with his brother against me? Had he been doing so the entire time?

My mother soothed me, seeming to know, without a word from me, the emotions that were crashing within me like waves upon a rocky shore. She stroked my hair and handed me a cup filled with warm blood, to nourish and sustain me. I had no idea where she'd gotten it, and I didn't ask.

I thanked her, though, and she said the most peculiar thing to me. She said, "There's no need for thanks, Lilith. This is what mothers do. They care for their daughters. They stand by them in times of trouble and need. They do anything within their power to help. And I have a lot of lost time to make up for with you."

I wondered, as I studied her beautiful face, if that were true. Was that really what mothers did? All of them? I'd never known a mother before and had no reference for comparison. But she hadn't lied to me so far, so I decided to believe her.

Mothers must be the most exceptional beings in existence, I thought. And mine, in my mind, stood above them all. I was a vampire. And she loved me still.

The leader, Ginger, opened the secret panel to one set of tunnels and called out to us to hurry, so we did. I was led through a snake's nest of tunnels, over a distance of what had to be several miles. I could see perfectly in the darkness, but I knew that the other women couldn't, yet they moved with confidence, without hesitation. I found myself admiring their sureness and lack of fear. My mother and I were in the midst of the group, moving single file and slightly stooped, due to the tunnel's low ceiling. She held my hand, walking directly ahead of me, as if she were strong and I were weak. As if she were the one who would protect me from harm, when I was, in fact, as strong as any ten of these women — maybe more.

And yet it felt somehow natural, so I let her lead.

The tunnels were dug deep, supported by braces every few yards. I felt as if I were traversing the arteries of the earth as I smelled the rich scent of soil all around me. It was as close to a grave as I would ever come, I thought. And then I realized that I hoped that were true. I wondered, with a pang of sadness, if any of these doomed mortals, with their abbreviated life spans, felt a sense of their inevitable end. And for the first time it occurred to me that my mother, a mortal, would grow old. Would die. How could they live with that certainty ever present in their minds?

How could *I?* I had only just found my mother. The thought of losing her, even at some distant point in the future, was painful, far more painful than I would ever have expected.

Eventually the ground began to slope upward, and we emerged through a wooden door that was completely hidden on the outside by moss and weeds. When it closed behind us, you couldn't even see it, so brilliant and natural was its disguise.

I turned and looked from the women

around me to the area where we now stood. It was an open field, bordering a glimmering lake. There were cabins in the distance, dotting the shoreline. Lights burned in some, while others remained dark and felt uninhabited.

"Here were are," Ginger said.

My mother, still clasping my hand, drew me forward. "This cabin is owned by the Sisterhood. It's for emergency use only, since we don't want to draw attention to it. And it really wasn't designed for fourteen of us, but I think we can make it work."

I looked at her steadily, holding back as she tried to pull me forward. She stopped and faced me again.

"You know that I can't stay here."

A look of dread came into her eyes, and her face seemed to go a shade lighter. "Of course not — not permanently — but stay just for now," she said, although I think she knew, even then, what my answer had to be.

I shook my head sadly.

"Just until we figure out what to do," she rushed on. "We can make a plan and —"

I cupped her face between my palms. "I already know what I have to do."

"Please don't go there alone." She blinked at the dampness that swam in her eyes but could not so easily hide her fear. "We'll get more help. We'll get reinforcements. We'll get —"

"You need to tell me where it is. How to get there."

She closed her eyes, bit her lip. "If I tell you, and you die in your attempt, how will I ever live with that, Lilith?"

"And if I don't try and just leave all those prisoners to their fate, and some of them die, or even just one of them dies, how will *I* live with *that?*" I asked her, then swallowed hard, because her tears spilled over, and the sight of them caused me pain. "What if this is what I was born to do?" I asked her. "What if my entire purpose in being conceived, being born with the antigen, being taken from you to be raised in that place, escaping alive — what if all of it was to enable me to do this? To save them? What if this is my destiny? Would you deny me my destiny?"

She blinked away her tears. "Does it really feel that way to you?"

I could only nod.

"I guess I can understand that. Though I joined this organization with only my own self-interest in mind — my desire to find you — I came to realize that it was so much more. It was meant to be. This cause is one I was destined to serve. So how can I deny you the chance to serve your own?" She sniffled and wiped at her eyes. "But be careful. Promise me that."

"Extremely careful. I'll just look around the place at first, see if there are any weaknesses I can exploit." I realized I was proposing to her the same plan that Ethan had earlier proposed to me. To take it slow, to be careful, to know all I could before risking myself. He'd been right about those things. Even if he had only said them to delay me.

"If they catch you —" my mother began, but she left the sentence unfinished. And I thought perhaps it was too horrible for her to contemplate what might happen to me if I were caught.

I smiled to reassure her. "You haven't seen me run, have you?"

She allowed a small smile in return. "There's nothing I can do to talk you out of this, is there?"

"No. I'm sorry, I really am. I wish we'd had more time together. If all goes well, perhaps we will." I took my palms from her cheeks and leaned close to press my lips to them instead, a gesture of love that was as spontaneous as it was sincere.

She sighed and nodded gently. "Give me a moment, then. We have maps inside, and the coordinates, as well. I'll write the directions down for you. It will be faster — well, at least safer — if you take one of the boats."

"Thank you."

While the other women headed into the cabin and began lighting lamps and building a fire in the hearth, my mother led me around to the side that faced the nighttime lake. For a moment I let the natural beauty of this place touch me and its peace soothe me. Then she left me there and went inside to get me the information she had promised.

There were two long docks, with several small boats tied alongside them. One or two had small outboard motors, but most had only oars.

As I stood there, listening to the gentle lapping of the water against the hulls, staring out at the way the stars were reflected on the surface of the lake, I thought again of Ethan. I felt again his arms around me. His mouth on mine. The delicious weight of his body on top of me, and the blissful pleasure of him inside me. And in spite of everything, I wanted him again. I ached for him. And I felt tears brimming in my eyes, but I blinked them away when I heard my mother reemerge from the cabin. Her footsteps crossed the dock to where I stood, and I turned to face her, hoping she

342

wouldn't see the pain and longing that seemed to be crushing my heart.

"Take this one," she said, pointing at one of the boats. "It has a motor, in case you need it. But don't use it unless you have to. You'll want to row," she told me. "Otherwise, the noise will give you away."

"All right."

"You start it by flipping the switch, there, and then pulling hard on the cord." She showed me what she meant, and told me how to steer the thing, as well. She told me how to speed up or slow down, and how to kill the motor when I no longer needed it. She checked to be sure it was filled with gasoline, and advised me to wear the life jacket that lay across the seat.

And all the while I thought she was only delaying the inevitable moment when I would leave her. I understood. I felt the same.

At last she handed me the folded scrap of paper on which she had scribbled directions, at the same time reciting them aloud, in case I should lose the note.

I took it and dropped it into a pocket. Thanks to these women, I had fed and rested and now wore fresh, practical clothing. Jeans, a tank top and a light hooded sweatshirt, currently unzipped. I had socks and running shoes. I had more than that, too. I had a small army of women who would grieve if something should happen to me. My mother most of all, of course, but I did not doubt that the other members of her odd secret order would weep for me, as well.

It was a foreign feeling.

I wondered if Ethan would mourn me if I were killed. I wondered if he would regret taking his brother's side against me. Or whether he even knew that was what he had done by betraying our mission to James.

James was evil. I had no doubt of that. No matter how much I'd thought on it, I couldn't see any other answer. Someone had told those DPI bastards that we were on our way. And no one else had known.

"I love you, Lilith," my mother told me, then hugged me hard. I hugged her back almost fiercely.

As we pulled apart, she pressed a key into my hand. I frowned at it. "For the locked case you'll find under the seat cushion in the boat. There are weapons inside. Tranq guns for vamps, regular ones for anyone else. Just in case."

"Thank you, Mother," I whispered, then found it difficult to speak any louder, due to the constriction of my throat. "I . . . No matter what happens, I —"

"Don't say that."

"No matter what happens," I repeated, insistent now, "I'm so glad I got the chance to meet you, to know you a little. And to understand what an extraordinary thing it is to have a mother, to know her love."

"I'm glad, too," she said softly.

I hugged her again, then pulled away and turned to climb into my boat. My mother leaned over to untie it from its moorings, then tossed the rope to me.

I waved once, then took the oars and began to row, watching my mother as I went. She remained right where she was, standing on the dock, a cloak wrapped around her shoulders. The night breeze lifted its fringed edges and tossed her hair. And I drank in the sight of her for as long as I could, until a bend in the shoreline hid her from my sight.

Then I lowered my head and let the tears flow.

This caring for other people was new to me. Oh, I'd thought I understood it. I'd thought that my desire to save the others at The Farm was because I cared for them — and I did. I had cared for them before I'd left. I remembered it clearly now. And I cared for them still.

But that caring was nothing compared to what I felt for my newfound mother. And nothing compared to what I felt for Ethan.

As I dipped the oars and rowed ever farther from them, I feared I had lost them both. And the possibility that I might die in my efforts this night paled beside the thought that I might never see either one of them again.

I wondered briefly if I'd been better off before I'd known what it was to love. For to lose that love was a pain beyond anything I could ever have felt had I never known it.

And yet, despite the pain and the loss, I realized I wouldn't give up any of it. Not the touch of a mother's love, and certainly not the joy I'd found in Ethan's arms. No, I wouldn't give up any of it, not for all the world.

Serena watched her daughter go and hoped to God it wasn't the last time she would ever see Lilith alive. She was so filled with love for her that it seemed to be nearly bursting from her heart. There was very little she could do to ensure her daughter's survival.

But there was *one* thing.

It would mean breaking her oath to the Sisterhood, the order to which she had pledged her very life. It might very well mean harsh punishment when they found out what she had done.

When a woman joined the Sisterhood of Athena, she joined for life. No one left, and betrayers . . . well, betrayers vanished. There was an unspoken understanding that for the greater good, no one must be allowed the chance to reveal the secrets of the order.

She didn't know for sure that traitors were summarily, if humanely, put to death. But it was what she believed happened, in those extremely rare instances. And it was, at that moment, what she believed would happen to her.

It didn't matter. She would gladly give her life to save her daughter's. There was no hesitation, no fear in her heart. "It's what mothers do," she whispered.

Pulling the cell phone from a pocket, she checked the screen, relieved to see that there was a signal in this remote place. It was Ginger's phone, not her own. She'd switched the phones while Ginger slept. She'd learned long ago of a forbidden contact Ginger had hung on to, despite orders from above to the contrary.

She found the list of phone numbers and scrolled down until she found the one she wanted. The one belonging to the only person in the world who might be able to help save Lilith and the other captives being held at The Farm.

She was one of only a handful of her kind who knew of the Sisterhood's existence. She and her friends had vowed to keep the order's secret, but the powers that be had forbidden any future contact, and though they hadn't said the words "on pain of death," that had been fully understood.

And yet Serena pressed the button, and the telephone placed the taboo call. She felt a chill rush up her spine as she listened to the woman's phone ringing. Once, twice, three times.

And finally, sounding extremely irritated, the woman herself answered the phone with a curt, "Who are you, and how did you get this number?"

Swallowing hard, Serena forced herself to speak. "My name is Serena, and I know what's been happening to the Chosen. I know where they are. The missing ones. My daughter is among them, trying to save them, though I fear it will cost her her life. I can't hope to help her, but you can. And I'm begging you to provide that help . . . Rhiannon."

18

"Where are you, Lilith?" Ethan demanded to the sky and the air and the emptiness around him.

But naturally, none of them answered his plea.

He'd followed his sense of her through a vast library and into one of several tunnels, then emerged from the underground passageway and spotted the amber glow coming from a cabin on the shore of an extremely large lake. There were other cabins, but his eyes were drawn to that closest one. There was a lot of movement inside, but more important, he felt that Lilith had been there, and quite recently. It was incredible, his unseen, undeniable bond with Lilith, begun in captivity, empowered by sex and the sharing of blood — but not even all that seemed capable of explaining the intensity of their connection. Nor did it explain his urgent need to find her. To protect her. To touch her again.

He'd followed his awareness of her through those tunnels, finding her trail unerringly. He didn't think he could have done that with anyone else, mortal or vampire. He didn't believe he could have done it even with his own brother. God knew he'd tried.

He let the trapdoor in the ground fall closed behind him and strode down the grassy slope toward the cabin. And with every step, his sense of Lilith grew stronger and he moved faster, until he was running.

His instincts led him not into the cabin but past it, toward the lake itself, and his feet hit the dock, pounding across it.

She stood with her back toward him, tall and slender and regal as a queen, staring off into the distance, over the water. Her hair was concealed beneath the cloak she wore around her shoulders. He wondered where she'd gotten it even as she heard his approach and turned to face him.

Her profile made his heart jump in his chest, but then she faced him fully, and his elation became disappointment. He came to an abrupt stop on the shore end of the dock, staring at her. This was not Lilith. And yet she resembled Lilith in a way that could not be coincidental.

"Who are you, and where is Lilith?" He spoke softly, though he wanted to shout.

"I'm Serena," she said, folding the cell phone she'd been holding and dropping it into an unseen pocket. "I'm her mother."

The words stunned him, and he rocked backward as they reached his ears. "That's a lie."

"It's the truest thing in my life," she told him. "Are you Ethan?"

He nodded, noting the tears on the woman's cheeks and the resemblance that seemed more evident with every second that he looked at her. Even her voice was like Lilith's.

"She was taken from me on the day she was born," the woman said. "I've been searching for her ever since."

He narrowed his eyes, probing her mind in search of any sign of deception. "All the children taken to be raised on The Farm are orphans," he told her, even though he'd had his own doubts as to the veracity of that bit of his so-called education.

"Is that what they told you?" she asked, and then, with a shake of her head, she went on. "They told me my daughter was still-born, even though I heard her cry. Lies, Ethan. All lies. That's what they do, they lie. And worse."

"But you . . . and all those other women who were with you — you shot at us. You took her —"

"Would have taken you, too, if that other vampire hadn't beaten us to it." She tipped her head to one side, coming closer to him as her eyes roamed his face. He felt as if she were trying to discover everything about him in one thorough look. He sensed no malice emanating from her. Moreover, her mind was wide open to his probing. She wasn't trying to hide anything from him.

"The keepers knew you two were on your way to The Farm, Ethan. Someone told them you were coming. They were waiting in ambush. You would have been killed. So *we* ambushed you instead. We couldn't think of any other way to save your lives."

"We?" he asked, glancing nervously back at the cabin, reminded again that this woman had a dozen or so others with her, and that they had been armed with tranquilizer guns the last he knew.

"They're no threat to you," she told him. "They're just a group of women dedicated to a common cause. A good one. And you really don't need to know more than that."

"I'm not interested in knowing more than that." He shifted his gaze back to hers. "Where is Lilith?"

The woman — Serena — studied him. "Why do you want to know?"

"So I can get to her in time to save her life!" he said, much more forcefully than he had intended. "My God, woman, do you know what she intends to do? She needs my help."

Serena tipped her head to one side, staring hard into his eyes. "You love her," she said softly.

"Just tell me where she is." He didn't even try to mull her words over in his mind. Not here, not now.

The woman nodded toward the water. "She's on her way to The Farm. Just to surveil it, for now, or at least, that's what she promised me. But you know how unpredictable she is. Probably better than I do."

He nodded. "She went by boat?" he asked, realizing now why Serena had been staring out at the water.

"Yes. From here, you just follow the shoreline until you see the waterfall, where the river empties into the lake. Bank the boat there, but hide it well."

He looked down at the boats lined up along the dock.

"Take that one," she said, pointing. "There are weapons under the seat. I'm sure you can get to them without the key. Take care of her, Ethan. Try not to get yourselves killed. I've asked for help, although I have no idea whether my request will be granted. Please try to keep her alive."

"I will." He climbed into the boat and stood in the bow, untying the rope that held it. He felt the woman's anguish, her worry, her grief. It was pouring from her in waves, and it felt to him a lot like his own. Looking up at her again, he said, "You really are her mother, aren't you?"

"I am," she whispered. "And while you're rowing, think about how the DPI knew you were coming. Ask yourself who could have told them."

He frowned hard, averting his eyes as he coiled the rope and dropped it to the floor of the boat. "You say that as if you have a suspect in mind."

"Lilith said she didn't tell anyone. Did *you,* Ethan?"

He looked up at her and held her eyes for a long moment. He knew exactly what she was suggesting and told himself it wasn't her business.

"Where is your brother, anyway?" she asked. "I'm guessing he was the one who took you from the road where we intercepted you and Lilith. Why aren't you with him now?"

"I thought it would be better to come alone."

"So you don't trust him, either?"

He sat down hard, grabbed the oars and dipped them into the water. "He's my brother."

"I see. I should probably tell you that Lilith believes you and he are working together, against her, and perhaps have been all along. So don't be surprised if she's not overjoyed to see you."

"She thinks . . . ?" He closed his eyes, shook his head. "How could she think something like that?"

"Well, she knows you told *someone* your plans, after giving her your word that you wouldn't. You tell me why she should trust you." She looked at him straight on. "Doesn't that make sense to you?"

He wanted to say it didn't, but he knew it did. Lilith had never trusted anyone in her entire life until she'd trusted him. And he'd betrayed that trust, even though he felt she'd been wrong to demand what she had of him, and even though he'd been trying to save her life with everything he'd done. That wouldn't change things in her eyes. He had broken his promise to her by telling his brother of their plans. He would be lucky if she *ever* trusted him again. Assuming, of course, that they lived long enough for her to have the chance.

As Ethan rowed away from the dock, Serena waved a gentle hand. "Be careful, Ethan. Bring my Lilith back safely."

"Or die trying," he muttered, but not loudly enough for her to hear. She was worried enough without that dire proclamation ringing in her ears. She was grieving again for the loss of the daughter she had only just found. He didn't doubt her story. The resemblance between the two women was so complete that it even included their auras. Their energy. He'd believed she *was* Lilith, standing there on the dock.

Now he had to focus on catching up to Lilith. He had to protect her. And he had to get his head straight about his brother. Was James on their side or not? Had he betrayed them to the DPI? Was James's loyalty to his trainers, his former captors, more powerful than his loyalty to the Bloodliners? To his own *brother*?

Ethan rowed around a bend in the water, moving beyond sight of the ethereal woman who stood watching from the dock. He used the power of his arms and his preternatural strength to propel the boat far and fast with each stroke. He opened his mind and honed his senses to search for any trace of Lilith.

He listened for her to call out to him but didn't dare call out to her. Thinking what she did, she might just run from him.

God, the idea that Lilith might actually be *afraid* of him, might actually believe that he wanted to capture her and return her to The Farm, when all along he'd been trying to prevent her from going back there . . . the thought of it almost made him physically ill.

But she couldn't believe that. Not really. Could she?

All at once he felt her, and his awareness quickened. Twisting around in his seat to see if he could catch a glimpse of her, he rowed even faster. A roaring sound filled his ears — the waterfall of which Serena had spoken — and he applied even more power to the oars. No one would hear his approach, not with the pounding waterfall covering the sounds of his oars cutting into the water.

He rounded a curve in the shoreline and then he saw it: the waterfall and, just this side of it, a boat resting on the shore.

Lilith's boat?

But why hadn't she hidden it? Surely her mother would have given her the same advice she had given him.

Frowning, he turned his boat toward shore, then stroked hard toward the small boat that rested on the water's edge. He was only about twenty yards out when he heard Lilith scream.

I rowed my boat ashore just beside the waterfall my mother had described to me. What she'd failed to mention was how the sight of the cascade would take my breath away. It tumbled from a cliff high above the lake, shooting outward before arching and tumbling down, so I could row right underneath it, if I wanted to.

And I did want to, because it would be magical. But there was no time to indulge in whimsy. Not then. Instead, I turned the boat before I reached the waterfall, and once pointed toward shore, I rowed hard enough so that my boat shot its nose up several feet onto the dry land before it came to a stop. Which meant I didn't have to get my feet wet getting out.

Before I debarked, though, I crouched and pulled my seat cushion aside. Then I inserted the key in the lock and opened the lid. The inside of the bench seat was lined in plastic, to make it waterproof. I reached inside and closed my hands around first one handgun, then another. One, I saw, was designed to fire tranquilizer darts, the other to fire bullets.

I set the tranq gun aside and felt for the box that contained ammunition, then pulled that out, as well. And as I crouched there, holding the gun in one hand and the box of bullets in the other, I felt another chunk of my past come rushing back to me. I knew how to use these weapons. I knew how to load them, how to aim, how to fire, how take them apart and put them back together.

I opened the box of bullets and set it aside, then turned the gun in my hand, depressed the release and caught the magazine in my free hand as it dropped from the hollow handle. Just cradling the gun in my palm had been enough to open the floodgates of knowledge and ability. I was delighted with that feeling of knowing, of confidence, of skill.

I felt empowered and strong and capable — right up until I felt the razor-sharp edge of a blade pressing against the skin of my neck.

"Don't move, Lilith. Don't move one little bit, or I'll slice your jugular clean to the bone, I promise."

I blinked and remained very still. He stood behind me, one arm at my waist, pinning my own arms to my sides, the other holding that knife to my throat.

"Drop the gun," he commanded.

And since I had little choice but to obey, I did, letting the handgun clunk onto the floor of the boat. I released the magazine from my other hand, and it, too, fell noisily.

"Now come with me. And don't try anything, Lilith. You'll bleed out faster than you can believe. I've seen it before in our kind. One slip of my hand and it'll be all over for you. Even if it's accidental, I wouldn't be able to save you. Nor would I be likely to try. They'll be just as happy to get you back dead as alive."

I nodded very slightly, lest my neck get sliced by that blade. I believed him. He was a vampire, that much I knew. He'd managed to sneak up on me partly because I'd been so involved with what I was doing, and partly, I suspected, because he'd been blocking his essence from me.

And now it was too late.

"I assume you're James," I said softly. "Ethan's brother?"

"Does it matter who I am?"

"It does to me," I told him. "I'm still going to kill you, you understand. I just might do it a little more humanely."

As I spoke, he forced me to walk ahead of him, keeping his blade pressed so tight to my throat that I could feel it scraping bits of my skin away with every step I took.

"Where is he?" I asked, barely moving my jaw as I spoke, fearing that any movement, no matter how slight, might result in the blade's pressure increasing. And it hurt. It hurt a lot. I shifted my eyes to the left and then to the right. I scented the air and felt the vibrations all around me. But I detected no sign of Ethan. "I thought he was with you."

"He sent me on a mission, a false one, just to get rid of me so he could come to you alone."

He spoke near my ear. I had yet to get a good look at the man, but I could tell that he was solidly built and several inches taller than I was, and his arm around my waist was like a band of steel.

"Fortunately for me," he went on, "my little brother has never been able to lie worth a damn. I saw right through it, hid myself and watched him, blocking my essence, then followed him. Once I knew that your path — and his — would end here, I cut through the woods to intercept you."

My blood was thrumming with the new knowledge that Ethan was coming for me. It made me hold my breath, wary and hopeful. But all I said was, "You must be good at blocking. I didn't sense you here."

"It's a gift." He shrugged and continued

propelling me along in front of him, into the woods that lined the shore, into darkness and the unknown. I waited for him to grow careless but held out little hope he would do so. The man was as sharp as the blade at my throat.

"So Ethan didn't know you were after me the whole time?"

He didn't even slow his pace, answering without even a pause, unshaken by my question. "I think he had an inkling, there at the end. Why else would he have tried to give me the slip?"

"He might just have tired of your company."

"No. He wanted to protect you." I felt his disapproval. "But I can forgive him that. He wouldn't be the first good man to be ruined by falling in love with a woman."

Falling in love . . . Those words echoed in my ears, but I didn't question them, even though I wanted to. Was it possible that Ethan . . . truly *loved* me? I tried to quell the surge of hope within my heart and to keep the conversation going. "And what ruined you, James?"

He did stumble then. Just one foot over a loose stone, knocking him off balance. I felt him shift to one side to regain his balance and took advantage of what might be my only opportunity, jamming both hands against his forearm and pushing it hard, away from my neck, even as I ducked low, somersaulting away from him. I sprang to my feet in a crouch, facing him now, ready.

He waved the knife in gentle arcs meant to draw my attention. He reached for me, and I ducked. He sliced at me, and I dodged. He lunged, and I leapt away, only to trip on a tree root and land on my back on the ground.

He was on me instantly, jabbing something into my breast. My first thought was that I was being stabbed with that huge blade, and I panicked and screamed. But almost instantly I realized the pain was far too small, and, glancing down, I saw him depressing the hypodermic's plunger. I felt the sleep rising in me in direct proportion to the plunger's descent.

I blinked up at him. "James, please don't take me back there," I whispered. "Please."

"It's my duty. And why do you beg? It's where you were going anyway."

"Not as a captive."

"It would have ended up the same. You never stood a chance, Lilith. At least this way, I redeem myself in their eyes. At least this way, *I* do my duty and get to go on living."

"No. It's not your duty, James," I said, though my words were beginning to slur. "They've warped your mind. How can you possibly believe that you owe your loyalty to the mortals who once held you captive, rather than to one of your own kind?"

"You are *not* my kind. You're nothing like me," he muttered, as if in disgust.

"I'm your sister as surely as Ethan is your brother." I blinked slowly, fighting the damned drug as hard as I could.

I felt him scooping me up into his arms and marching through the woods, and I had time to marshal my strength just once, just enough to cry out mentally, *Ethan! James ambushed me. He's taking me back to The Farm. He's betrayed us both!*

Then I was gone, sinking into darkness, my pain and my fear fading far behind me.

Ethan heard her scream, felt her terror, and then received her mental message as she cried out for him, mind to mind, the way he'd taught her. But he couldn't believe — didn't want to believe — what she'd said. James had taken her? *James?* His own brother?

But he knew then that she had been right about his brother all along, and that his own skewed judgment had, just as he'd begun to fear, cost her —

No. He wasn't going to think it had cost her her life, not while she still lived. He beached his boat and set off through the forest, weaving around tree trunks, ducking limbs and jumping roots. He moved fast, and as soundlessly as he could manage, blocking his thoughts as he ran. And yet, he never caught sight of them. Not until he finally emerged from the forest to see a chain-link fence with a gate looming large in front of him.

A sentry stood in a boxlike structure inside the gate, and Ethan ducked behind a tree as he saw James stride right up to it, Lilith slung limply over his shoulder. Her long coppery curls hung to the ground, trailing in the dust. Her arms dangled, and her essence had gone silent. Ethan couldn't see her face, and could not, for the life of him, sense whether she was dead or alive.

The sentry pushed a button, spoke to someone, then hit another button that opened the gate. It slid sideways on some sort of track, and James stepped through. The gate remained open behind him, but Ethan thought it would be easy enough to clear the thing and follow, should it close before he could gain entry. He would be seen that way, however, which meant it had to be his last resort.

He was itching to go right then, to race through the gate, with fists flying. He hadn't even taken time to bring the weapons from the boat, he'd been in such a hurry to get to Lilith. He hadn't been thinking clearly.

But he had to think clearly now, he told himself. Getting himself captured would only take away Lilith's only chance. So he remained hidden amongst the trees, and was glad of it a moment later, when two armed guards stepped calmly up to James, aimed their weapons and told him not to move.

James's head snapped up, and Ethan felt his brother's sudden tension as the shock of the moment caused him to briefly lower the blocks on his mind. None of it came through in his voice, though, when he spoke with seeming confidence. "I work for you, so you can put those down," he said. "I've brought the captive I was sent for."

"We can see that, Bloodliner. Drop her."

"Drop her, my ass," James countered.

"Drop her, James." The command came in a voice used to being obeyed, and a moment later Ethan could see its owner, the commandant. White hair looking windblown, face like an aged baseball mitt. Ethan remembered that face. Seeing it never meant anything good for those in his care.

James had gone still, and Ethan felt the cockiness leaving his brother, saw some of the steel leaving his spine. He bent forward and let Lilith's body flip off his shoulders. She hit the ground hard, faceup, and Ethan winced at the sight of it.

"I've done nothing wrong, Commandant, sir," James told him.

"Perhaps you have. Perhaps not. Tell me, then, James, where is your brother?"

"Ethan?" James asked dumbly.

"Do you have any other brothers I should know about, James? I'd assumed there was just the one."

"No, sir. No other brothers. That I know of, I mean." He was nervous, stammering. "I just — I'm surprised by the question. I haven't seen my brother in more than two years."

"According to those we've had watching you, that may not be true. Until recently, this . . ." He tapped Lilith's rib cage with the toe of his boot. Ethan lunged, but caught himself and pulled back, biding his time. "This . . . sorry excuse for a Bloodliner was reportedly traveling with Ethan. So how is it you found her and not him?"

"She was alone when I found her." James stood there, at the ready, and Ethan feared for his brother in spite of himself.

"We'll see." The commandant snapped his fingers, and the guards stepped up, rifles pointed at James's head, while two more came out of nowhere to grip him by the arms.

He began to struggle, but the working of a rifle lever stilled him without a word. Lowering his head, he said, "You're making the biggest mistake of your entire life, Commandant."

"I think you lost the right to argue with me when you chose loyalty to your brother over loyalty to me, James. I'm extremely disappointed in you, but I can't honestly say I'm surprised."

The guards began leading James away, even as two others stepped forward and lifted Lilith off the ground. One held her beneath the arms, the other just beneath her knees, as they carried her away, but Ethan heard her groan and rejoiced to know she was still alive. As they moved farther into the compound, the sentry turned to watch them go, even as he hit the button that would close the gate.

Ethan saw his chance and sped from his hidden vantage point, running at full vampiric speed, which would render him no more than a blur to mortal eyes. And yet it was a blur these mortals were trained to notice.

The gate was nearly closed when he skidded through the gap sideways, came to a stop at the bottom of the sentry house and sat there, silent, willing the dust to settle as he pressed his back to the wood. The gate banged shut.

Ethan closed his eyes. He'd done it. He'd come back, willingly, to the one place where he'd sworn he would never set foot again. And he hadn't done it for his brother, who'd betrayed him, he'd done it for Lilith.

It was his fault she was back here in captivity and likely condemned to die in short order. He had to save her.

Or die by her side.

19

Moving slowly, keeping to a crouch, his body close to the ground, Ethan moved behind the sentry house to get a clearer view of what lay beyond it. Not that he didn't already know. This place was as familiar to him as his own ranch — no, more familiar. He'd spent his entire life imprisoned within the boundaries clearly marked by the electrified fence.

He'd once seen one of his fellow captives, in a fit of desperation — or perhaps it had been madness — rush at the fence, as if he would climb it or burst straight through somehow. But as soon as he'd touched it, there had been a terrible shower of sparks and spiraling smoke — and then he'd been launched like a man shot from a cannon. Airborne, he'd sailed in an arc that ended only when his back slammed into the ground some fifty yards from where he'd begun.

His hands had been burned black. His eyes had been wide, and his hair singed and smoldering at the ends. He was dead, of course, his life burned from him in one burst of electricity.

Ethan had never known his name. But he *did* know not to touch that fence.

There were areas that had been deemed forbidden, places he and the other captives had never been allowed to go and would have been punished for even daring to look at for too long.

But now Ethan needed to know everything about this place. He had to learn more than just *what* was there. He needed to know *who* was there, and where they had taken Lilith, and how many keepers and guards stood between him and Lilith now, and whether they were armed.

And so he crouched in the shadows and looked ahead to the first building on the grounds, the motor pool. Rows of prefab metal buildings, olive-green with white doors standing open, ran along both sides of the blacktopped roadway. Jeeps, minivans and high-performance sedans filled every spot available.

The compound was huge — three miles from end to end. A vehicle would be an added bonus. Ethan glanced up at the guard in the sentry house. The man stood still, his head bowed over a book. Silently willing him to stay that way, Ethan darted across the compound to the motor pool. As soon as he reached the first vehicle he ducked behind it, then peered back at the sentry.

He was still involved in his book. He hadn't noticed a thing. Good.

Ethan crept from one car to the next in search of one with its keys still in the ignition, but there was none to be found. He suspected the keys were kept inside one of the buildings, but he had no time now to search there for them.

He had to find Lilith. His reaction to seeing that she was still alive had been enough to fuel him for the battle to come. His bitter disappointment at seeing proof, beyond any doubt, that his brother had betrayed them could easily have crippled him, but he wouldn't allow that. Lilith's life was in his hands.

He sped from one point of cover to the next, moving faster than human eyes could detect. The entire time, he was searching with his mind for Lilith, hunting for that sense of her that had become so much a part of him that he was lost without it.

He wove and dodged from one building to the next, skirting the barracks where most of the captives lived out their lives of indentured service and indoctrination, and heading for the educational area, the part of the camp reserved for brainwashing, mind-altering and torture.

Torture.

God, the thought of them hurting Lilith —

No. He forced the thought away, because it would do nothing to help him find her. And it made him ill, made him weak, to dwell too long on the nightmarish fears of what might, even now, be happening to her.

He crept around to the side of one building, his sense of her failing miserably — probably because she was still unconscious. He had to peer through each window, and he stopped short when he heard the unmistakable sound of electricity zapping into something.

Or someone.

Lilith?

"Leave off, Griz," a voice said. "There's no point while she's drugged."

"There's a point, all right." The man sounded irrationally eager.

Ethan was itching to put his hands around the bastard's throat, but he had to wait. He couldn't even tell for sure which room they were in. The building's acoustics — designed to keep the screams of the tortured contained — made it impossible.

"We're under orders to keep our hands off her until further notice. Sorry, but you won't be having any fun with this one."

"Humph. When's the next dose due?"

There was a pause, then, "Three hours."

"I'll be the one giving it, then. Alone, this time."

The other one said, "Griz," in a tone that made the word a warning.

"Hell, it's not like I can hurt her any."

Damn right he wasn't going to hurt her, Ethan thought, and he eased himself farther, closer to the door.

As the two keepers left the building, Ethan watched. And more than that, he *felt.* He could feel others nearby and could probe their thoughts, could probably even communicate with others of his own kind, just as he could on the outside. He was relieved to learn that the barrier blocking communication between this place and the outside world had no effect within the compound itself. He'd left this place immediately after his transformation, so he'd never had the chance to test it before.

He waited until the two keepers were out of sight, then edged nearer the door. He felt inside for others, guards, keepers, mortals, prisoners — *anyone.*

He felt no one. If anyone else was inside, they must be as unconscious as Lilith was, and therefore they were harmless to him.

He looked in every direction, grateful for the mortals' inability to see as well in the dark as he could, then quickly gripped the doorknob, twisted it until the lock gave and pushed it open. Ducking inside, he closed it behind him and kept moving. The building consisted of two rows of rooms, separated by a narrow hallway. Each steel door was locked, and he had no way of knowing what lay on the other side of any of them. Or which one might hide Lilith.

Glancing behind only once, he realized there were no guards here. The captives kept in this building must not be considered much of a threat. As he moved along the hall, his feet tapping over the institutional-gray tiles of the floor, he stopped at the first door. It was a rectangle of pale slate-blue, breaking up, just barely, the otherwise unbroken gray of the walls and floor. Even the ceiling was gray, though it looked like it had been white once. But now it was coated in layers of grime in between the lighted panels.

He stopped outside the first door, licked his lips nervously, dreading what he would find beyond it. Lifting his palm, he pressed it to the steel. With his mind, he called out to her. *Lilith?*

But he heard no reply.

There was no time for finesse, he decided. He had to find her. He was *desperate* to find her. He drew his hand back, then drove it forward again, palm hitting the door just above the knob.

It smashed open and crashed against the wall behind it, making more noise than was probably wise. Ethan ducked inside, his gaze sweeping the room in search of Lilith.

But there was only one person in the room, and it wasn't her. A young man, maybe in his late teens, lay bound to a set of bedsprings, with no mattress between his flesh and the metal. His jeans were torn, his feet bare, no shirt in sight. He was one of the Chosen, of course — everyone here was either one of the Chosen and a captive, or an employee of the damned DPI. This kid's essence was weak, too weak to be felt beyond that steel door, even by a vampire. But Ethan felt it now, compelling him closer.

The electrical wires attached to the bedsprings told Ethan of the way in which the boy had been tortured. His stomach convulsed at the thought of it, and he had to close his eyes briefly. "Good God," he muttered.

When he dared to look again, the young man's eyes had opened, huge and brown, unfocused and swollen, a plea in their depths. "Please . . ." he whispered, his voice as dry as a wind over straw.

Vampires, Ethan had been told, were compelled to protect the Chosen. And now he felt it. He couldn't turn away, even though he wanted to. Even his drive to find and save Lilith couldn't prevent him doing what every cell in him was demanding that he do. He had no choice.

Quickly, he moved forward, ripped apart the bonds that held the boy, hauled him off the bed and over his shoulder and quickly turned and strode out of the room.

No time now to mess around. No more time for pondering or wondering or searching with his mind. He set the kid on the floor, leaning him back against the wall, and moved to the next door. One kick and the door banged open.

This room was empty. So he moved to the next, and then the next, kicking open each door in turn. All were empty, except the final one, where he found a young woman. He couldn't begin to guess her age. She was on the thin side of healthy, and had platinum-blond hair that was as straight and smooth as satin. It hung to her shoulders and was cut in bangs over her forehead. She was strapped to a chair, her eyes were taped wide open and duct tape covered her mouth — screaming captives, Ethan thought furiously, were probably bad for morale. In front of her, a huge television screen flashed images at strobe speed. She wore headphones, and Ethan knew they were blasting DPI propaganda into her ears and her mind, and probably drugs into her bloodstream. This was how they "programmed" their future killers.

He moved into the room, and her huge, blue, drug-veiled eyes darted in his direction, fear in them, though she couldn't turn her head. He felt her stiffen in terror, and he felt awful for it. He tried to send calming thoughts to her mind, but he had no idea if she could hear him, and there wasn't time to spend finding out. Instead, he walked right up to her, blocking the television screen with his body, and gently removed the headphones, then dropped them onto the floor. Carefully, he peeled the tape from her eyelids, and then he removed the straps that held her wrists and her head to the chair.

She let her head fall forward but didn't try to get up. He bent closer, gathering her up in his arms, and whispered close to her ear. "I'm not one of them," he told her. "I'm going to take you out of this place. You can take that tape off your mouth, but please, be very quiet."

She was peeling the tape from her face as he carried her into the hallway and bent to reach for the boy.

"Ellie?" the boy muttered, his gaze on the girl in Ethan's arms.

"She's going to be okay," Ethan said. "Can you walk?"

The kid nodded and got to his feet. "Who are you, anyway?" the boy asked, and then, with eyes narrowed, "*What* are you?"

"There's no time," he began, but then he heard a siren in the distance and swore. His entire raid on the building had taken no more than three minutes, but already an alarm was sounding. He shifted the girl to one side, slinging her over his shoulder, then scooped up the boy and tossed him over the other one. There was no time to let him walk. He wasn't a vampire and couldn't hope to move like one.

Ethan took off running as fast as he could go while carrying two humans, knowing it was far faster than any mortal would ever be able to match, though slower than he could have gone without the added baggage.

He sensed keepers rushing toward the

building he'd just left, but he was already long gone. He reached the fence and then pushed off for all he was worth.

He cleared the fence, barely managing to keep the kids from making contact on the way over, and then he landed hard on the other side. He hit the ground feetfirst, then fell forward. His passengers tumbled every which way, but he pulled them to their feet again.

"Come with me, and hurry," Ethan said.

"Where are we going?" the young man asked.

"Not far, I'll bet," the girl said. "I can barely walk. And besides, he hasn't got what he came for yet."

He glanced at her only briefly, wondering how she knew. Even now, keepers were swarming through the building where the two captives had been held. They would search the compound next and, he hoped, would have no reason to believe they could have escaped. He scanned the area. "There," he said, pointing. "Quickly!"

He dragged them toward the shelter of a fallen tree, diving behind it. The tree's root plate was thirteen feet in diameter, at the very least, and it was packed with earth and brush. It leaned at an angle over the depression it had left in the ground, and formed a shield between him and the compound.

"We have to hurry," Ethan told them. "In minutes they'll be on us. Turn around," he said to the boy, who, being already shirtless, was the easiest one to approach first.

The boy turned, and Ethan looked at his lower back, saw the barcode tattooed there and touched it with his fingertips. "Dammit," he said, when he felt the telltale lump just beneath the skin.

"What?"

"You've got a tracking device implanted here. I've got to cut it out. It's going to hurt, but it's your only hope. Bear with me, kid."

The boy nodded and braced himself. Ethan got out his pocketknife, opened it and wished to God for some alcohol to sterilize it. The kid wasn't a vampire, but he would still be prone to infection.

"It's one snip, it'll be fast."

On the plus side, not yet being a vampire, the kid wouldn't feel pain the way the undead did. But he would be just as prone to bleeding out.

Bracing himself, Ethan poked the blade underneath the lump, making an incision rather than just slicing off the skin entirely. The boy arched his back and hissed. Quickly, Ethan squeezed the device, and it popped out. Then he tore a strip from his shirt and wadded it up. "You can hold this there, keep the pressure on," he said.

"Wait." The girl handed him something. A strip of cloth torn from her own shirt, bearing a gob of some sticky substance.

Ethan looked at her, his question in his eyes.

"It's sap, from the tree. It's a pine, so it's antiseptic and should help with the bleeding." She held up the duct tape she had pulled from her mouth. "This might help, too." Her speech was still slurred, but her mind was clearly sharp — even with the drugs they'd given her.

"You're amazing," Ethan said, sincerely impressed by her. "But save some of that for yourself — you're going to need it."

"No, I won't," she said. And, turning, she lifted her shirt and showed him that she bore no tiny lump at the small of her back. "I've only been here a little while. They hadn't got around to tagging me yet probably."

He nodded and looked at the electronic chip in his hand. "Patch him up, and stay right here. I'll be back, I promise. Don't move, don't make any noise, cover yourselves in brush. I think you'll be all right until I return."

She nodded and turned to do as he had

asked of her.

Ethan dashed out of their shelter, running as far and as fast as he could, circling the compound until he estimated he was on the opposite side, then dashing directly away from it into the forest. Once he got far enough to satisfy himself, he began listening for a stream or the river, and once he homed in on one, he raced toward it.

It was a winding and deep river, not a stream at all, and he was glad of it. He took enough time to peel a shell-shaped bit of bark from a nearby tree and test it to be sure it would float. Finally he set the tracking chip in the middle of it. He set the little boat adrift on the river, then turned and raced back the way he had come.

His entire mission took, he estimated, around twenty minutes. And then he was back with the others again.

They looked up at him with surprise in their eyes, as if they hadn't really expected him to return. At least, that was the feeling he got from the boy. The girl had a more knowing expression in her eyes, and Ethan sensed that there was a reason for it.

"We have to move," he told them, and helped them to their feet.

"You're a vampire, aren't you?" the girl said softly.

He nodded. "This way, it's more than a mile. Can you make it?"

"I'd make it if I had to crawl, as long as it meant getting out of there." She turned to glance at the boy. "How about you?"

"I can make it," he muttered.

"You're really a vampire?" the girl asked. Ethan nodded.

"And you're obviously not working for them. So — you have to be Ethan."

Ethan glanced back at her but never slowed his pace. "What makes you so sure I'm not James?"

"James works for them. Everyone knows that," she said.

"You know a lot for a newly acquired captive, Miss . . . ?"

"I'm Ellie. He's Jeremy."

"And what happened to your family, Ellie?"

"My parents were archaeologists, on their way to a dig in South America. Their plane went down in the jungle."

"And then these jerks showed up to take you in," Ethan said. "Veer left up here. Try to hurry."

"You came for Lilith, didn't you?" Ellie asked.

He frowned hard at her this time, pausing only briefly. "Have you seen her?"

"No, but I heard some of the keepers talking. They said she'd been brought in, and that something big was going to happen."

"Something horrible, I'll bet," Jeremy said. "They'll try to make an example out of her. We have to try to stop them."

Surprised, Ethan stopped walking and turned around. "I have every intention of trying to stop them. I just need to get you two to safety first, as fast as possible, and then I'll go back."

Jeremy held his gaze, lifting his chin though it seemed to require a great effort. "We should go back together. We could help you."

"Why would you want to?" Ethan asked.

Jeremy frowned, as if that were a ridiculous question. "You're legends, you and Lilith. The only two ever to escape and survive."

"How did you know we had survived?" Ethan asked him.

"It was all over camp as soon as they brought her in."

Ethan reached for the kid so suddenly it frightened him. He jumped as Ethan's hand clasped his shoulder. "Do you know where she is? Where they're keeping her?"

The kid blinked, regained his composure and lowered his head. "No. I'm sorry."

Ellie shouldered her way between them, staring up at Ethan a little defiantly. "We're on your side, you know. We want to help."

Ethan felt a tightness in his throat, one he was unaccustomed to feeling, and he found himself absurdly glad he had found and rescued these people, even though it had delayed him in saving Lilith. "I'm sorry," he said. "It's just — I have to get to her before it's too late."

"We want that as badly as you do," Ellie said. "She's a hero. Her escape is what inspired our entire movement."

"Movement?"

She nodded, and Jeremy said, "We're . . . well, I guess you'd call us the resistance. We stopped letting them believe they'd broken us. We became as rebellious as Lilith was, modeled ourselves after her. No more pretending to accept their bull. We meet in secret and plan for the day when there will be enough of us to make a real difference."

Ellie said, "The keepers don't know about the meetings, or how organized we've become, even though it's only been a few days. They just see us rebelling. That's why we ended up in the torture rooms."

"So there are more of you?" Ethan asked.

Ellie nodded. "Sixteen. Before long we'll have enough to overthrow this place."

"We're going to overthrow this place now," Ethan said.

Ellie gripped Ethan's arm. "Never mind getting us to safety, Ethan. We can't leave her there. I heard she was coming back for us, so we have to do the same for her. Let's go back — right now. Let's go back and get Lilith out of there."

He hesitated, then glanced at Jeremy, his brows raised in question.

"I'm with Ellie," the young man said.

"Lilith won't settle for us just getting her out," Ethan told them. "She won't leave that place unless we can take everyone with us. You should know that before we go in."

The two exchanged a worried look, but then Ellie sighed and nodded. "We'd better connect with the rest of our group and organize something as fast as we can. We're going to need all the help we can get."

I woke in chains.

Lifting my head slowly, I tried to focus, to get my bearings, but it wasn't easy. I was upright, I realized slowly, my wrists and ankles spread and shackled to the wall at my back. I was still wearing the clothes given to me by my mother.

My mother.

My heart twisted a little at the memory of

her, because I was terrified that I would never see her again. But I had no time to dwell on that regret at the moment.

Instead, I let my gaze scan the room. The wall at a right angle to mine — brick. No windows. The one across from me, also brick, and in its center . . .

"James."

He was shackled just as I was. His shirt had been torn open, and I saw welts crisscrossing his chest and tiny streams of blood trickling from them. I could only hope they weren't deep enough to cause him to bleed out.

"How much did you tell them?" I asked him.

He met my eyes. "Nothing."

I searched those eyes of his, and was reminded sharply and painfully of the last time I'd looked deeply into Ethan's eyes. So similar, physically, and yet so very different, too. I felt relief, not heartache, when I thought of Ethan now. Relief at knowing he hadn't betrayed me the way I feared he had. His brother had been working without his knowledge. All of that was clear to me now. Oh, Ethan had indeed lied to me — he had broken his promise and told his brother our plans after vowing he wouldn't.

But that was a far cry from conspiring

against me, from plotting my recapture and even my death.

"I told them nothing. But you don't believe that, do you?" James asked.

"Why would I believe anything you have to say to me? You've already proven yourself a traitor against your own kind."

"But not against my own brother."

I stared hard at him, trying to read his thoughts.

"If I'd told them what they wanted to know, do you think I'd still be here?" he asked.

I shrugged as best I could with my arms stretched in a V above me and held in place by manacles and short lengths of chain. "Maybe," I said. "Or maybe they left you here to see what you could get out of me."

"They don't want to get anything out of you, Lilith. You won't be questioned, and you won't be tortured."

"No? And how do you know that?"

"They're making no secret of it. You're simply going to be executed. They're calling an assembly on the parade grounds. Everyone here, captives and keepers alike, is going to watch it happen."

His words, each one of them, hit my nerves like knives plunging into my flesh. Each one made me flinch in pain, tremble in fear, dread what was to come. "How am I going to be killed?" I asked him, unsure whether I really wanted to know.

"They didn't say."

I lowered my head, stared at the floor. "When?"

"I don't know. I heard one source claim it would be before sunrise. Another said tomorrow night. Either way, it's soon. You won't have long to wait."

Raising my head, I looked for a window, but there were none, so I couldn't judge the time by the stars in the night sky. And then I realized how they would kill me, and I went rigid with fear. I felt my eyes widen. "They'll stake me out to await the sunrise, won't they?"

James shrugged.

"God, I don't want to burn alive."

"I can't think of anyone who really does."

"Are you *joking?* Are you being *sarcastic* about my impending death, James? Has it even occurred to you that you're the cause of it?"

He blinked and averted his eyes.

"Your brother might just love me. Have you thought of that? He'll never forgive you for this."

"No, probably not. But at least he'll be alive."

"And he wouldn't have been otherwise? Is that how you justify what you've done, James?"

He shot me a look that should have wilted me. "Yes, that's how I justify it. If you'd stayed with him, someone would have found you sooner or later. They doubled their efforts to recapture Ethan when you escaped. They realized that more would follow unless they stamped out the spark of rebellion you two ignited. If it had been any of the other operatives — anyone but me — Ethan would be facing the same brutal end that you are." He looked me up and down, then looked away, turning his head hard, as if he couldn't stand the sight of me. Or maybe it was his own guilt that made looking at me impossible for him. "I had to capture *you* to save *him*. I had no choice."

"You really believe that, don't you?" I was disgusted. "Why is it that their brainwashing works with some people but not others? How is it that you couldn't see any other option? Like turning against them. Like sowing the seeds of rebellion the way I —"

I blinked then, as I remembered the few bits of my past that had still been missing. "As I tried to do. I thought I could ignite a spark and then feed it until it became a full-blown flame that would devour this place whole. Why wasn't something like that an option for you, James?"

He looked at me with such a puzzled expression that I knew he couldn't imagine it as an option even now.

"I *work* for them," he explained. "I can't work *against* them. They *made* me."

"And they can unmake you. You were created for one purpose only — to serve. To kill on command. To follow orders — to the point of death, if necessary. I know," I said. "I know because they tried to imprint my brain with all that nonsense, too, James, but I wouldn't listen. I wouldn't believe. I wouldn't give in. And you did. Think about it. How much sense does it make that you should obey them without question just because they say so?"

He blinked, shaking his head. "It's our purpose."

"Is it?"

He wasn't responding to me anymore. It felt as if a wall had come down between us. He wouldn't look at me, wouldn't listen. There was nothing but emptiness in his eyes. I lowered my head and sighed, giving up.

The door burst open then, and several keepers came inside. And I knew, with a gut-deep horror, that they had come for me.

20

The keepers, four of them — two men and two women — armed with tranq guns, marched straight to me. But only one met my eyes, and I remembered her. She was Callista, the one who had always been as kind as she could without being discovered. And now I knew why that was. She was not truly one of them, never had been. She was a Sister of Athena, working here undercover, to learn the DPI's secrets.

I met her eyes, felt her anguish and, I hoped, let her know that I knew who she was. Then I quickly lowered my head again, not wanting to risk anyone else seeing any hint of a message passing between us.

Callista was blond, blue-eyed and small in stature. Her movements were quick and sharp, and I sensed a strength in her that wasn't readily apparent. The other woman had straight brown hair, very bad skin and no hint of such inner power.

"Shouldn't we drug her again?" one of the men asked.

"She's still plenty weak from the first dose," Callista said.

"You sure?" The men looked at me closely. Perhaps too closely. These bastards, I realized, were used to dealing with the Chosen, not with the Undead. They were afraid of me, as well they should be. Given half a chance, I would gladly tear out their hearts.

Callista shot their curious looks right back at them. "I'm the medical officer here, gentlemen, but if you think you know more than I do, feel free to drug her again. Guidelines, however, state that four hours between injections is sufficient to keep a vampire weakened and unable to fight. And it's only been two."

The men looked at each other. One said, "They want her conscious for the end. I suppose we'd better not tranq her again so close to dawn."

"I thought we were taking her to the holding cell and the execution would take place tomorrow," Callista said.

"That was before the latest . . . incident," the brunette said. And I heard her mind as she recalled that two prisoners she thought of as rebels had escaped within the past hour. "Now the powers that be want to move things up."

In case those rebels had help, I suspected. And I opened my mind to feel for him — for Ethan. Was he here? Had he come after me? Would he, when coming back here was the last thing he had ever wanted to do?

"How close is it to dawn?" I asked.

They all looked at me as if shocked I had spoken at all. I hadn't meant to, but I had to know.

"A couple of hours," Callista said softly. She approached me, and I tensed. But I sensed something. I saw the intensity with which she looked at me while her back was turned toward the others. As if she were trying to speak to me with her mind — the way vampires could do with each other.

Frowning, I probed her mind with mine and found the message waiting there.

I'll slip you something before it happens. I promise you won't suffer. I'll slip you something before it happens. I promise you won't suffer. I'll slip . . .

I met her eyes and nodded once, by way of thanks. It was a small kindness, but all she had to offer.

She unlocked the shackles that held me to the wall, but I was still too weakened from the drug to break free and run for my life, though it was what I wanted more than anything else to do.

Another keeper came close, and knelt, intending to attach the chains that dangled from my wrists to the ones that held my ankles, but I wasn't too weak to deal with that. I brought my hands down fast on the back of his head, forcing it downward just as my knee came up to connect with his chin.

When I let go, he slumped to the concrete floor. Not just unconscious. Dead.

I lifted my gaze to the others. "You really shouldn't get too close. I'll take as many of you with me as I possibly can."

They all kept their distance after that, even Callista, who had no cause to be afraid but was anyway, and stuck to pointing their weapons at me.

I glanced at James as I shuffled out, but he only watched me go. Mindless twit. The man must have the will of a grapefruit. Thank goodness Ethan wasn't so weak.

They led me through the compound. It was a fair distance to the parade grounds, not that there had ever been any parades there — at least not within my memory. But this had been a military base once, and the name, I supposed, had stuck. We passed things that were familiar to me. The barracks where I had once lived. The school building where I had spent my days. The gymnasium where I had learned kickboxing and tae kwon do and swordplay. The firing range where they had only let us use blanks.

Then, finally, they led me onto the parade grounds, and I saw that a pole stood upright in the very center. Its bottom was embedded deeply in the earth. And there were iron rings high and low.

They led me right up to that pole, motioned with their guns for me to turn around and told me to raise my hands above my head, so they could fasten my shackles to the rings.

I shook my head. "I'm not aiding you in any way. Come and do it yourself, if you have the nerve."

One of the men did just that. With an angry sigh, he yanked something from his rear pocket, lunged at me and jabbed me in the belly with it. It sent a jolt through me that had me screeching in pain, then sinking to the ground as my entire body vibrated.

"Stun gun. And I'll use it again if you keep up with the bull," he said. He gripped my wrists, lifted me and slammed my arms against the pole, over my head. With a quick snap the chain between my manacled wrists was anchored to the ring. A moment later and the chain between my ankles was attached to the other.

"There, bitch. Enjoy the sunrise." He smiled slowly, and then, before I knew what he was about to do, he jabbed me with the device again, sending another shock through my body.

I screamed as tears of helpless rage ran like rivers over my face.

Ethan lunged at the sound of Lilith's scream, only to feel himself gripped by four strong young hands and tugged back. It would have been easy to overpower them, of course. They were only mortals.

But he let them pull him back behind the metal-sided building where they'd been crouching. He knew he would be killed if he dashed into the open, as he had nearly impulsively done. And if he allowed himself to die before Lilith was safe again, she would never survive.

"That came from the other end of the compound," Ellie whispered. "God, how did her voice carry so far?"

"We're vampires. Everything's . . . intensified. Strength, speed, every sense, and the volume and resonance of our voices."

"We need to get closer, see what's going on," she said.

"*I* need to get closer," Ethan told her. "You two need to go gather your band of rebels and get them ready to fight their way out of here. We'll meet in, say, thirty minutes."

"Okay," Ellie said. "At the far end of the compound, by the fence. We'll find you there. Thirty minutes." She gripped Jeremy's hand, but he pulled it free.

"I'm going with Ethan," he said.

"No," Ethan told him. "You'll only slow me down."

"I'm going with you. You might need my help, and Ellie won't. Rounding up the group is an easy job. All she needs to do is stay out of sight and tell one or two of them. They'll spread the word and meet us. But you might have to fight, and if you do, I'm going to fight at your side."

"You couldn't even begin —"

"I'm going, so stop wasting time."

Ethan sighed but gave in, then turned in the direction from which the scream had come. "Try to keep up, kid."

"Try to outrun me," the boy said with a cocky grin.

Ethan took off at full preternatural speed, rendering him no more than a blur, there one moment, gone the next, to Jeremy's mortal eyes. And all to make a point. He stopped near a tree a few hundred yards away and waited, watching with undisguised amusement, for the kid to catch up.

Jeremy came running, carefully keeping himself concealed from view, using trees and brush for cover.

When he got there, he braced one hand against Ethan's tree, let his head hang and sucked in breath after breath.

"That was pretty fast — for a mortal," Ethan said. "Well, for a mortal who's been tortured for the past couple of days, at least. Which, actually, isn't very fast at all."

"Yeah, yeah. You were . . . right."

"You've never seen a vampire before, have you?"

"No. Only other Chosen Ones, like me. Once they change you over, they . . . we never see you again."

Ethan nodded. "I remember."

"I had no idea you could move that fast."

"You can climb on my back for the rest of the way."

The kid's brows went up questioningly.

"Our strength increases just as much as our speed when we become . . . what we are."

"It seems to me that I'd be a lot more help to you if you — you know, transformed me."

"There's no time. You'd need a day to

sleep while the change fully took hold, and I'd need a day to recover from the blood loss, or a ready supply at hand to replenish myself."

He nodded, but Ethan could tell he was still thinking about it. Craving the power, the strength, the illusion of immortality. And that was all it was: an illusion. They could die — quite easily, in fact — which was why he was so afraid of losing Lilith right now. If he hadn't already lost her.

Perhaps that pain-racked scream he'd just heard had been the last sound she would ever utter.

The thought made his stomach heave. "Climb on." Ethan turned, presenting his back to the scrawny boy. Jeremy wrapped his arms around Ethan's neck and his legs around his waist. "Hang on," Ethan said, and then he launched into motion.

By the time they stopped again, they were crouching in some scrub brush behind a metal building that was surrounded by its own fence, a smaller, shorter version of the one that encircled the entire compound. A sense of Lilith's presence there brought Ethan to a grinding halt.

"This is where they would be keeping her," Jeremy said. "The few who've ever been put to death have been kept here beforehand. Though — we're not supposed to know that."

"I didn't know they'd ever put anyone to death."

"Only in the past six months. One prisoner who tried to escape. Two keepers caught breaking some rule or other."

"They're getting desperate," Ethan mused. "Your resistance movement, my escape and then Lilith's. They must sense they're running out of time."

"Good," the kid muttered. "I hope they're scared shitless."

"Crude turn of phrase. Not that I disagree."

"Do you . . . you know, sense her inside?"

"I sense something. I don't know."

"How do we get in?" Jeremy asked.

"*We* don't. *I* do." Ethan looked around, spotting a barrel nearby. Sniffing the air, he frowned. "Do you have a lighter? Or some matches?"

"I know where to find them," Jeremy said. "Why?"

"I want you to give me five minutes — then I want you to twist up a rag, stuff it into that barrel over there and light it. Then get under cover."

"Five minutes."

"Count them off. One, one thousand, two,

one thousand . . ."

The kid picked up the count. Bending his knees before giving the boy a chance to get to four, Ethan pushed off and cleared the small fence that surrounded this one building. He landed near the rear of the building, pressed a hand to the window, wiped the pane clear of the accumulated dust and stared inside.

At his brother.

He scanned the rest of the room, but he saw no one else. Nor did he sense anyone else inside, though the essence of Lilith teased his senses, and he realized that she must have been there recently but had clearly been moved elsewhere.

Ethan! James called mentally. *Ethan, is that you? What the hell are you doing here?*

Ethan drove a foot through the window, then dove inside, rolling over the floor and springing to his feet, ready to defend against attack.

"It's all right, Ethan," James said. "There's no one here. They've all gone."

Ethan's eyes focused on James, first in fury, and then that eased when he saw the marks of torture on his brother's face and body.

"I thought you worked for them, big brother. So why are *you* in chains?"

Lowering his eyes in what appeared to be shame, James whispered, "I only gave them half of what they wanted. The DPI doesn't like to settle for partial portions."

Ethan blinked. "You gave them Lilith — the woman I . . . a woman I care about. You deceived me in order to get your hands on her. You used me — used my love for you and my trust in you — to capture her for those DPI bastards. You betrayed me, James."

It hurt Ethan beyond measure to speak the words, but they had to be said. His throat convulsed painfully, and he could barely force air through it. But as hard as it was to speak those truths, it was harder yet to know them beyond any possibility of doubt.

"I didn't betray you," James insisted. "I betrayed *her,* but dammit, Ethan, that's my job. It's what I've been trained —"

"Programmed, you mean."

"Fine. It's what I've been programmed to do."

"Lilith was right about you all along," Ethan said as he strode closer to his lying excuse for a brother.

"They wanted you, too, Ethan. They tortured me. But I didn't tell them where to find you. I *didn't* betray you. The only

404

person I betrayed was a woman who means nothing to me."

Ethan gripped the front of his brother's shirt and jerked him against his chains. "She means something to *me*."

James couldn't meet Ethan's stare. "I didn't have a choice," he said. "I tried to talk myself out of handing her over for your sake, Ethan. Again and again I tried to convince myself that I didn't have to go through with it. But in the end, I knew I had to." Lifting his gaze at last, he looked Ethan in the eye, and there was regret in his own gaze. "I was afraid of what they would do to me for disobeying orders again."

"I don't blame you — when *this* is what they do to you for *obeying*." Ethan shook his head. "Where is she?"

"Set me free and I'll take you to her."

Ethan couldn't believe his brother thought he would leave him imprisoned, whether he promised to take him to Lilith or not. But he said nothing, just pried the manacles away, using both hands and all the strength he could muster.

"The only guards are out front. And they're most likely distracted."

"If they're not," Ethan said, "I can assure you that they will be." He led his brother to the exit of the otherwise empty building, gripped the knob and opened the door just slightly.

As James had predicted, two keepers stood outside the door, cradling their automatic weapons.

Closing his eyes, Ethan listened for the thoughts of his young cohort and heard, *Two-ninety-nine, one thousand, three hundred. Now!*

As the explosion rocked the grounds, James drew back, instinctively ducking and raising his forearms, as if to shield himself from falling debris. Ethan gripped his wrist. "The guards are running off, just as planned. Come on."

"That — that was *you?*"

"It was a friend." They trotted down the steps, and Ethan asked, "Which way?"

"A vampire friend?" James demanded.

"I'm not going to tell you who it is, James. But if you don't guide me to Lilith, I'm going to blow *you* up next. So where the hell is she?"

"That way. Parade grounds."

Ethan felt his stomach twist at the words. "Why?"

"Hurry, Ethan. It's too close to daylight as it is. Just go." And with that, James pulled free of him and ran in the opposite direction.

Ethan's eyes were powerful enough to follow the blur that was his brother as James darted behind the building in which he'd been held and leapt the perimeter fence. Then he ran straight at the larger electrified fence that surrounded the compound and leapt that.

And then he was gone.

Ethan was surprised, even after all he'd learned about his brother, that James had abandoned him. He'd half expected his brother to offer his help — to try to redeem himself by finally doing the right thing. But he hadn't.

The disloyal, addlebrained bastard.

Squaring his shoulders, Ethan shook off the bitter disappointment he felt in the brother who'd been his lifelong hero. Instead, he focused dead ahead and continued striding toward the parade grounds, alongside the guards and keepers who continued spilling out of buildings and racing toward the explosion.

No one even noticed him as he moved with the flow of bodies, and when he veered off to the right and cut around to the parade grounds, he kept under cover by moving between buildings until he neared the edge of the open expanse.

And then Jeremy was beside him, running

to keep up. "Was she in there? Did you find her? I couldn't see when you came out, but — Ethan? Ethan, where are we going?"

The buildings ended abruptly, and the well-worn dirt track they'd been following curved away, looping to form a complete circle around a large grassy area about an acre in size. On the far side of that circle stood a bare flagpole, its cords snapping in the night wind. At sunrise, Ethan knew, an American flag would be hoisted as the captives stood at attention and the national anthem played over the loudspeakers. It was the way they began each and every day here.

But tonight the view included a different, heavier pole, erected in the center of the circle, with a woman chained to it. Her arms were stretched over her head, her ankles bound, as well. Her hair, coppery curls tumbling free, fell around her shoulders, strands flying with every touch of the breeze.

"Oh hell," Jeremy whispered.

As Ethan stood there in the last of the cover provided by the alley between two buildings, staring at Lilith, aching for her with everything in him, she lifted her head and met his longing gaze. Her lips trembled into a small smile, and a tear spilled onto her cheek.

You came for me.

408

He only nodded, then stepped toward the open ground, eager to get closer to her. Jeremy reached for him. "Wait, Ethan!"

You really came for me.

"Take her back to the holding cell!" someone shouted, and Ethan automatically drew back, still unseen, as men in uniform surged forward around Lilith.

"Double the guard," the ranking officer commanded. "Anything goes wrong, it's on your heads."

"Yes, sir."

As Ethan watched, two of the uniformed men moved closer and began fumbling with Lilith's bonds. Others took up sentry positions, bearing rifles and watching in all directions as the first two released Lilith's bound wrists and ankles. A few of the guns were pointed at her, others aimed outward, as the leader gripped Lilith's upper arm and jerked her roughly across the open grounds toward the buildings.

Keeping to the shadows, Ethan followed, with Jeremy sticking close to his side.

"The explosion bought her some time," the kid said in a harsh whisper.

Ethan nodded. "Let's just hope it's enough."

21

I was returned to a room much like the one I'd been in only a short while before. This one, though, was empty. No sign of James, and I wondered briefly whether he had escaped. It seemed likely. Ethan wouldn't leave his brother in captivity, even though he knew about James's duplicity and betrayal by now. I had no illusions about his feelings. If he was here trying to save me, then he must already have rescued his black-hearted brother. I knew where Ethan's priorities lay.

I strained to feel Ethan's presence anywhere near me, but I felt no hint of it. Had I only imagined seeing him moments ago? Or had he given up, left me here to suffer my fate alone, now that his brother was safe?

A blade twisted in my chest at the thought, even though the logical part of my brain told me it was unlikely. Ethan would try to save me. Even though I was here because of my own stubborn insistence on returning to this place. Even though I had brought every bit of my suffering on myself. And even though he might very well die in the effort, he would try to save me. He was too decent a man not to.

That, I told myself, was true. And even if Ethan had freed his miserable brother before he'd come after me, and even if his brother came first with him and always would, that didn't mean Ethan had changed sides. It didn't mean he'd abandoned me.

I bit my lip, willing that belief to overwhelm the doubts that tried to squelch it, and worked to keep my emotions well hidden as the keepers chained me to the wall. Their movements were short and quick, their nervous energy zapping from them like electric sparks. They feared me. They weren't used to working with vampires, only the harmless Chosen Ones, far less able to defend themselves.

I was weak from drugs and hunger, from the pain they'd inflicted, from the fear of my impending death and worry for Ethan. I was weak. But I was also wise. Trying to fight them just then would have been a waste of my limited energy. I would wait and bide my time. Ethan was here — somewhere. He would help me, and I would need every bit of strength that remained in me to fight by his side when the time came. Because he wouldn't just leave me here. He wouldn't save himself and leave me behind. He wouldn't run away for his brother's sake and abandon me to the brutality of the keepers.

Not again.

Finally the nervous mortals exited the building, leaving me alone. I leaned my weary head back against the wall, closed my eyes against the hot tears that burned in them and realized that I could still hear the humans. They were talking softly outside my door. They really were unused to working with the Undead, I thought, to speak — even softly — so close to someone with preternaturally enhanced hearing. My head came up, my attention focused to glean whatever information I could from their words.

"What's happening, sir?" one of the younger ones asked. "What was that explosion?"

The leader replied slowly, and with great care. "We believe someone has breeched the perimeter of the compound."

"Someone got out?" the same voice asked, sounding alarmed.

"Someone got *in,* Jeffries. We believe

they're attempting to rescue certain residents. James — the vampire assassin we had chained inside — is gone. So are the two rebels we had in the punitive programming barracks, and I've heard a handful of others have vanished. Though if they're still inside, we'll find them, and I'd bet my right arm they *are* still inside. And it's probably this one they're after, her they came for to begin with."

"Is it Ethan?" Jeffries asked.

"Seems a likely bet."

"Then wouldn't it be better to execute her at dawn, as planned, and get it over with?"

"It's not our job to question orders, just to carry them out. Besides, by keeping her alive another day they can use her as bait to get their hands on Ethan and James, and on those they've already rescued."

"I think they should kill her now," Jeffries said. "The sooner the better. Take away Ethan's reason to hang around before some of us end up hurt."

"We're not going to end up hurt, kid."

"Ethan's a *vampire,*" the kid said. "So is James. And so is the one we just chained up. That makes three of them, and I've heard what they can do."

The other man was silent for a moment.

When he did reply, he said nothing to re-assure his younger comrade-in-arms, only, "I'm putting you in charge of security for this prisoner. It's your only job tonight. I want two men guarding each side of this building. I want all of you awake and alert. Keep your radios on, and report anything even remotely unusual. Don't hesitate to use the tranquilizer guns you've been is-sued. Understood?"

"Yes, sir."

"Good."

I heard footsteps as the two men dis-persed, the elder moving beyond the range of my hearing, while the younger moved only a short distance and spoke to a number of other men. When he returned, there were other sets of feet stomping the earth along with his own. I heard them clearly, splitting into pairs and moving around the small building that housed me to take up their as-signed positions. I felt surrounded, closed in.

And mostly hopeless. I had no reason to be hopeful, after all. Those men outside were more certain Ethan would come for me than I was. And now that I was so well-guarded, I wondered if he would be able to get to me even if he tried.

I hung my head, trying to remove my

focus from the chafing and pressure in my wrists and ankles, bound too tightly and too long within the metal jaws of my shackles.

But my head came upright when I heard a very soft sound above me. Tipping my chin up, I stared at the ceiling, and the soft sound came again. Someone was moving around — on the roof.

I closed my eyes, opened my senses.

Are you all right, Lilith?

A sigh of utter relief was wrenched from my chest, and I struggled to blink back a rush of scalding tears. *Ethan.*

Are you hurt?

Drugged. Weak. Starving. But unharmed. I wanted to say more but bit it back. This was not the time.

I'm coming in.

Ethan, don't! There are at least eight guards surrounding this building. You'll be captured if you try.

I'm coming in. He repeated the thought with a firmness that brooked no argument, and then I heard the sounds of nails ripping free of the rafters and metal bending. It wasn't loud. It wasn't likely to even be heard by the mortal guards outside my building. But *I* could hear it.

And it wasn't long before I felt Ethan moving closer as he landed somewhere amid

415

the rafters in the ceiling above me, and a moment later he was on his feet on the floor.

He turned until he faced me and then just looked at me. His face showed a thousand emotions, none of which was clear to me, so fast did they move from one to the next. And then he was rushing toward me, clasping my face in his palms and kissing the dampness from my cheeks.

"Lilith. God, Lilith, I was so afraid I'd be too late."

I tipped my face up to his, hungry for his touch, his kisses, despite my lingering doubts. I wanted this. I wanted to believe. I wanted *him*.

He covered my mouth with his, giving me what I craved more than blood, or life, or even freedom in that moment. And when he lifted his head again, I held his gaze and whispered, "I didn't think you would come."

"I don't believe that. You had to know I would come for you."

I lowered my eyes. "I hoped you would," I admitted. "But then, when you freed your detestable brother first . . ."

"I came for you, not him. I freed him, yes, but only in hopes he could help us."

"He'll never help us."

Ethan cupped my chin and turned my face to his. "He proved that when he ran off and left me on my own the second he was free. He did tell me where to find you first, though."

"Then let's forgive him for putting me here." If my tone was sarcastic, good. I intended it to be.

"It's you I came for, Lilith."

"And the others I heard you've rescued?"

He slid his hands along my left arm, giving me chills all the way, until he reached the manacle at my wrist and snapped it open. "I found them in the first building where I was searching for you. A pair of teens, Bloodliners, the Chosen. I found them in the torture rooms, and I — well, I couldn't leave them behind."

I raised my eyebrows, then bit my lip as he slid his talented hands along my other arm, freeing my right wrist as he had the left. "I wonder what crimes they committed."

"They've started a movement, Lilith. Inspired by your constant rebellion and eventual escape, they've begun some kind of resistance movement. They insisted on helping us. The girl is gathering her group together. We're supposed to meet them at the compound fence. I sent the boy on ahead to wait for us there."

"Despite my guards?"

"Despite anything." As he spoke, he bent his head to my neck and pressed his mouth to my skin, and I shivered and clasped his head in my newly freed hands.

"Ethan," I whispered.

"I'm here, Lilith. I'm not leaving without you."

"You really did come for me?"

"Only for you. The others were happenstance. I only came for you."

"I want you, Ethan."

"There's no time," he whispered. And yet he kissed a path over my throat and down my breastbone, to my belly, to my thighs. Kneeling, he dropped his hands to my ankles and snapped the shackles free.

I fell quickly to my knees, as well, twisting my arms around his neck. "I *need you,* Ethan. We might not survive this. This could be our last chance to be together."

"I know, but, Lilith —"

"I need you *now.*"

Ignoring my words, he pressed my face to his neck.

"Drink," he whispered. "You're weak. You need blood. Drink from me."

I couldn't stop myself. My lips tasted his skin. My tongue lapped a slow path over it, and I felt the blood rushing in his jugular, felt it pulsing hard against my mouth.

Grimacing in torment, I denied my raging hunger. "No. Not until you're inside me." I nipped at his neck. "I'll *die* without it, Ethan, I will. I need it more than I need blood. Please."

With a low growl, he shoved my jeans down to my ankles and, still kneeling, loosened his own. I sank down onto him and felt such relief that I very nearly cried out. I bit his shoulder to keep myself from moaning in pleasure, and I know I bit hard enough to hurt him, yet he didn't flinch away.

Instead he pulled me down, arching into me, holding my hips captive in his large, powerful hands as he drove himself deeper. I took all of him and loved it.

And as we moved together and I neared climax, I sank my teeth into his neck and drank him into me. When I came, he did, too, and I suckled and swallowed and tried to be silent as his magnificent body drove mine into spasms of shivering ecstasy. I felt him shudder and clutch me tighter, drive into me harder, and as he held himself there, pulsing into me, it was sheer bliss.

Finally, slowly, our bodies still entwined, our muscles relaxed.

Lifting my head from his sweat-slick shoulder, I licked my lips and smiled into his eyes. "So good," I whispered.

"So *very* good," he replied. "Now, if you're feeling stronger . . . ?"

"I'm feeling invincible."

"Then let's get you the hell out of here."

I nodded hard, quickly pulling my clothes back into place and getting to my feet. He led me to the hole in the ceiling and took me by the hand. With a single push, we both leapt up into the rafters, and in a moment, we were emerging onto the building's roof, the stars twinkling in the fading purple night above.

"We have to leap and clear the guards below without a sound, and land on the far side of the next building," he said, pointing. "Ready?"

I nodded, and we crouched low — only to go utterly still when a voice from the ground below shouted up at us, "Don't try it. You're completely surrounded, and every gun in this place is aimed right at your heads."

I blinked and peered down at the keepers and guards below, dozens of them. And every one pointing a weapon at us. We were outnumbered, and, I thought, we had no chance.

"That's what I was afraid of," Jeremy said.

He had gone to the farthest end of the

compound to meet Ellie and the other members of the unofficial resistance.

And now he and Ellie and the other sixteen Chosen were lurking behind one of the nearby buildings, fully aware the entire compound was being searched for them, but also aware that most of the keepers in the immediate vicinity were focused solely on the two vampires trapped on the rooftop.

"How long before sunrise?" Ellie whispered, leaning in close to him.

Jeremy looked at the sky, reading the stars. "Maybe an hour."

"What are we going to do?" She glanced back at her fighters as she spoke, worried, Jeremy knew, about every last one of them. There were seven boys, nine girls. He and Ellie were the oldest among them. The youngest was all of eleven.

"We've got to get inside that building," he said. "If we can't fight our way out before dawn, maybe we can at least protect them while they sleep and try again at nightfall."

Ellie shook her head. "We'll end up trapped, just like they are."

"What are our other options?" he demanded, growing angry. "Give up and return to captivity? Or maybe run off and leave them to die, when they came back here, risking their lives, for us?"

Ellie pressed a hand to his cheek. "I wasn't suggesting either one of those options, Jeremy. I was going to say we should get some weapons before we charge in there to join them. It'll at least give us a fighting chance." And as she said it, she nodded toward the building adjacent to the one providing them with cover. "They keep the guns in there."

Jeremy smiled slowly. "I should have known better than to think. I'm sorry, Ellie."

"I'll forgive you if you get me out of this alive." She turned and, with a small hand motion, told her resistance fighters what she wanted them to do.

Ethan caught movement from the corner of his eye and, seeing perfectly despite the darkness, noted the small band of Chosen Ones darting from one building to another. Frowning, he looked quickly back at the guards and keepers surrounding them.

"How did you know I was here?" he called down, because he wanted to keep their attention right where it was: on him. God, why hadn't Jeremy and Ellie led their little band to freedom? Why had they brought them back here?

"Someone saw movement on the roof," a

keeper said. "It didn't take much to figure out that you had come to try to rescue her. It was a stupid thing to do."

"It was the only thing to do," Ethan replied. "I got my brother out. I assumed it would be just as easy to rescue Lilith. You people may be pretty adept at intimidating the Chosen into submission, but you have no clue what you're dealing with now. We're not mortal. We're vampires. And if you don't back off and let us go, I promise you, a lot of you are going to die."

The man on the ground hesitated, and Ethan saw some of the others exchange worried glances. A bit of muttering broke out among them, but the leader held up a hand for silence.

"So what happens now?" Ethan asked, at the same time silently telling Lilith what was happening and asking her to watch the rebels' actions, smiling when she reported that their cohorts had entered the building to the right, and that she'd heard the sound of glass breaking.

The keepers, though, hadn't. At least if they had, they gave no sign of it.

"You two need to jump right back down through the roof, Ethan," one of their captors said from the rear of the building. "Then stay put until we get our orders.

Though given this latest attempt, I don't imagine you're going to live past dawn."

The Chosen Ones are coming this way at a dead run, Ethan. And they're armed!

Ethan stiffened at Lilith's mental news bulletin. But the man on the ground, clueless as to what was happening, kept on speaking.

"You two will make fine examples to the youngsters around here," he said. "Some of them have been getting some pretty radical notions since Lilith's escape, and —" There was a lot of shouting, followed by a crash, from the front of the small building, and the man's head jerked to one side. "What the hell was that?"

Ethan knew exactly what the hell *that* had been. It had been Ellie and Jeremy cutting through the guards and kicking open the door of their prison. Their little army surged inside, even as the keepers raced to see what was going on.

Ethan grabbed Lilith by the hand and leapt through the hole in the roof, landing just in time to see the tail end of Ellie's band dash inside and Jeremy slamming the door closed behind them.

"Good God, Jeremy, what were you thinking?" Ethan asked.

He couldn't see what was happening

outside — there were no windows — but he could feel and hear it. The guards were massing just beyond the front door and surging forward. In a moment they would burst through it.

"They're coming in," Ethan warned.

"Not alive, they're not," Jeremy said, and he leveled his rifle and blasted a hole through the door with a single shot.

Ethan smelled blood and felt the surge grind to a halt. He sensed the keepers and guards scattering — seeking cover, he was sure.

Sighing, he looked at the newcomers. "You got one of them. But, Jeremy, just what is your plan here?"

"We don't really have one. We just thought you'd have a better chance of fighting your way out of here with some help."

"Yeah, and you've got a better chance of dying," Ethan told the kid. But then he turned, sensing something behind him, and saw that the other members of the band were all staring at Lilith, awe and admiration in their young eyes.

Hell, he couldn't really blame them.

"You're the one," Ellie said. "You're the reason we found the strength to stand up for ourselves. We *couldn't* leave you behind."

"I would have preferred it," Lilith told the

girl, and Ethan knew it was nothing but the truth. "At least my death would have served a purpose then."

"We're not dead yet," Ethan told her softly, though he had little hope this could turn out any other way.

A voice from without cut the adoration-fest short, jerking every head toward the door.

"We're going to give you ten seconds to throw out your weapons. All of your weapons."

"Yeah, and what if we don't?" Jeremy shouted, defiant and angry.

"Then we're gonna torch the building. You got any other questions you want to ask before we do?"

Ellie's eyes went wide, and she took a step backward. "T-torch the building?" She shot a look at Ethan, then lifted her chin and said, "We've got to make a break for it. We've got no choice."

"They've got weapons, and we're surrounded," Jeremy said. "Dammit, Ellie, a lot of us will die."

"And maybe a few of us will live," she said. "It's our only chance, Jeremy. And frankly, I'd rather die free than live in captivity." She turned and eyed the rest of the rebels. "What about you?"

Before any of them could answer, the lights in the building flickered and went dark.

"They've cut the power," Ellie shouted, aiming her rifle at the door. "They're coming in. Get ready!"

There were shouts from outside, but no one stormed the building.

"That makes no sense," Lilith said in a whisper. "Even they must know vampires can see perfectly in darkness."

"You can," Jeremy said. "But we can't. Why aren't they coming? What are they waiting for?"

22

Serena stood in the woods just outside the compound with Terry and Ginger when the vampiress she had summoned arrived.

She was stunning — tall, regal, powerful — and the energy she gave off was one of raw fury and danger; though Serena knew none of it was directed at her, she couldn't help being afraid of this creature.

Eyes snapping, Rhiannon said, "You should get your people farther away. This isn't going to be pretty."

Serena nodded. "My daughter's in there."

"We know."

At the word *we* Serena frowned, and then she looked around and realized that there were vampires all around her, emerging from the woods, moving toward the electrified fence of the compound as if intent on climbing it.

"Wait! It's electric, it will —" But even as she said it, the lights inside the compound suddenly went out and the entire place sank into darkness.

"I told you, we have this covered. Go someplace safe." Then Rhiannon turned, raised a long, slender arm above her head and snapped her fingers just once.

The rest of the vampires surged forward, bursting into blurs and appearing to vanish before Serena's eyes. She stared, stunned, as Rhiannon joined them, leaping the tall fence with apparent ease.

But rather than running to safety, as the vampire queen had advised, Serena ran to the fence, too, touched it gingerly once, and then, when she wasn't jolted, gripped the wire mesh and began to climb.

"Serena, no!" Ginger shouted, chasing after her. "You could be hurt!"

"My daughter's in there. I'm going." And she continued climbing.

I was as puzzled as Ethan and the others, who were crouched and ready to fight an enemy that never appeared. And then I sensed violence, smelled blood. I heard shouts, and then gunfire broke out.

I ran to the door and opened it slightly, only to have Ethan rush to my side to stop me.

"Careful, Lilith," he whispered.

Together, we opened the door and peered outside. Bodies littered the ground. Keepers, I realized, and as I watched, a beautiful dark vampiress with an aura of age and power grabbed a female keeper by the neck and lifted her right off her feet.

It was Callista!

"No, wait!" I surged from the building without thought, running right up to the powerful female before finally realizing I was risking my life. Around me, vampires I did not know wreaked havoc, killing every keeper they found without mercy. Ethan was beside me, a protective arm around me, his entire body quivering with readiness.

"Wildborns," he whispered. "They have to be."

I shifted my gaze, locking it with that of the tall vampiress who held Callista in a death grip. Swallowing my fear, I said, "She's not one of them. Please . . ."

The vampiress lifted one perfect brow and lowered Callista to the ground, where she lay trembling, curling into herself. I quickly bent over her, assuring myself that she was unharmed. "It's all right," I told her. "We know who you are."

She rubbed her neck but did not speak.

Looking at the vampiress again, I asked, "What's happening?"

"You're being rescued," she said, her tone heavy with sarcasm. "Apparently by those you call 'Wildborns,' though it's a term I've never heard before."

Things around me were beginning to go quiet, but I felt death everywhere.

I swallowed hard and held her eyes. "We've been told that you — free vampires, Wildborns — would kill our kind on sight."

"And why would we do that?"

I blinked. "Because you're . . . uncivilized savages."

She smiled then, and it lit her face and immediately eased some of my fears. "Thank you for the compliment. But no, we don't kill our own kind. Actually, your mother sent us. Assuming you are the one called Lilith? And I'm guessing you are. There's a strong resemblance."

I nodded. "What about the other captives? The Chosen? Will they be harmed?"

She rolled her eyes. "Clearly you have a lot to learn, fledgling. I'll attempt to be patient in the face of your ignorance. My name is Rhiannon, by the way. You'll do well to remember it." She looked past me then, and I turned and saw the little band of rebels hovering near the door, watching, wide-eyed and shaken to the core.

"It's all right," I told them. "These vampires are good. They've come to help us. They won't hurt you."

And then I heard a voice I knew, one that filled my heart with warmth and relief. My mother's voice, calling my name.

I saw her through the darkness and the trailing smoke of dying gunfire, coming closer, looking for me.

"Mother!" I ran to her and wrapped my arms around her, and she held me with a fierceness I'd never known. Her entire body trembled as tears streamed down her face, wetting my hair.

When she finally released me and I lifted my head away, I found Ethan standing right beside me. Sniffling, I said, "This is my mother, Serena. Mother, this is Ethan. He's . . . he's . . ."

"He's the man who loves your daughter," Ethan said, sliding an arm around my waist.

Blinking in shock, I turned to stare up at him. "L-loves?"

Staring into my eyes, he nodded once, but then I heard a commotion and saw Rhiannon at the center of it. The keepers' bodies littered the ground, and now there was silence as vampires led captives from the barracks and buildings where they'd been huddled. Each vamp seemed to have collected a group to themselves, and they were

432

leading them from this place of horrors.

One stood in a doorway, an infant in his arms, and called out, "There are babies here. Nine of them, some newborns."

Rhiannon nodded, and though fury sparked in her eyes, her voice remained calm. She addressed my mother. "I hope your . . . organization . . . can take charge of the Chosen for the day? They need shelter, protection and education, and *we* —" she nodded toward the vampires around her "— need to retire before the sunrise."

"Of course," my mother said.

To the Chosen, Rhiannon said, "This woman and others like her will help you. And later, so will we. Until then, please believe that your captors are no more, and that you will never again be held anywhere against your will. And *you,*" she added, looking directly at me, "know that we so-called *Wildborns* are your family. Now get yourself to shelter before you burn in the sunrise. I assume even *you* understand the necessity of that."

"I do," I told her. "You should know that there are other vampires who were made as we were, to serve the DPI. They've been programmed to kill us — and you, too, I imagine."

"How many?" she asked.

"I don't know."

"Mmm, a roving band of assassins, without guidance or a clue." And then she smiled. "Sounds like fun."

I gaped, but she just waved a hand in the air. Instantly the vampires surged toward the now-open gates of the compound, their mission accomplished. She waved to me only once before dashing off to join them.

"Thank you!" I called after her, but I never knew if she heard me.

And then I turned. My mother's sisters were arriving now in droves. Vans full of them pulled slowly into the compound, each one beginning to load up the newly freed captives to take them away from this place — even the babies, in a group led by Callista. I knew they were in good hands.

"Here's the address where I'll be — the nearest Athena House," my mother said, handing me a small card from her pocket. "Will you be all right for the day?"

"Yes," I told her.

"I'll see to it," Ethan promised. "Thank you, Serena. We wouldn't have made it out alive without your help — and theirs." He nodded toward the woods, where the vampires had vanished only seconds ago.

My mother nodded and climbed into the final van. I waved as it drove away.

And then the place was deserted. No one else remained — no one alive, anyway. There were bodies everywhere, but only Ethan and I standing upright, arm in arm, as we walked toward the exit and through it, leaving the place in ruins, and for the very last time.

We walked along the dirt road that led from the compound to the nearest town, and found a vehicle waiting there, keys in the switch. The Bronco we'd been driving all along. Somehow, someone had left it for us.

I smiled when I saw it, and then turned into Ethan's arms, smiling at him. "Say it again, Ethan," I whispered.

His eyes intense, he parted his lips to utter the words I so longed to hear. But before he could speak, another voice cut him off.

"Step away from her, Ethan."

Startled, we both turned. James stood there, between us and the Bronco, and he held a handgun, its barrel pointed squarely at my chest. Gently, Ethan pushed me behind him and stood facing that barrel.

"It's over, James. The compound is destroyed. The people giving you your orders are all dead. There's no reason to continue this."

"No reason? Ethan, she got everyone

killed! The people who raised us, who *made us!* All of them lying dead in the dirt — because of *her!*"

"They're killers, kidnappers, abusers, James. They deserved to die, and they brought all this on themselves."

"She has to pay," James said. "Step aside, Ethan. I don't want to kill you, too."

"That's the only way you're going to get to her, brother."

"So be it." James steadied the gun, tightening his grip as he stared down the barrel at Ethan's chest.

But even as I sensed his finger beginning to tighten on the trigger, Ethan surged forward, straight at his brother. His body hit James like a rocket, and I heard the gun go off as the two of them flew twenty feet before landing on the ground. They struggled, and I ran to them, smelling blood, feeling Ethan's pain as if it were my own.

The gun went off again, and the two men went still on the ground.

Terrified, I gripped Ethan's shoulders, rolled him onto his back and stared down at him.

Blood was pouring from his chest at an alarming rate, and I tore off my blouse, wadded it up and pressed it hard against him to stanch the flow. He was conscious, but only barely.

"James?" he whispered.

I looked at James, who lay on the ground, even as I pulled Ethan to his feet and half carried, half dragged him to the waiting Bronco. James was dead. The bullet had gone straight through his neck, blowing the jugular open. He'd bled out already, and there was no life left in him.

Ethan would soon follow unless I took action. I eased him into the Bronco and drove to the barn where we'd found shelter once before. He kept pressure on the wound, but the bleeding hadn't stopped, only eased.

I got him inside and laid him gently in the hay, closed the doors and knew we would be safe there from the sun. And then I curled beside him, cradling him in my arms. "Drink from me, my love. Drink now, and then the sun will rise and the day-sleep will heal you. Please."

His eyes mere slits, he said, "I didn't say what you asked me to say."

"There's no need. You've shown me, Ethan. You love me. There's no question in my mind anymore. No more doubt. I believe you, and I trust you as I've never trusted anyone before. You love me, Ethan. And I love you. Only you, now and forever. So please, drink from me. Don't let me live out my days in love with a dead man."

His lips pulled into a weak smile, and then he nuzzled my neck. His teeth sank into my flesh, and I closed my eyes in ecstasy as I felt him drinking me into him. My strength, my essence, my endless, powerful love.

And I knew that was what would save him. My love. Just as his had saved me. "Tonight," I whispered, "we'll return to the ranch. The horses will be there waiting. And we'll be safe there. We won't have to hide anymore."

He swallowed, kissed my wounded neck and laid his head back in the hay. I snuggled close beside him, my hand pressing against the fabric that stanched the blood flowing from his chest. "I would have come back for you," he said. "I always intended to."

"You *did* come back for me," I told him.

"I'm sorry I left you in the first place." His words were slurred, and I felt the power of the day-sleep tugging him into its embrace, just as it did me.

"Everything happened as it had to happen, Ethan. If you'd stayed, perhaps neither one of us would be alive today. None of the innocent would be free, and that place wouldn't be reduced to rubble. You did what you had to do."

"I loved you even then," he whispered. "I'll love you forever."

And it was with that whispered promise that he drifted into sleep.

I laid my head on his chest and whispered, "And I will love you forever, my Ethan. My hero. Forever and ever . . . and ever."

And then I slept, too, and knew that the nightfall would bring with it a future I had never even dreamt of. A future of bliss, of freedom, of newfound family . . . and of perfect, endless love.

ABOUT THE AUTHOR

"Tension packed," "haunting," "bewitching," "tasty" and "better than chocolate" are just a few of the ways *New York Times* bestselling author **Maggie Shayne** and her award-winning novels have been described by critics and colleagues alike. Maggie is one of the hottest authors currently writing paranormal romance. Her works are fresh and sexy, carrying the reader into a darkly compelling and fully realized world where vampires are creatures of the heart, not just of the night.